The Stamp of Beauty

Fionola Meredith

Dalzell Press

First published in 2023 by Dalzell Press

Dalzell Press
54 Abbey Street
Bangor, N. Ireland BT20 4JB

ISBN 978-1-8380871-5-9

Cover artwork: Neisha Allen

Author photo: Charles McQuillan

The Stamp of Beauty is a work of fiction. Names, characters, businesses, places, events, locales, and incidents are either the products of the author's imagination or used in a fictitious manner. Any resemblance to actual persons, living or dead, or actual events, is purely coincidental.

For my friend Peter, who made all the difference

Chapter One

Leni Moffett knew that if her mother came to stay, she would not be able to breathe.

Patti was tiny, with the body of a doll, but she had a way of expanding her presence so that the whole house seemed full of her, with no escape possible. She filled the place like a gas. Everywhere you went, there she was in front of you, confronting you, her huge peacock-blue eyes demanding – no, requiring, insisting upon – your full attention. Your full compliance.

But why was Leni even thinking about Patti right now? Why was she allowing her mother to take up precious minutes of her time when she was supposed to be writing this bloody email? She had promised Theo she would send it today, and he was sure to ask her about it as soon as he came home.

Half an hour earlier, Leni had put Ann down for her after-lunch nap. She'd walked purposefully into the hall and retrieved her laptop from its bag, taken it to the kitchen table, plugged it in and opened it, all in one seamless, determined motion. She'd sat down squarely in front of the computer and twisted her hair into a scrappy but business-like bun on the back of her head. If she'd been wearing a top with sleeves, instead of one of Theo's vintage Grateful Dead T-shirts, she would have rolled them up. But suddenly all her impetus dissolved. Since then, she'd been gazing out the window at the whitewashed wall of the backyard and watching the swaying, shifting shadows cast by the honeysuckle vine, lost in dread about Patti.

Oh God, no, was that Ann stirring already? Leni thought she heard the distinctive half-cry, half-cough her daughter usually made when she started to wake up. She experienced a familiar sinking weight in her chest, a sudden body-heaviness which she instantly denied to herself that she felt.

Tiptoeing back down the hall, Leni peered into the living room. No. All was well. Ann had kicked off her blanket but she was still fast asleep, snuggled deep into the sofa, knees drawn up under her padded corduroy rump, carrotty top-knot tied with a purple ribbon, a silver thread of saliva trailing from her determinedly out-thrust lower lip. Ann was almost two. Even in sleep, she was formidable.

Leni returned to the kitchen and sat down again at her laptop. The afternoon house was quiet. Every surface was pristine, gleaming, no trace of the multi-coloured splatters from this morning's finger-painting activity. Ted, Leni's old black spaniel – she'd had him since she was twelve – was curled up in his usual spot under the table, and Leni now eased her bare feet into the warm, familiar crevice under his shaggy haunches. She had perhaps twenty minutes, half an hour if she was lucky. She launched her email app and began to type rapidly:

Dear Mr Riseborough
My name is . . .

Wait, should that be, 'Dear Roddy'? No, too familiar, she'd never even met the man. Give him his full name instead, that would seem more professional, as well as showing respect for him as the editor-in-chief of the newspaper. Leni picked absently at a patch of rosacea on her cheek – she had fragile, blue-white skin, easily inflamed, the redhead's curse – then erased the words and started over.

Dear Roddy Riseborough,

My name is Leni Moffett and I am an aspiring freelance writer. I'd like to pitch a feature idea for publication in The Sentinel.

Since giving birth to my daughter, I have adopted the attachment parenting technique, which, as its name suggests, is all about keeping babies as close to their mothers as possible. For example: carrying them in slings during the day, sleeping with them in the same bed at night, and of course breast-feeding entirely on demand.

What I'm proposing is an article explaining what is involved in this kind of parenting, drawing on my own direct experience, in the hope that other young mothers – I am 24 years old – will be inspired to try it for themselves. For me, it has been a revelation and I am keen to share some practical advice about how to make it work.

Leni paused and went back to toying with the itchy spot on her face: she was a very 'picky' person, and could never resist a scab or a flake of dry skin. A trace of red appeared on her fingertip. Ugh, no, she'd made herself bleed again. She jumped up and grabbed a piece of kitchen roll, ran it briefly under the cold tap, then clamped the damp wad to her face and continued writing.

> *I would also like to counter the negative publicity which attachment parenting often gets in the media, particularly the claim that it puts a strain on a mother's relationship with her partner. Far from driving us apart, I have found that it has actually enhanced my relationship with my husband. He uses the same techniques and we both enjoy the same deep bond with our daughter, Ann. Although we sometimes sleep in separate bedrooms, he understands that this is a temporary measure, necessary to facilitate successful mother/baby co-sleeping, and he is fully supportive of raising Ann in this way.*

Was that too much information? It sounded sort of self-justificatory, as if she was protesting too much. But it really was true. Theo couldn't be a kinder, more loving partner, totally on board with the attachment philosophy – even the nights he spent on the lumpy futon in the nursery. And he was devoted to Ann, willing to play endless giggling games of chase and hide-and-seek. His dog-like patience was almost miraculous to Leni; she was in awe of it.

> *My own upbringing was completely different. I grew up in my grandmother's house, and rarely saw my mother. I think that experience made me realise how vital it is for a child's wellbeing to have the constant*

presence of a parent, especially her mother, in the formative years of her life. This builds a deep-rooted sense of confidence that she is safe, protected and always loved.

Her mobile, plugged in and sitting on top of a stack of second-hand Ottolenghi recipe books beside the kettle, began to ring and vibrate simultaneously. She could have got up and silenced the phone, but instead she started to type faster, faster. Ted slipped out from under her feet and paced the floor whining, getting himself worked up. Phone, doorbell, even the manic tunes of Ann's baby keyboard – all of these noises made Ted howl.

After five rings, the phone stopped, the dog subsided into a series of protesting groans, and Leni exhaled sharply, unaware until then that she'd been holding her breath. Within a few seconds, though, the insistent buzz-ring resumed. Ted sat down, threw back his head and let out a long, plaintive, high-pitched warble.

Moments later, Ann appeared at the kitchen door. Red-faced with sleep, brows lowered, thumb wedged in her mouth, she hung briefly on the doorframe, then charged full force against Leni, struggling to climb on to her knee.

'Come here, Baba.' Leni hoisted Ann up with her left arm and straddled the child across her thigh, bouncing rhythmically. 'Hush-a-bye, hush-a-bye, hush-a-bye,' she murmured. She continued to type with her right hand, rattling it out now, not weighing her words anymore, determined just to get the damned thing finished.

The phone rang for a third time, and this time it didn't stop. Ted's howling became operatic. Ann fretted and squirmed, pulling up Leni's T-shirt, wanting to be fed.

Her tiny sharp nails, each one rimmed with paint from that morning's activities, left pink claw-marks on the pale skin of Leni's inner arm.

It was no use. Automatically, obediently, Leni shut the laptop, stood up with Ann still clinging to her chest, walked across the kitchen and lifted the phone. She knew exactly who it would be.

Yes, there was the usual warning message flashing up, the one she'd programmed into her mobile contacts instead of Patti's name: 'Brace Yourself!'

'Hello, Mama,' she said.

Her face was completely blank as she spoke.

Chapter Two

'Darling?'

Weak, croaking voice with a flinty bite in it. This could be bad.

'How are you, Mama?' No, no, no, she'd said exactly what she shouldn't have. Never ask Patti how she is, not when she's full of self-pity and looking for somebody to blame. Leni knew that, from long experience – yet still she parroted the expected response, as though someone else had taken charge of her brain.

'Oh . . . you know. These migraines. Every day now. They – they kill me, Leni . . .'

Last month it had been agonising back pain, and pins-and-needles in the tips of her fingers – a sure precursor of total paralysis, according to Patti.

'It sounds horrible, Mama. What does Dr Khan say?'

'Well, I don't want to worry you, darling, but he thinks it *might* be something worse than a migraine. He's talking about getting one of those CAT scans for me. To take a look inside my head and see what's going on in there. I dread to think what they'll find.'

'But you've only been having these headaches for a week or so. Isn't it a bit soon to be getting a scan? Maybe it's just stress. They might settle down by themselves, you know.'

Patti's mournful tone changed instantly. 'Oh, so now you're a medical doctor, are you?' she snapped.

Leni imagined her mother crouched in the darkened Notting Hill flat, curtains drawn, perennial glass of rum and Coke to hand, the shock of white hair falling forward as she darted her head to strike in that blind, reptilian way she had.

'You have X-ray vision, do you, special magic glasses to show me I'm wrong, yet again, always wrong? You have no idea, no fucking *idea*, what I suffer.' Her Germanic inflections, from the years spent in Berlin, came out more strongly when she was angry.

'No, Mama, of course not,' Leni said. 'I'm sorry. But look, the thing is, I'm actually pretty busy right now, I'm just about to feed the baby and—'

Ann, momentarily distracted by trying to pull the lid off the jar of homemade granola, had gone back to yanking fretfully at Leni's bra. 'Milky, milky, milky,' she wailed. 'Want my milky. Now!'

'Fine, fine, go to her, spoil her as you always do,' cried Patti, her voice trembling. 'I see where your priorities lie. You're obsessed with that child – you don't care about anyone else, even your own mother. Go, go – don't let me stop you!' A guttural sob echoed down the line.

'Wait, Mama, no, it's alright, just hang on a second—'

Propping the phone against her ear, Leni lifted Ann on to the bench, pinning the child awkwardly into place with her hip, then unhooked the front clasp of her bra, releasing her left breast. Ann grabbed it greedily between both little hands and clamped on to the nipple, swinging her legs over the edge of the bench as she sucked. Leni could have sat down comfortably to feed Ann, but she rarely sat when she was speaking to Patti. It felt too dangerous. You had to be on your feet, alert and ready for whatever came flying at you next.

'I'm back, Mama. Sorry about that.'

'Ok. Let's try again.' Long, shuddering sigh. 'Leni,

darling, the thing you must understand is that it's so hard for me being here on my own. Ever since Conrad abandoned me, I have been entirely alone. It's alright for you. You have your perfect little life in Belfast, everything all sweet and friendly and peaceful, no bombs and bullets anymore. You have your Theo, and you have your Ann – but I have nobody. And London is a cruel city. They walk through you on the street as though you don't even exist. It crucifies me, Leni.'

Leni's gut tightened, sensing the inexorable direction this conversation was taking.

'I've been thinking, Mama, would it help if you started taking pictures again?' she asked. 'It might make you feel happier.'

Useless, really, to attempt to deflect Patti, but some flailing sense of self-preservation made Leni try it all the same. A long time ago, Patti had been a famous – no, a notorious – photographer. Her shocking work was displayed in galleries all over the world. But after she left for Berlin, the exhibitions stopped. As far as Leni knew, her mother hadn't picked up a camera since.

'I want to come home. How many times must I say this? I want to be back where I belong, among my own people. My family. That is the only thing that could possibly help me now.'

'I – I know, Mama. And of course, you're always welcome here with me.' Leni swallowed hard, then rushed on before Patti had a chance to speak. 'It's just that we have so little room, now that Ann is getting older, you'd hardly believe a toddler could take up so much space, it's chaos . . . and then there's all the noise she makes, she's up before 6.00 a.m. every morning, singing at the top of her voice and, well – I really think you'd be happier if you had a place of your own.' She leaned her chin against Ann's shining head, panting a little, heart fit to burst out of her throat. Why did saying no to her mother feel so impossible?

'It's alright, darling,' said Patti, suddenly sympathetic. Leni had never got used to the speed of Patti's emotional U-turns: they always left her off-balance, scrabbling to find her footing in the conversation. 'I understand what you're trying to tell me, you don't have to be embarrassed. Look, it's about the money, isn't it? I know you and Theo don't have a lot to manage on. So I've been having a little think, doing a little research. I reckon I'll have to pay at least a thousand a month to rent a really nice place in Belfast, but it will probably take me a while to find something just right. How about I give that money to you, for the short time I'm staying with you – just two or three months, say four at the most – and that can be my rent? You can be my landlady. Then I will be paying my own way, and you won't have to worry about a thing. It will all be wonderful.'

Prey – that's what Leni felt like. Something very small and helpless. She knew it was absurd. Her mother was far away, she couldn't touch her, but her scintillating eyes, her beak and her talons seemed to be right here in the room, the circling wingbeats brushing ever closer.

'I don't know, Mama. I'll have to speak to Theo.'

'My God, I cannot believe this. I offer you a gift and you fling it back in my face,' cried Patti, instantly enraged. 'That's always been the problem with you, Leni. You're so fucking selfish!'

The phone went dead.

~

After her mother hung up on her, Leni flew madly through the house, grabbing piles of washing, straightening cushions, scooping up bits of Ann's random detritus – a velvet green frog, a waterproof book about fish, a half-chewed rice cake – and slinging them into their proper places: toy-basket, bath, bin. She kicked Ted's horrible pink rubber bone out of sight behind the long hall curtain. Then she spent a full half hour scrubbing traces of mildew off the grouting around the shower, the reek of bleach burning in her lungs. Every few minutes she burst out of the bathroom to check on Ann, who was plopped down in her playpen, sucking dreamily on a normally forbidden bar of milk chocolate.

Leni always had this impulse after a bad encounter with Patti: a ravening need for order and space and control. Pulling soap-congealed hairs out of the bath plughole, the forensic attention required to extract the yucky, slippery mess, suspended by just a single strand or two: these actions physically soothed her.

Leni loved her house. She had created it out of almost nothing. When Theo's parents put down the generous deposit for the red-brick Victorian terrace, 42 Isthmus Avenue, and it finally became theirs, the first thing she did was to get rid of the ugly plastic front door and replace it with a mahogany one she'd found in a skip. The door was a bit battered, and there were crowbar marks on the side where somebody must have previously tried to prise it open, but Leni covered it all with a thick, delectable coat of lilac paint, the colour of Parma Violets, and added a bright brass letterbox. After that, she felt she owned the place. True, she mourned for the sash windows that must once have been, the lovely underwater distortions of the old glass replaced by utilitarian double-glazing, no doubt by the same philistine person who poured concrete over the tiny front garden. But she forged on regardless, hiring a sanding machine to scour the floors, sending up clouds of wood dust to reveal smooth, bone-white boards underneath.

Every wall in the house was painted white too, she and Theo working away with brushes and rollers like something out of a Dulux commercial, as happy and unreal as that. She bought a second-hand pair of long, slumberous, smoke-blue sofas on Gumtree and – this was her one extravagance – a floor lamp from Ikea with a glass globe, deep orange in colour, suspended from a curved metal stem like the head of a flower. In the evenings, Leni liked to stretch out underneath the lamp, letting its kind light pour over her face.

Above the tiled fireplace she hung a framed fly-poster for Theo's schoolboy band, The Troubles. It was a rough, blocky screen-print, Theo skulking with the others in a rubbish-strewn alleyway, looking as lovely as a girl. Leni's books lived on shelves to the left of the fire, Theo's records were stacked in shelves on the right. Upstairs, the main bedroom was almost empty except for the pale, inviting expanses of their king-size bed, a gift from Great Aunt Caroline, who believed in investing in quality.

On a breezy Saturday morning in April, not long after they got married, Leni had sent Theo out with a pickaxe and he swung and smashed and tore at the concrete covering the front garden – he was stronger than he looked – until it was broken into pieces, and after the mess was cleared away, they planted a cherry tree there. That autumn, in the days before Ann was born, the sight of the russet leaves dancing against the backdrop of her lilac front door gave Leni a startling jolt of pleasure. She had made herself a home.

By the time she'd finished cleaning the shower, and given Ann another quick feed, it was almost 5.30 p.m. She slipped her phone from the back pocket of her jeans and texted Theo.

You on your way?

She watched for the set of three bouncing bubbles beneath her text that showed Theo was replying. He was usually a very quick responder, but they didn't appear.

I'm cooking something fancy for dinner, she wrote. *Garbage soup. Know what that is?*

Ten minutes later, still no reply.

You make it with random veg, anything you've got hanging around. It'll be better than it sounds, honest :)

Nothing, even after twenty minutes.

Hey. Is everything ok?

No reply to that, either, which was very strange, and a bit worrying.

If Granny June were here, she'd tell her to keep busy and get on with making the dinner, no use in fretting, so that's what she decided to do.

There wasn't much left in the wooden vegetable box. Theo brought home lots of lovely organic produce from Grow-a-Pear, the community garden for ex-offenders which he co-managed with his former bandmate, Gav Thornton. But this week's supply of spinach, tomatoes and rainbow chard had already been eaten. The late raspberries had lasted less than a day, disappearing like sweeties, pop, pop, pop, one after the other, into Ann's red mouth. Now there were only a couple of tired-looking carrots, an onion, and an elderly whiskered turnip left. Luckily, she had some homemade stock on standby in the freezer, and a handful of parsley – proper, flat-leaf parsley that she'd grown herself in the kitchen window-box, never the supermarket kind – which would liven things up.

When Theo came in, the soup had been ready for ages, and she was frying some tiny scraps of bacon to sprinkle on top, just to give herself something else to do. Normally he would rush straight to Ann and swing her up in his arms, making a smacking sound against her neck which made her wriggle and shriek with glee, before placing a gentle kiss on Leni's forehead. Tonight he simply stood there, arms hanging down uselessly, and Leni knew something bad had happened, but all she could think of at that moment was how filthy his hands were, all crusted and smeared with mud. Theo liked to be clean, and always got washed at the sink in the Grow-a-Pear shed before he came home.

'Hi,' she said, smiling uncertainly. 'Did you not get my texts?'

'I've lost my gig at the Riveters,' said Theo, and started to cry.

Chapter Three

The Riveters was a working men's club in East Belfast which had been turned into a vintage music bar after the Troubles ended. The red plush-lined walls still smelled of cigarettes and sweat and chicken-in-a-basket. It was where Leni and Theo had met, three-and-a-half years ago.

Leni was on a rare night out with some sort-of friends from university. She didn't have much space in her life for real friends. She was at the end of her final year studying English at Queen's, and she spent almost all the rest of her time with her grandmother at Ascot Court, the nursing home where she'd gone when Leni couldn't cope with looking after her at home anymore. By then, Granny June was in the last months of her life, her once-resolute mind completely desiccated by Alzheimer's, her brain as full of holes as the white lacy doilies she used to crochet with such quick, impatient fingers. The doilies had been kept in a special drawer in the dining-room sideboard, where they slowly went yellow with age. They were meant to be placemats, for special celebration meals, but Leni couldn't remember them ever being used.

At the club that night, Cara McCullough, who sat beside Leni in Renaissance literature class, had been gushing about a trip to Rome with her new boyfriend; they were flying from Dublin the following weekend. 'Oh my God, I just checked the weather and it's gonna be, like, forty degrees – we are gonna fuckin' fry! We'll be getting naked in the fountains! Bring on the gelato, that's all I can say . . .'

Leni was watching the DJ, a dense-browed, startlingly beautiful young man with a silky black ponytail. He looked up at that moment and met her gaze with an answering stare of such profound intensity that she blushed and turned away. A few minutes later, she stole another glance at him, but he was busily flicking through his records, head nodding rhythmically, one headphone crushed against his ear by a raised shoulder. Maybe that serious stare was just his natural expression, nothing to do with Leni. Far too good-looking for the likes of her, anyway.

Cara insisted that everyone had to stay until the end of the night, since it was the last time they'd be out together as students. At 2.00 a.m., when the music stopped and the overhead lights came on, showing the ancient cigarette-burns in the velvet seats, and the dancefloor wet with spilled beer, Leni discovered that her coat was missing. It was a little bolero jacket with a gold clasp, made from nubbly black merino wool. She'd left it under a pile of other cast-off coats and bags behind the speaker-stacks, but when she went to retrieve it there was just an empty space: everything was gone.

The bolero was far too small for Leni, it pinched her terribly under the arms, but it was precious and irreplaceable because it had belonged to Granny June. Leni had a photograph of her grandmother wearing it, chic as Coco Chanel, with a steely glint in her eye and ankles as thin as a blackbird's leg. It was nearly impossible to believe that the young woman in the picture was the same person who sat shrivelled, lost and muttering to herself, in a wing-backed chair at Ascot Court.

The others were already outside the club, drunkenly

trying to flag down a taxi. Leni tried to dart into the women's toilets, in case the coat had found its way in there, but a puffa-clad bouncer intercepted her and shepherded her away towards the exit, stolidly ignoring her explanations. At that moment, the DJ, who had been putting away his records, came out of the booth and asked her what was wrong, and when she told him, fighting back tears, he said to the bouncer, 'It's okay, Freddie, I'll take care of this.'

He helped her look in every possible place, but it quickly became obvious that someone had stolen the jacket. He insisted that Leni take his own coat, which was a grey suede one with long fringes. It had an earthy scent, like woods in autumn. When he helped her on with it, it felt comfortingly heavy over her light summer dress. The tender weight across her shoulders, the sensation of being held, safe inside the DJ's coat, was something almost like peace. Even when she got home to the dark, empty house, Granny June no longer there to leave a lamp on for her, she found that she didn't want to take the jacket off. She liked the way the sleeves were so long that they completely covered her hands.

'I could tell you were different, from the moment you walked into the club,' said Theo, later, after they got together.

'Did you? In what way?'

'You looked like a proper adult woman. Grown up, you know. Not some silly little girl.'

They had their wedding party at the Riveters, a year after they met there. Since Leni was pregnant, and everybody was making such a big deal of the fact they were so young – she was twenty-two and Theo was only twenty-one – she half-jokingly suggested a shotgun wedding theme. And that was what they ended up doing, Leni kicking up the froth of her petticoats in a pair of cowboy boots, Theo unwittingly thrilling in a tightly fitted suit and Stetson. They had Waylon Jennings, Loretta Lynn and Dolly Parton on the turntable, everyone clapping and singing along. Well, everyone except Patti. She had arrived resplendent in highly corseted bridal white, slipped on a spilt drink and fell down a flight of stairs, spraining her ankle, before being borne off wailing to casualty by Conrad, the wealthy West German art collector who Leni thought of as Patti's zookeeper. Patti was a zoo in herself.

By the time she married him, Leni had realised that Theo was pretty different too. He took everything literally, was confused by ironic jokes and held himself to gallant, old-fashioned codes of behaviour, like never swearing in public. But he was doggedly, devotedly loyal. Leni could be sure of him, she trusted him absolutely, and that was all that mattered.

~

Theo sniffed and carefully wiped away his tears with the cuff of his shirt, to avoid getting dirt on his face. He hardly ever cried, but when he did, like the time when his granddad died, he wept openly; he wasn't ashamed of it. It was one of the things that Leni loved about him.

'Jimmy called me earlier. He said they're knocking the old place down, selling the land for apartments. The demolition won't actually happen until after Christmas, but Jimmy said he's letting me go now, because there's no point keeping me on. So that's it over. I'm gone.'

'Ah T, I'm so sorry, that's awful. I can't believe it. The

club's been there so long, I thought it would go on forever.' She took both his hands in her own and squeezed them tight. The dried mud felt soft and dusty.

'Every Saturday night, since I left school,' said Theo. 'The only time I missed a night was when Ann was born, remember?'

'Yeah,' said Leni, stroking his fingers: piano-playing fingers, long and delicate. 'I told you that you could go if you wanted, but you said no.'

Theo smiled sadly. 'Just that once. I was back the next week. It was like . . . my time, you know? Four hours where I could just disappear into my music. Be somewhere else.'

Leni nodded. 'I get it, T. I really do. Look, sit down, have some of this soup. You'll feel better.'

'Wait, Len. It's not only the music,' said Theo, keeping hold of her hand. 'It's the money. We're not going to able to make it on my salary from the garden. We're dipping into the overdraft every month as it is, but without the Riveters, we're sunk.'

'Yes, I know, Theo,' Leni said, turning away. Without thinking, she lifted the hot metal lid of the pan then dropped it with a crash. 'Shit!' Pushing her scorched fingertips into her mouth, she sucked them hard as she bent over the oven, pulling out the bread.

Normally Theo was instantly attentive if she hurt herself, however slightly, but tonight he didn't seem to notice. He sank heavily into his chair and slumped there, inert, his back to Leni. Ann stopped banging the tray of her highchair with a plastic spoon and regarded Theo with frank, almost anthropological interest, her round blue eyes wide. She picked up a grape and offered it to him, and he took it and ate it automatically.

'Did you send that email to the editor of *The Sentinel*?' Theo asked, over his shoulder.

Leni pressed her lips together. 'No. My mother called and interrupted me when I was halfway through, and then Ann woke up from her afternoon nap, so I didn't get the chance to finish it.'

She set the bowl of soup down in front of him. It was perfect: rich, green-freckled, golden, with a curl of crème fraîche melting into it, and crisp snippets of bacon floating on top. But Theo ignored the soup and stared up into her face.

'Leni, you have to do it. You said you would. Things are getting desperate here. We could lose our house!'

'Oh, what's the fucking point?' cried Leni. Theo looked horrified. Bad words were banned, by mutual agreement, for Ann's sake. But knowing that she had the means, through Patti, to relieve all their money worries, right this very moment, had suddenly filled her with unreasonable rage.

'Sorry, I shouldn't have – sorry, Theo. It's just – this man is not going to want my article. He'll think it's a weird subject. He has no idea who I am. I have no journalistic qualifications. The only publication I've ever written for was *The Owl*, and that was just a student paper. And even if, by some miracle, it did get printed in *The Sentinel*, a single article won't make any difference to anything, will it? What do you think he's going to pay me for it – a thousand pounds?'

'You've got to try,' said Theo earnestly. 'And if you get one piece in the paper, then Mr Riseborough will see how brilliantly talented you are, and he'll offer you loads more work. You're so clever, Leni, I know you can do it. Tell him about coming top of the degree class in English, and that prize you won – you know, the Mabel Whatshername award.'

'But what about Ann? She has to come first. The whole point of the attachment thing is that I'm there for her, at all times. We both agreed on that.'

'You can write in the evenings when she's asleep. Look, Len, you've got to help me here. I – I can't do this all by myself.'

Dinner felt painful, dragging along from silence to silence. Afterwards, Theo roused himself and took Ann upstairs, as usual, to get her ready for bed. Leni cleared the table, noticing that Theo had eaten barely half of his soup. She had eaten even less. Using a curved rubber spatula, she scraped the remains into Ted's dish, concentrating with great intensity on each slow, accurate sweep through the yellowy sludge, leaving the bowls as white and clean as if they'd been washed already. She could bring her whole attention to a simple task like this. Like pulling hairs from plugholes, it was another way of shutting out chaos.

Bedtime, and its many associated rituals, belonged exclusively to Theo and Ann. First came the bath, with its high-pitched squeals and splashing, and when the scent of Johnson's baby powder came floating down the stairs, it meant that Ann was out of the tub and getting into her pyjamas, Theo having lovingly dried the gaps between each tiny pink finger and toe with a soft warm towel. Then there was the sound of two pairs of feet on the landing floor, one comically heavy, one light and scurrying, as Theo chased Ann into bed with a loud, mock-scary cry of 'Fee-fi-fo-FUM!', like the giant in *Jack and the Beanstalk*. Though of course he never included the rest of the gruesome rhyme, the parts about smelling the blood of an Englishman, and grinding bones to make bread, just as he always skipped the page with the evil troll hiding under the bridge in the *Billy Goats Gruff*.

And then Theo would play his guitar for Ann, and there would be stories, endless stories, until at last he would gently, slowly, pull his arm from beneath her sleeping head and leave her there, a cosy little bundle in the gigantic bed, until Leni came up and joined her later.

But tonight there were no giggles coming from behind the bathroom door, and no pounding feet overhead. Leni's heart pinched sharply when she heard a small, puzzled voice ask,

'Where's fum, Daddy?'

Chapter Four

When Theo didn't appear again downstairs that evening, Leni went to investigate. She found him in their bedroom, lying fast asleep on top of the covers beside Ann, one arm flung over his face, and a book called *Bad Babies* on his chest, rising and falling with the rhythm of his breath.

It was noticeably chilly in the big room. For the last four months, their oil boiler hadn't been working properly. This hadn't been a problem in the summer, but it soon would be, now that the nights were drawing in. Housed in its own brick shed in the back yard, the boiler was an antique fixture of the house, cobwebbed, wheezy and stinking of burnt kerosene. It was badly in need of replacement, but they couldn't afford the vast expense. Lately, rusty water had been gathering in a pool around the base of the boiler on the concrete floor of the shed. Clearly the end was near.

Leni lifted the book and touched Theo lightly on the hip.

'Theo,' she whispered.

He stirred. 'Whuh?'

'Theo, if you doze now, you won't be able to sleep later.'

He woke with a start and sat up, blinking and bewildered. 'Sorry. I must have completely conked out.'

'It's understandable. You've had a hard day.'

'What time is it?'

'Just gone eight.'

Theo groaned quietly, rubbed his eyes, and swung

round so that he was sitting on the edge of the bed.

'Listen, I called Rafferty while Ann was in the bath,' he said, speaking in the hushed voice they both used when Ann was sleeping. 'Wanted to see if there was anything going at The Echo Chamber – Raff looks after the bookings there. He said there was nothing right now but there could be a chance in the New Year because Ryan, the guy who does Thursday nights at Echo, might be going back to Dublin. So that's at least a possibility.'

'Ok, good, T, that's good. But look, there's nothing more you can do right now. Why don't we both try to forget about it all, at least for tonight, yeah?' Leni knelt beside the bed and rested her head on Theo's lap, wrapping her arms around him. He laid his hands wearily on her back. Their warm, familiar pressure made her move closer, nuzzling her face into his denim thighs.

They stayed like that for a while, swaying together slightly, Leni rubbing her cheeks every now and then against the rough material, bumping the ridges of the stitched seams over and back against the line of her jaw. Then, very slowly, button by button, pausing cautiously between each, she began to undo Theo's jeans. Once the fly was fully open, she reached inside, fumbling gently for his cock, and found it curled, soft and mouse-like, in a fold of his pants. She eased it out of its hiding place and lowered her mouth onto the delicate thing. Moving her head back and forth, she could feel the life in it starting up, a sparkling below the skin, responding irresistibly to the taut pressure of her lips. Up above, Theo shifted uncomfortably.

'Don't, Len,' he murmured.

'Why not? Ann's out cold, she won't wake.'

'It's not that. I just think it's ... demeaning.'

'Oh, Theo. Not this again. I've told you, I don't mind.'

'Well, you should. You're – look, you're the mother of my child. It's not right for you to be on your knees in front of me, doing . . . that.'

'Theo—'

'No, Len, I mean it. Please stop. I don't want it. Really. I respect you too much.' He whisked his cock out of sight, like a magic trick in reverse, and buttoned up his jeans again.

Leni sat back on her heels. She wasn't exactly surprised: since Ann was born, Theo had been funny about sex, especially when she went down on him. She thought men were supposed to love that, but Theo didn't seem keen. And he never – ever – went down on her. Sometimes she had the impression that he'd prefer to avoid sex entirely. It wasn't as though she really wanted it tonight herself, in all honesty. Comfort: comfort and sweet escape, a temporary reprieve from anxiety, that was all she was offering him. But the rebuff made her feel ugly and ashamed, and powerless too. Intolerably cut off from Theo, and all the love and safety he provided.

She had to get that safety back. So right there, before she knew what she was doing, she told him about Patti's offer of money – helplessly sicking it up in front of him on the carpet like a guilty little dog.

Theo looked stunned. 'You're joking me. She's actually willing to give us a grand a month to stay here?'

'Yes.'

'But that's amazing!'

She'd known he would say that. He never understood about Patti, who was unfailingly charming to him on the few occasions that they had spent time together. To Theo, Patti was eccentric, unpredictable, a bit free with her tongue, but essentially harmless, and he treated her with the same quiet reverence he extended to all women.

'I don't think I could stand it, Theo. If she came here. I've explained it all before.'

'Hang on a minute, why didn't you tell me about this earlier, when I came home? I've had the most hellish night, Len, trying to work out how we're going to manage, and you didn't even think to mention this massive amount of cash we're being offered?'

'Because I knew that this was exactly how you would react! You would want to have Patti, and her money!' The words came out in a childish wail. Ann stirred in her sleep. She made a rhythmic sucking sound, dreaming of milk.

'Listen, Leni, listen. Would it really be so awful? It's only for a few months. It could tide us over until I get a new DJing gig. And she could help you look after Ann.'

The idea of Patti cheerfully changing nappies and rolling out Play-Doh was so painfully absurd that Leni didn't even bother to respond to it.

'Theo. Do you not remember the last time she stayed here? When Ann was born?'

It had been a long, drug-addled birth, and Leni spent much of it borne along uselessly, a seasick passenger on her own trip. Afterwards she felt ripped, torn, turned inside-out. More or less indifferent – whisper it – to the tiny, red-raw alien in the plastic box beside her. All she wanted to do was go home and lie very still in her own bed, gradually reassembling her smashed and shattered forces, and working out how to start the impossible business of being a mother. But when Theo brought Leni and Ann back to Isthmus Avenue, Patti was there, standing on the doorstep with two massive suitcases, looking through the letterbox.

Leni had retreated upstairs and spent the next three days holed up in her bedroom, teaching herself to breastfeed Ann, with the help of YouTube videos and a leaflet from the hospital called 'Latching On'. It was then that she discovered 'the Seven B's' of attachment parenting – breastfeeding, baby-wearing, bedding close to baby . . . Oh, she could never remember them all off the top of her head, but it didn't matter, the wonderful thing was that there was a set of rules, something sure to cling to.

Meanwhile Patti, having given Ann a cursory glance, sat in state in the living room, grandly receiving well-wishers, Theo dancing attendance on her with coffee and shop-bought buns. Every so often, Leni could hear the rum-saturated rasp of her mother's laugh break through the murmur of polite conversation below.

When Leni finally emerged, she found that Patti had moved one of the sofas to the other side of the living room so she could sit and smoke out the window, and had added a fake fur throw flecked with angular silver sequins, 'just to liven the place up, darling – it's so bare and dull.' The glass floor lamp had been relegated to the hall, and there was a cigarette burn on the mantelpiece. Leni had trembled with unspoken rage.

'It wasn't that bad, Len,' said Theo. 'She just shoved the furniture around a bit, didn't she? Easily fixed.'

Leni sighed. 'Theo, look, the reason you don't understand any of this is because you had a nice, normal upbringing. Bill and Dorothy are nice, normal parents. But I didn't have that. What I had was a mother who saddled me with the name of a Nazi filmmaker, then abandoned me when I was two years old. I have no idea who my father is because Patti, by her own admission, had so many drunken one-night stands that she couldn't remember his face, let alone his name. And I know I've only got her attention now because she has nobody else to lean on, since Conrad's finally had enough and gone back to his wife.'

~

When Leni turned seven, Patti had sent her a Leica camera for her birthday. Leni was ecstatic with the gift, but Granny June took it away, tutting with disapproval, because it wasn't suitable – far too valuable to be used as a toy. A ridiculous present to give a child, she'd said. Typical of Patricia's thoughtlessness.

Leni's most vivid childhood memories of Patti were of travelling in the car with her, after being picked up from the airport, when she went to visit her mother and Conrad in England. The gut-gripping, fearful excitement of being in Patti's presence again: she seemed so much sharper and brighter than other people. Roaring fast along the packed English motorways, with Leni sitting illicitly in the front passenger seat (Granny June would have been appalled), Patti would tell her how to be a good photographer. She said it was all about learning to see, which made Leni giggle nervously because of course she knew how to see – didn't everyone, except blind people?

The window frames of the car were like photograph frames, said Patti: snapshots of all the places and people that you saw on your journey. You could use your hands as a frame too, Patti said, letting go of the wheel for a moment to demonstrate.

On one of these airport drives, Leni had seen a young swan – she knew it was young because it was brown, not white – suddenly framed in the front windscreen. The bird was forging along above the road ahead of them, flapping as hard as it could, its long neck straining forward. But there was a motorway bridge coming up fast, and Leni was horrified to see that the swan wasn't flying high enough to get over the bridge, in fact it was headed straight for it.

As they passed beneath the swan, Leni let out a cry of anguish, dropped the can of 7up she was clutching, and jerked round frantically to peer out the back window. She saw a brief flutter of tumbling wings crash-land on the central reservation before a lorry closed in and blocked off her view.

Patti was angry because Leni had spilled her drink on the new leather seat cover, and Leni's tears wouldn't stop, which only made her mother angrier. There was shouting, and screaming, and no matter how hard Leni tried to choke back the babyish sobs, they came jerking noisily out of her raw, hurting throat. They were speeding faster and faster, with the sound of her mother's rum-soaked voice too loud and too close to her face, and the car was driving by itself because Patti wasn't looking where she was going. . .

~

Well. That was all a very long time ago. Leni was an adult now, safely grown up, with a home, a husband and a daughter of her own. Nothing like that could ever happen to her again.

'Honestly? I think it's just a case of making your mum feel wanted,' Theo was saying. They were back downstairs in the kitchen now, sitting at opposite sides of the table. 'Leni? Are you listening to me? What I mean is, if Patti feels like she's actually welcome here, that we care about her, I bet she'll behave herself. She'll settle down, I promise.'

'You just don't get it, do you, Theo?' said Leni.

Theo twisted the wispy end of his ponytail round his index finger, a habit he had when he was perplexed. 'Not really, no,' he said.

Leni shook her head wearily.

'Look, I know Patti's been difficult in the past,' said Theo. 'But things are different now. She's older, she's all on her own, and she needs our help. And, well, she's your mother. You only get one of those. Don't you pity her, even a little bit?'

'God, no! I can't risk it.'

'Why not?'

'Because she'd eat me alive.'

Theo laughed. 'Leni. Come on. Patti is many things, but she is not a cannibal.'

The discussion – you couldn't really call it an argument – went on for the rest of the evening, looping in ever-diminishing circles over the same ground, but long before it ended, Leni was already preparing to give in. It was the money that sealed it, that made Patti's visit definite. Yet even if Patti hadn't offered the cash bribe, she was always going to be coming to stay. Leni was no match for her, and they both knew it.

That night she asked Theo to sleep in the big bed with Ann. She wanted to be on her own, for once. But after two-and-a-half fretful hours on the nursery futon, Leni got up, crept down the stairs and opened her laptop. Suddenly it seemed imperative for her to send that email to the editor of *The Sentinel*.

Before, she was only doing it to please Theo. Now, with Patti on the way, it took on new urgency. It was a flare, a flag, a statement of selfhood, a proud manifesto for Leni's chosen way of life. It was a riposte to the lonely past. She had somebody, was somebody: a mother. In the expansive night silence, the words came easily, and the email was soon finished. As an afterthought, she attached a photograph of herself with Theo and Ann. Just a simple selfie, snapped last weekend at the play park, all three of their laughing faces squashed in tight together to fit into the frame. Leni's perfect little family. If her eyes looked a little sad, it was only because she was squinting into the sun.

Chapter Five

Roddy Riseborough was alone in the firelight. The curls and chips of the wood he was carving fell around him softly like snow. It was a little bird he was making tonight – a robin. The knife knew exactly where to go, sliding instinctively through the green willow, and the rounded breast soon took shape in his hands. How to whittle animals from wood was one of the few things he'd learned from his father, the Judge. Other skills, such as how to keep out of the Judge's way when he was in the mood for one of his sadistic teases – needling, goading provocations that made you feel you were going mad – Roddy picked up for himself.

He turned the half-formed robin so that the light from the turf fire fell directly on it. He needed to give the pointed wings that lively, flicking quality that robins always have, and the head had to tilt at exactly the right angle, curious and questioning. He was driven, in pursuit of perfection: the essential 'robin-ness' of a robin, that was what he wanted to capture, the quick, brave life of the bird rendered in wood. The staff at *The Sentinel* would have been amazed to hear it, but Roddy loved all wild animals, with a tenderness entirely absent from the fierce, laughing, autocratic way he ran the paper (punctuated with occasional outbursts of searing rage, all the more terrifying because of their rarity).

The squirrels, for instance, swinging by their tails to raid the birdfeeders he'd hung on the washing line behind the house: he could watch those canny buccaneers for hours. The sight of a fox tracking purposefully across the wet grass in the silence of the early morning had, for him, the power to suspend time for one exquisite moment. And his heart still lifted, creaking on its moorings, when he saw the slow, solitary flight of a heron setting out across the bay at dusk.

But it was the lowliest creatures that Roddy cared for most of all. The slimy ones, the crushable ones, the ones that everyone else despised. On a rainy night, arriving home late after the long drive from the city, he'd stop and pick up every single slug or snail on the front path, depositing them carefully in the wild tangle of nettles and brambles that had once been Mummie's flower garden. If he missed one, and heard the ominous crunch of a breaking shell, he felt a lurch of remorse so strong that it was almost as if it wasn't the snail, but he himself who was being crushed to death underfoot, sharp shards piercing his exposed, painfully vulnerable body.

Roddy kept working at the robin for some time, sculpting and smoothing, but gradually his zeal for the task began to ebb. Boredom started to nibble at the edges of his concentration, causing the knife to falter and pause. He could feel the familiar echo of emptiness invading his chest cavity, taking unsolicited soundings in his gut. He knew the forbidden places that emptiness could lead him to, the things it could make him crave and do, once it got a hold, so he forced himself to press on with the carving. But soon it became obvious that it was too late, he'd lost that lovely, easy flow, the sheer mindlessness of it, and now it was just a job like any other. Worse than any other, really, because he had failed in what he set out to do. He wanted to create a thing of simple truth and beauty, not this sightless, legless lump of mutilated willow tree.

He leaned forward and carefully balanced both bird and knife on the hearthstone, beside the plate containing the remains of his dinner: two bacon rinds and the lacy, frizzled white of a fried egg (since childhood, Roddy had only ever eaten the yolk).

What was the point of carving wood if it didn't keep him busy and occupied? He needed work for his hands, a focus for his thoughts, to ward off that gnawing feeling in his chest, and the seamy antidotes his mind suggested. Crouched over the fire, he sat powerless as temptation rose in him, sly and definite and irresistible.

What time was it anyway? The blameless face of his watch said 7.32 p.m.

Still far too early for anything like that.

He leapt up fretfully from his chair and flung the curtains open, sending them jangling and clashing the full length of the pole on their broken brass rings. Red western light flooded the vast room, illuminating the flaking pattern of palm trees on the wallpaper and igniting the gilt rims of the cocktail glasses on the bar cart. Dust motes, set free from the thick folds of the curtains by Roddy's savage yank, danced around his head like a cloud of golden midges. The September sun was going down in splendour beyond the lough.

It would be dark in half an hour, but probably not dark enough for his purposes. He would have to wait. Leaving the curtains open, he sank back into his chair and took up the knife again. Slowly twilight crept around him as he worked, head bowed diligently, like a boy at school. He didn't stop until the air was thick as ashes and he could no longer distinguish the silver blade from the pale wood.

He was calm now because he had accepted what he was going to do. It was always like this: once the little crisis of conscience was over, and he'd given in, he felt fine. Better than fine, actually. Bright, alert, restored to himself. No longer empty and alone.

He stood up, weighing the robin in his hand, rubbing his thumb around the smooth curve of the bird's throat, and then dropped it casually into the fire. It landed beak down, its jaunty tail poking out between the glowing banks of turf. Roddy watched it for a moment. Then he called Terence, his Staffordshire bull terrier, put on his coat and went out into the night.

~

Honolulu was the name of Roddy's home. Mummie's idea, of course, to call it that: a lush fantasy of tropical warmth and decadence on a bleak little Irish island. It was originally intended as the Riseborough summer family residence, but she used it all year round, often leaving the Judge under armed guard back at home in Belfast – after the Troubles took hold, and they started killing judges, he was given round-the-clock police protection. The whole island belonged to the Judge; it had been in the family for generations. He built the house in 1965, to a design by Paul Brophy, the famous modernist architect. But it was Mummie's kind of people who came to visit there: for picnics, midnight bathes, boat trips to the bird islands. The parties were legendary, everyone said, but all Roddy could remember were lanterns in the trees, laughter in the garden, and the bath suddenly full of ice and wine.

Sometimes old comrades visited from Mummie's time at Le Cirque, the gentlemen's club in Soho, where she'd worn a brown velvet leotard trimmed with cream lace, very decorous, and tipped forward prettily to pour the drinks for the men. That was in the days before his father met her. On the island, Mummie asserted all the parts of her personality that the Judge was intent on quelling.

Fleeing the city on a winter evening, the sky frosty with stars, she would stuff young Roddy into the back seat of her little Renault. He'd sit there, already in his pyjamas, alongside a dozen champagne bottles wrapped in a blanket, and the bottles would roll and clash as she flew round impossible bends on the country lanes, and he'd feel sick and delighted and terrified all at the same time. 'Hold tight to the fizz, Rodders,' she'd laugh. 'Precious cargo!' Everything she did made life a thrill. Then at last they shot across the causeway, rattled over the cattle grid, and the headlights swept the long glass and stone front of the house, conjuring it out of the salty dark. Ta-da! They were there: Honolulu.

~

Tonight, Roddy stood patiently outside the house as Terence snuffed and grubbed in the drifts of rotting seaweed that had been washed up on to the grass by last winter's storms, tugging the dog's lead every now and then until he consented to trot on. The air was very still and soft. Clouds had come down low to meet the sea, and the moon showed itself only as a faint luminescence in the northern sky, like a reflection of the lights of the distant city. As usual, Terence paused to cock his leg importantly on the Judge's old flagpole. A few trailing strands of discoloured blue and red thread still hung from the pole, the last remains of the flag that once flew there, many years ago. Roddy remembered how it used to crack sharply to attention whenever there was a stiff breeze.

On a night like this, all hushed and gathered in on itself, the past felt almost palpably close to Roddy. He found himself walking with a slight limp, as he often did when he thought of his father. The Judge had been wounded in Italy in 1944, while on active service as an officer with the Royal Inniskilling Fusiliers. He'd been shot in the right ankle, of all places, during the battle for Monte Cassino. 'Worse than Stalingrad,' the Judge would mutter, if anyone asked him about it, refusing to say anything more.

Passing under the thicket of overhanging fuchsia bushes at the corner of the drive, Roddy allowed his limp to become more pronounced, and he dragged his right foot a little too. The ghost-pain in his shattered ankle felt satisfyingly real. Funny how his father haunted parts of his body, thought Roddy, permitting himself a twisted smile. It was only when the old man died, 16 years ago last May, that he'd felt able to return to Honolulu, this time to stay for good.

The pebbles on the beach were slippery with algae, so Roddy stopped limping and began to walk normally again, watching his step. Terence followed gingerly, nails scrabbling for grip on the smooth, rounded stones. Roddy didn't have to walk across the beach to leave the island, he could have followed the drive until it reached the causeway. But this was the way he often went. His feet, acting of their own accord, took him to the exact spot where he needed to be.

This was where he'd seen her, that August night in 1975, the fiery red corona of her head rising fantastically above the bent thorn trees. A slim Roman candle in a shimmering dress, bare arms raised and swaying, firelight licking round her girlish shins. As he stared, she shrugged her shoulders and the dress disappeared, like magic. He'd been fifteen years old. The sight would never leave him.

Muffled whoops, clapping and cheers had woken him from a light sleep, shortly after midnight, and he knew it was the voices of the police protection squad. When the Judge was in residence, as he was at that time, the police parked their armoured grey Land Rovers on a flat stony outcrop at the far end of the beach, partly screened from the house by a windbreak of whitethorn. They would build a bonfire on the shore, as much to keep themselves occupied, Roddy supposed, as to keep themselves warm. The men seemed bored. Sometimes they threw bits of dried-out bladderwrack on to the fire, and the sharp pop of the pods exploding resounded like gunshots. Feeling shy and embarrassed, Roddy steered clear of them. His father had told him that they had installed hidden surveillance cameras in every room in the house, including Roddy's bedroom, as an additional security measure, but Roddy was sure that was just a tease. Well, almost sure.

Roddy's room was on the ground floor, in the south wing of the house, looking out towards the police encampment. When he had heard the commotion among the men, he got out of bed and gazed across the dark garden. What he witnessed made him gasp with wonder or horror; he didn't stop to think. He simply had to get closer, to make sense of what was happening, and to be able to see more. So he'd grabbed his dressing gown from the chair, knotted it hastily around his waist and climbed out of the window. The grass was cool and wet on his bare feet as he ran towards the whitethorns. Peering through the contorted branches, he felt the heat from the great bonfire strike him like a blow. Heard 'sha-la-la' crooning and a slow, suggestive drumbeat from a crackling radio. Saw Mummie, mother-naked, dancing on the roof of one of the police Land Rovers, her face a blur of giddy joy.

Chapter Six

Roddy's head was a jumble of other people's sayings. Picking up pace as he crossed the causeway, Terence pulling ahead on the lead, Roddy chanted an old favourite of Mummie's: 'I must, I must, I must improve my bust, my bust, my bust!' Crossing her arms, she would grab the inside of her elbows with each hand and squeeze sharply, causing her breasts to jump like frogs under her brown cashmere jumper. 'Don't stare, Roddy, it's rude,' she'd snap when she caught sight of him behind her in the mirror, toying with the amber beads on her dressing table. Mummie loved amber, she said it set off the copper highlights in her red hair. It was all very confusing because sometimes she seemed to want him to look at her, and even to sit on her knee while she told him her secrets, but sometimes she didn't, and Roddy was no good at telling the difference.

The Judge was a defiant atheist and an admirer of B.F. Skinner's behaviourism – particularly the idea that human beings were best understood through a system of reward and punishment. He was given to declaiming random bits of the Bible, thundering them out during dinner for some private amusement of his own. Roddy let one fly now, in a stentorian bellow: 'Which were born, not of *blood*, nor of the will of the *flesh*, nor of the will of *man* but of *GOD*!' The words were instantly swallowed up in the sea mist. Somewhere far out over the tidal flats, a seabird cried – a harsh, lonely sound – and then the soft silence closed in again.

That was the great thing about living on an island, thought Roddy. You could rave away like a lunatic as much as you liked, and nobody could hear you. But he was getting close to the mainland now, so it was time to go more carefully, and quietly.

The McQuistons were Roddy's nearest neighbours. They lived in a white cottage with a tin roof and red-painted window-frames, opposite the gate at the end of the Honolulu causeway. Set back from the road in its own small square of clipped grass, the house was blank-faced and plain. A satellite dish, cocked skywards against the stovepipe chimney, was the only visible adornment. Advancing towards the cottage, Roddy felt himself gripped by a renewed intensity of purpose; it came on as strong as hunger. But he took care to stroll casually, letting Terence linger over an interesting smell he'd discovered in the ditch. It must have been a particularly pungent one, because Terence paused to savour it, drooling and clacking his teeth together, as if chewing the scent to extract the full flavour.

'Come on, boy, that's enough, let's go,' murmured Roddy at last, keeping his voice low. He crossed the road and walked past the cottage, towards the little fir wood beyond. 'Just Mr Riseborough, taking his dog for an evening stroll,' he wanted the McQuistons to think, should any of them happen to look out as he went by. He kept his own eyes averted from the house.

Once he was inside the wood, the darkness was much denser. It was stuffy too, dry and resinous underfoot. Roddy quickly tied Terence's woven leather lead around a tree-trunk and tested the knot to check if it would hold. Terence sighed and sat down, accepting the inevitable, his tiny bat ears folded back with disapproval. 'Won't be long, sir,' Roddy whispered apologetically. 'You stay here and keep watch.'

The trees pressed in close and unfriendly as he forced his way through, and he had to duck under several low-hanging branches, but the floor of fallen fir needles muffled his steps more completely than the softest carpet slippers. When he arrived behind the McQuistons' cottage, he was certain that nobody knew he was there.

In the square of light from the kitchen window, close to the back door, Roddy could see three saucepans sitting on the grass. That was Joan McQuiston's doing, he knew. He'd seen her before, rushing down the steps with a smoking pan and ditching it with a sizzle on the lawn. She was forever burning things. The pan would stay there for days, filling up with rainwater, the charred contents still inside, until Joan eventually retrieved it, sluicing the blackened mess into the fir wood before she went back into the house. On one occasion, a blustery evening last February, she'd actually hit the tree behind which Roddy stood. His grey whipcord blazer, the one he liked to wear with a mauve handkerchief tucked carelessly into the top pocket, was still stippled with tiny grease spots from the splash. Somehow, he'd never found the opportunity to have it cleaned since then.

Monday night was the time to visit the McQuistons, because Monday night was bath night. He hadn't been there for months – not since he'd finally ended things with 'Chelle, in fact, back in the spring, but he was confident that the family's unbreakable routine would not have changed: dinner, dishes, bath time, bed. Always Joan's turn first, and then her daughter, Darlene, would go in afterwards, using the same water, topping it up with a fresh blast from the hot tap and lots more bubbles.

Darlene was growing up fast, she must be nearly seventeen now, Roddy told himself, though he knew her real age was fifteen, because he remembered her birth. A surprise late baby for Joan and Arthur, she'd been born the summer after the Judge died, the summer he came back to Honolulu. Still, he allowed himself these little delusions, they kept things somehow decent.

The McQuistons' bathroom was at the side of the cottage where the rubbish bins were kept. This was Roddy's customary hiding place. The sudden dash from the cover of the woods to the safe shadow of the bins was the only moment when he was fully exposed.

Afterwards, he crouched low, hands on thighs, placating the uproar in his chest with deep lungfuls of slightly foetid air. But he wasn't worried about his heart, he was superbly fit, ran five miles every other day, not a peck of fat on him. Roddy was proud of his hard, lean body in its close-fitting pink or lavender shirts, proud of his still-full head of hair, even though there were more grey threads than dark ones now. 'Silver fox,' he often whispered as he looked at himself admiringly in the full-length bedroom mirror. 'Silver fox.'

Tonight, he'd timed everything to perfection. The steam from Joan's bath was already misting the window with an enticing rosy glow when he arrived beside the bins. The larger pane on the left was frosted with a swirly *fleur-de-lys* pattern, but the narrower one on the right was plain glass. Roddy guessed that the smaller pane had been broken at some point and replaced with cheaper, ordinary glass; because the bathroom was so private, well removed from the road, frosting wasn't seen to be necessary. Fortunately, there wasn't a curtain either, probably for the same reason. As he waited, he heard the taps stop running.

Now there was no fear, no rush, only a delightfully buoyant sense of anticipation. Roddy knelt under the window, like a supplicant, and slowly raised his head above the sill. Frosted side first, of course - he wasn't entirely reckless. Yes, she was safely in the bath: he could make out her wavery shape, distorted by the patterned glass. Her head was immediately under the window, facing away from him. Staying on his knees, he shifted to the right, and looked through the clear glass at Joan McQuiston. Took her all in – lard-white stomach, sad tuft of greying pubic hair, vast sagging breasts.

It wasn't desire that drove him, obviously. Or at least not the ordinary sort. It was more like an overpowering urge to see into the private world of women, to get a glimpse of their real, hidden selves. He was fascinated by Joan's flesh, the way it quivered and undulated beneath the bathwater as she turned the page of the gossip magazine she was reading. She did not revolt him. He felt a remote sort of pity for her that wasn't so far away from his sympathy for slugs and snails, although perhaps less profound. He liked to see her things, too: a crumpled web of hair-net and two pink rollers by the sink, discarded pants and tights draped neatly over the bamboo chair. Her ample beige girdle. Soon she would sit up and wash herself, rubbing up a modest lather with a bar of pale green soap that was cracked down the middle and worn to a sliver. He waited avidly for that. The way she raised her arms to sponge her armpits was a poem: she did it so delicately, for such a large woman.

Joan stayed in the bath much longer than usual, and for once it seemed that Darlene was not coming to take her turn. Well, no real loss. There was something about the girl's brisk manner that alienated Roddy: the graceless way she whipped off her top and jeans and dumped them on the floor, right on top of the damp footprints Joan had left behind, or how she squirted in far too much lurid pink bubble liquid. The lovely, languorous movements that the mother made were entirely absent in the daughter. Where was the mystique, the womanliness? Her young body was all surface, it lacked any sense of suggestion. Truth be told, it was boring to watch her. For 20 minutes, she would lie inert like a floating log, listening to her music device through a pair of white earphones, then leap out again and towel off, not even rinsing or drying herself properly, Roddy would note fastidiously, observing the scurf of foam clinging to her sparse shoulders and small, unripe buttocks.

Normally Roddy sloped off again through the woods when bath time was over, after doing the initial dash across the lawn in reverse, but tonight he was struck by an impulse to peek at old Arthur, who was probably slumped over Sky Sports in the front room. Actually it had been a clear glimpse of Arthur's semi-prone form, flickering in the cold light of the television, as he drove home past the McQuistons' one night last November, that first gave Roddy the thrilling idea of spying on the old man's womenfolk. Arthur was a retired plumber who had been a moderately successful boxer in his youth, and he still had the wary gaze of a fighter, though he'd run to fat and his spine was buckled with what Roddy guessed must be Parkinson's disease.

It was much more risky to peep in at Arthur, Roddy knew, because he would have to break cover and walk round openly to the front of the cottage, in full view of the road. But the urge was upon him, and it would not be ignored. Just a little look, what harm could it do? To see Arthur, close up and unaware, without Arthur seeing him, that's what he wanted. And what Roddy wanted, he hardly ever denied himself.

Chapter Seven

In the event, it was disappointingly easy. He'd swiftly passed Joan and Arthur's bedroom, crunched once, twice, on the gravel path, and dropped down beneath the front room window. A glance over his shoulder: all serene. The road was empty, the potholes making indistinct black islands in the wet tarmac. The row of white-painted rocks that marked the boundary of the McQuistons' property looked like dirty lumps of snow. The cloud had lifted a little but the only lights Roddy could see were a cluster of pinpricks on the far side of the lough. That faint, high, soughing sound – eerie really, somehow unearthly, like a very distant choir of angels – was nothing to worry about: just the telegraph wires stirring in the soft night breeze.

Rising to a crouch, Roddy risked a sidelong peep, shielding himself behind the half-drawn curtain. The back of Arthur's bald head loomed out at him like a great white moon, inches from the glass, close enough for him to see a constellation of tiny pockmarks on the otherwise smooth skull. Roddy stepped back abruptly. His next peep was more cautious. He let barely a quarter of his right eyeball emerge from the shelter of the curtain.

Yes, there was Arthur, sitting with his back to the window, while opposite him, on the floor, sat Darlene, cross-legged, in furry purple pyjamas with white polka-dots, casually nursing a family-size packet of crisps. She looked different, younger, with her clothes on, Roddy noted. Between them on a low table was some kind of game with counters and a brightly chequered board. The room was harshly illuminated by an overhead light in a flounced satin shade, and the giant television in the corner was switched off.

Another quarter of an eyeball. Aha, look, they were playing Snakes and Ladders, exactly the same version he'd had as a boy in the sixties! He could see the familiar diamond-patterned serpents, lascivious forked tongues flickering at the pictures of children stealing birds' eggs from the nest or skipping heedlessly into the road, about to be crushed to death by a passing Morris Minor. Roddy couldn't remember anyone ever playing the game with him, but he'd devised a clever way of playing against himself. Forgetting to be careful now, he leaned in eagerly to watch.

Arthur reached for the brown cylindrical dice shaker, which was sitting on the edge of the board, on square 40, above a good little girl helping an injured cat. His big hand shook helplessly over the cup, then made a fruitless grab, knocking it down and spilling the two dice on to the floor. His head sagged miserably beneath the thick, ruined shoulders. Darlene immediately jumped up and retrieved both dice from under the table, scooping them neatly into the brown cup. Then she pressed the cup into the palm of Arthur's right hand, closing her small fingers around his, and saying something to him that Roddy couldn't hear. With Darlene's help, Arthur shook the dice and tipped them out on to the board. Two sixes.

Watching them together, Roddy was seized by a sudden wave of longing so powerful that his knees almost gave way. Unshed tears burned in the backs of his eyes and, absurdly, his nose began to run. Inside the house, Darlene smiled up into her father's face, a gap-toothed grin, full of bright, uncomplicated love. Nobody had looked at Roddy like that in his entire life.

Then she stared directly into Roddy's wondering gaze and her mouth changed shape.

Fuck, fuck, *fuck*!

Roddy leapt away from the window in confusion, brushing his trousers, wiping roughly at his nose. He was halfway across the McQuistons' lawn, when the front door opened and Arthur burst out, stumbling a little on the metal-rimmed mat.

'Who is that? Who's there?' A querulous old man, trying desperately for long-lost force.

Roddy stopped and turned back toward the house. 'It's only me, Arthur,' he called. 'Roddy Riseborough. My – my dog's gone on the run. Stupid wee bastard took off on me and I saw him head up past your place. I was just taking a look around, but there's no sign of him. Sorry to bother you like this, Arthur. I know it's late.'

Arthur stood stooped in the warm light from the doorway, assimilating this information, his hands fluttering uncontrollably around him like heavy, meaty moths.

'You've lost your dog, you say, Mr Riseborough?' he said slowly.

Roddy prayed to a God he didn't believe in that it was too dark for Arthur to see the wet patches on his trousers. What had that little bitch Darlene said when she saw him peering through the window?

'Yes, he charges off like that sometimes,' said Roddy, as levelly as possible. His voice sounded well-modulated and authoritative compared to Arthur's, and that was all to the good. 'I'll check the woods; he might have gone in there after foxes.'

In a moment of inspiration, he suddenly shouted, 'Terence? Terence!' Tied to his distant tree, Terence responded with a volley of high-pitched barks.

'There he is!' Roddy exclaimed. 'Excuse me, Arthur, I'll head on and grab him before he runs off again. Apologies once more for disturbing you.'

Shame. It was hot, unbearable shame that pursued Roddy down the road, dragging a chilly and reluctant Terence behind him, shame that lashed his back as he crossed the causeway, forcing him into a half-sobbing run, shame that made him fling Terence roughly into the kitchen and slam the door on his bug-eyed, reproachful face.

In the great room, the fire was almost out. The half-carved wooden bird still protruded from the barely glowing embers, charred but intact. Roddy seized the poker and flicked the bird on to the hearthstone, where it lay like a sorry little malformed corpse. Then he beat it and beat it and beat it until it was splintered into hundreds of tiny shards.

~

Hours later Roddy was sitting up in bed, wearing only a pyjama top and a pair of reading glasses, with a mug of whiskey-spiked Ovaltine at his side. He was resolutely refusing to think about the McQuistons. That was over, finished, done. No more Joan, no more Darlene. He could never go back again. It was like a bereavement, he thought – then snorted with contempt at his own histrionics.

The clock radio was set for 6:40 a.m., and he was making himself go through work emails on his phone.

The barrage of messages was relentless. A month ago, he had taken the experimental step of deleting his emails *en masse*, both read and unread, though mostly unread. His over-stuffed inbox, full of warning flags and forests of red exclamation marks, was suddenly, wonderfully clear. But the liberating purge meant that ten days later, he'd missed an important meeting about falling circulation figures with Sean and Mitchell Wallace, the Galway-born brothers who owned *The Sentinel*. Mitch, in particular, wasn't the type to forget a slight like that. Oh, he'd come rolling in, all ruddy-faced smiles, punching Roddy on the arm with a 'how-are-ya-pal?,' like a cheerful beef sausage in a suit. But his suspicious little eyes were always darting here, there, everywhere, seeking out trouble.

Worse, Jacqueline Shields-Maguire, his deputy editor – strongly fragrant, ostentatiously capable, with a supercilious smile that made Roddy want to wring her throat – had stepped in when he couldn't be found (on a whim, he'd gone to Millisle to view a motorbike for sale – a gorgeous 1981 Suzuki Kantana, in marvellous condition for its age), and she attended the meeting in Roddy's place. And I bet she made a damn fine job of it too, he thought bitterly. Roddy had come to *The Sentinel* in 1999, after twenty bizarre, squalid and terrifying years in the Royal Ulster Constabulary. The flatulent stench of frightened men – that's what he remembered most clearly about his time in the force, the sickly, all-pervasive gut-reek.

'Roderick, are you insane,' the Judge had said, when Roddy announced that he was joining the police, straight out of school, instead of going to university. It wasn't a question. 'Sergeant Thanatos', the Judge took to calling him, with a snigger and a mocking salute, which perplexed Roddy until he discovered that Thanatos meant death-wish.

His own deeper motives were initially obscure to him. Aged nineteen, he was attracted to the smart uniform, with its harp and crown on the lapel, and he liked the idea of avenging evil through the officially sanctioned use of submachine guns. But Roddy came to see that his father was not wrong. And although he rose to the modest rank of Detective Inspector, his face – or more accurately, his voice, and his privileged background – ensured that the force was never going to be a comfortable fit. He knew that he was filed under posh, bookish and almost certainly gay.

One small off-duty perk of the job was hobnobbing with the journalists who gathered in the bar of the Metropolitan Hotel, among them the Judge's cousin, Carson Carruthers. Roddy liked talking to the hacks, who were always eager for inside information, especially concerning the clandestine activities of Special Branch. When Carson became editor of *The Sentinel*, Roddy realised that this could be his passport out of the force. Carson took a qualified punt on him as an investigative reporter, and it was immediately obvious that this was what Roddy should have done in the first place. He excelled at challenging the murderous, the pious and the corrupt, even if he said so himself. Promotions came swiftly and often. When Carson experienced a massive coronary at his desk in 2005, Roddy was catapulted into the old man's chair before the imprint of his corpulent rear had even left the leather.

But then everything went fuzzy around the edges, and he realised that he'd left the great change in his life too late. Peace made the place soft and boring. Now

Roddy was expected to run stories about the opening of glossy new clothing stores, or the benefits of mindfulness for schoolchildren, and to respond rapidly to trends on Twitter. Roddy despised all forms of social media. *The Sentinel* that he presided over today had become a vacuous, tawdry version of its old, dignified self. He was glad Carson wasn't around to see it.

Roddy had just finished the last email, placating a tortoise-faced male columnist who was upset about the use of an unflattering photo byline, when a new message announced itself with a bright electronic chirrup.

He sighed. Who in hell's name was emailing him at a quarter to two on a Tuesday morning? Leni Moffett. Never heard of her. 'Subject: PARENTING FEATURE??' Unnecessarily shouty capitalisation and two question marks – Christ, this was precisely the kind of infantile disrespect for proper punctuation that made him gnash his teeth in despair.

He scanned the email. Wittering on about the best way to bring up baby, another one of these girls who thinks she's the only woman ever to have given birth. Not a badly written pitch though, to be fair. Jacqueline would probably love it. Well, tough shit, Jackie, because you're not going to see it. He tapped the lidded red dustbin icon on his screen and the email detached itself like a ripped page and disappeared into the trash.

But wait – what was that whizzing past at the bottom, a photograph? Roddy hit the 'Undo Delete' button and the message re-materialised. Ah yes, there they were: the preachy young Moffetts and their overindulged sprog. He stared at the image, took a sip of by now unpleasantly cold Ovaltine, and zoomed in on Leni's pale face and her copper-red hair, studying her closely for a while. Then he read the message again, more carefully this time. His finger hovered once more over the delete button. But then, on an obscure impulse, he hit reply.

Chapter Eight

Leni woke up stiff and disoriented. Groggily, she reached out for Ann and surged with sudden panic when she felt the blank space beside her, before subsiding with a groan beneath the covers again. She'd remembered why she ended up sleeping alone, on the nursery futon. Patti was coming to stay.

It must have been early because it was still dark outside. No thrum of traffic yet, just the odd fluting note from a nameless city bird and the distant bleep-bleep-bleep of a van reversing. In the big bedroom, muffled slightly by the closed door, she could hear Ann carolling her favourite song.

'Bananas in p'jamas, a-coming down de stairs, in pai-yers. . . you sing too, Daddy! Sing, Daddy! Daddy, sing!' Theo mumbled something unintelligible in reply before joining in with the tune, as Ann had commanded.

What time was it? Keeping the duvet swaddled around her, Leni felt about under the pillow until she found her phone. It was 5.35 a.m. Jesus. That meant she'd only had three hours sleep, not nearly enough to cope with a whole day of activities with Ann.

Then she saw that there was an email message waiting for her, from Mr Riseborough. Leni pulled the phone close to her face, the light from the screen blinding her for a second or two. Received at 1.59 a.m., barely fifteen minutes after she'd sent her own message.

Leni felt a warm pulse of pleasure. To get a response from the editor so quickly was very encouraging indeed.

Wait, don't read too much into it, she cautioned herself: he's a newspaper man, they work all sorts of unsociable hours, maybe even all night. He was probably sitting at his computer when her email came in. Still, the speed of the reply was satisfying; it made her feel validated, somehow – she had called out, into the unknown, and her voice had been heard.

But the editor's reply was curt to the point of rudeness. There was no greeting or acknowledgment, just a set of instructions. 'Write me 1,400 words on this subject and I'll consider it,' he said. 'Don't send the piece by email. When you're ready, contact my PA. Provide her with your full contact details and make an appointment to see me, then bring it by hand. I prefer to read hard copy when I'm evaluating new writers.'

Brusque as it was, the directive worked on Leni like a whip. She got up immediately and slipped downstairs to fetch her laptop, avoiding the creaky board on the top stair so that Theo and Ann wouldn't hear and realise she was awake.

Safely back in bed again, with the nursery door closed firmly behind her, she began to write.

~

For almost a week, Leni seized every spare moment to work on the article for Mr Riseborough. She couldn't get much done during the day, because of Ann, but the second that dinner was over, and Theo took Ann up for her bath, she opened the laptop at the kitchen table. As the week went on, she didn't even stop to clear away the dishes first, just pushed them aside and started typing, picking up where she'd last left off.

The first two drafts were no good, far too vague and simplistic, almost child-like, so she scrapped the whole thing and began all over again. The new version was an improvement, but Leni wasn't entirely happy. It was so difficult to get the right tone: she wanted to show that she had experience, she knew what she was talking about, but without coming across as arrogant, as if she had all the answers. At the same time, she had to be authoritative, and sound confident and in control, otherwise why would anyone else, including Mr Riseborough, be interested in what she had to say?

Theo reminded her that there was no rush with the article now, since Patti would soon be paying them rent, but she just nodded distractedly and kept on typing. She was driven; inspired; she could think of nothing else.

The momentum generated by the writing spilled over into the rest of Leni's daily life. It gave new energy to each of her little interactions with Ann, and boosted her over that treacherous, weary late-afternoon slump before Theo got home from work. Everything seemed to mean so much more now that it was part of a narrative she was telling: the story of how to be a good mother. Best of all, this new sense of purpose carried her through several long phone calls with her own mother.

Once it was agreed that she was coming to stay at Isthmus Avenue, as a paying guest, Patti wanted to have endless conversations about the practicalities of the move. What was the name of the best local doctor, where could she buy colloidal silver for her sinuses, how could her personal items be safely shipped, door-to-door? Leni had said nothing to Patti about the article she was writing, but the fact of it sustained her, like a secret amulet in her pocket.

At last, the piece was as close to perfect as Leni could make it. She called Mr Riseborough's personal assistant, explained who she was, and asked for an appointment with the editor. The assistant put her on hold while she checked his availability. In a few seconds, she was back on the line. Could Leni come in at 9.30 tomorrow morning? Yes? Fine. Mr Riseborough would see her then.

The meeting was far sooner than she had anticipated; she thought it would be days, if not weeks, before Mr Riseborough found time to fit her into what must be a fantastically busy schedule. She realised, too, that she'd agreed to the appointment without stopping to think what she'd do with Ann, and that sent her into a further spiral of stress. But Theo told her not to worry, he was happy to take Ann with him to work for the day. Special circumstances, he smiled. He was sure he could manage this once.

Next morning, as Theo drove her into town in the family Skoda, Leni felt weak with anticipation and nerves. Ann sat in the back, strapped into her car seat, wearing a pair of red wellies and brandishing a plastic trowel. She kept kicking the passenger seat, which made Leni want to scream in irritation, but she controlled herself: it wasn't the child's fault, she was just excited to be going to visit Daddy's garden – who could blame her?

When Theo dropped her off outside *The Sentinel* offices, at the corner of Linenhall Square, Leni stood in the street for a moment, trying to collect her wits. She craned her neck and looked up at the ruddy red sandstone building, standing tall and imposing against the blue morning sky. Its arched windows were crowned with dolphins and mermaids, sea-monsters and sphinxes, and it rose storey after storey to a single turret, which jutted out like the prow of a ship. The soot-blackened grandeur of the place only increased her apprehension, but she made herself climb the granite steps and go inside.

Even though Leni was ten minutes early, Mr Riseborough's assistant, Pam, was already waiting for her in reception. Pam turned out to be one of those brisk, blonde, hard-faced women that Leni both feared and secretly admired: she wished she had their blunt confidence. In the lift, Pam jabbed the button for the fifth floor with a red manicured claw, then stood in impregnable silence as they went up. Leni longed for a friendly word or two, but Pam didn't seem to feel the need to make casual conversation.

The lift opened on to a large open-plan office, littered with discarded takeaway cups. Important-looking people, mostly women, were striding about barking into their mobile phones, or battering away with great intensity at their computer keyboards. There was a jangling aroma of perfume and banana peel, with an unmistakeable under-note of used gym gear. A huge banner hung overhead, emblazoned with the familiar *Sentinel* logo: a stylised helmet of a Roman centurion, with a pair of frowning eyes peering through the visor. 'We Guard the Truth': that was the paper's motto, printed below the masthead every day.

Pam cut a fast path through the middle of the office, and Leni followed as best she could, awkwardly stepping over open boxes of printer paper and trailing electrical wires, squeezing past people having loud, stand-up conversations about God knows what, but it all sounded terribly urgent. Her bottom bumped against someone and she apologised, blushing, and rushed on.

Pam came to a halt in the far corner of the newsroom, beside a small set of stairs recessed into the wall. At the top of the stairs was a narrow mahogany door marked with the word 'Editor' in faded gilt paint.

'Go on in,' said Pam. 'He's expecting you.'

When Leni entered the room, Mr Riseborough was standing alone at the window, staring out. He wasn't as tall as she'd imagined he'd be, but even with his back turned he gave off a feeling of great energy. When he swung around, his expression was strangely sombre, as if somebody had died. He didn't speak.

He walked behind her and closed the door, then sat down at his desk, motioning for her to sit too. Leni perched on the edge of the chair he'd indicated, waiting to be told what to do. He stretched out a palm expectantly, still saying nothing. Leni was confused. Did he want to shake hands? Then she realised that it was her article that he wanted. She took it out of its plastic envelope, hoping that her sweaty fingers didn't mark the pages, and passed it across the desk. He placed the article squarely in front of him and began to read.

The minutes went by. She wished she could see his expression, to try to guess what he was thinking. But his head was buried deep in his hands, strong fingers pushing up tufts of hair like floppy horns. Every so often, he exhaled sharply with an impatient-sounding sigh, which did nothing to reassure her. How long could it take to read two-and-a-half pages? Since she'd given him the piece, he hadn't lifted his eyes once.

Leni looked around the editor's office, trying to distract herself. It was an odd shape, almost circular, but not quite. One wall was curved, with three ornate arched windows, and the early sun was slanting in, making a lacy, quivering pattern on the polished floor. There was a round pitched ceiling, very high, with a copper lantern suspended from a long chain. This room must be inside the turret, she realised, the one she'd seen from the street, right at the top of the building.

With its dark wood panelling, and rows of laden bookshelves, the office felt serious, austere, a world away from the hectic newsroom. Leni could imagine it belonging to a professor, or a bishop. There was a stuffed pheasant on the desk, its feathers dusty and faded. The bird's cold glass eye seemed to be fixed on her, as she sat there, waiting to be judged.

'Good,' said Mr Riseborough abruptly, looking up at last.

'Oh!' she exclaimed, flustered and relieved. 'Thanks, I'm really pleased you like—'

'But it could be better. An awful lot better.'

'Oh.'

'Yes, I'm afraid so. There's no doubt you have talent as a writer – raw natural talent. I caught a few tantalising glimpses of it. But it's been maimed, somewhere along the line. University, probably. That's usually where it happens. Did you go to university?'

'I did, yes, I – I came top of my year in English, actually. I won a prize.'

'A prize?' He made it sound like an embarrassing affliction. 'Ah well, there you have it. That's what's done the damage. Such a shame.'

'I'm sorry,' Leni faltered. 'I don't understand.'

Mr Riseborough took off his glasses and fixed her with an open, frank stare. Struggling to meet it, Leni felt exposed to a cool and unsparing intelligence. His eyes were seawater grey, melancholy, but the way the lids sagged at the corners gave him a rueful, wistful expression that was not unkind.

'What's happened is that you've been taught to over-write,' he said. 'To use ten words, when one precise, well-chosen word would be ten times – a hundred times – better. To say 'notwithstanding' and 'moreover' and 'nevertheless', and write sentences that go on for a century-and-a-half, until everyone's given up reading or died of boredom. To say 'narrative' and 'discourse', when you mean 'story' and 'ideas'. Hang on, I'll give you an example.' Replacing his glasses, he picked up Leni's manuscript and riffled through the pages.

'Ah yes, here's a howler: "Furthermore, while co-sleeping may appear to present a dichotomy between the needs of the parents and the benefit to the child, I contend that prioritising co-sleeping is ultimately beneficial to the family as a whole." I mean, yuck! That's just nasty. You see?' Mr Riseborough swept his glasses off again with a look of sorrow. His tired face was all bone, a series of intersecting planes and angles – jaw, nose, forehead – barely softened by the boyish fall of steely hair over his raised right eyebrow. 'I wish I'd got hold of you at seventeen, before they did this to you,' he said, with sympathy.

Leni was floored. Or maybe flattened was a better word for the way she felt at that moment. Flummoxed. Flabbergasted. Her brain automatically suggested a scrolling list of alliterations, as if trying to prove its nimble capability and worth. Mostly, though, she just felt ashamed. Nobody, going right back to her earliest schooldays, had criticised her talent for language, or at least never with such casual brutality. When Mrs

Magowan, her third-form English teacher, had questioned whether Leni's impressive analysis of *Dr Jekyll and Mr Hyde* could possibly be all her own work (which it was), Granny June had stalked into school, frosted helmet of blow-dried hair adding inches to her tiny height, cat's-eye spectacles glaring, and demanded that her granddaughter receive an apology. This Leni subsequently was given, in an awkward private encounter with Mrs Magowan, along with a superlative mark for the essay.

But the editor was waiting for a response. Leni nodded, her eyes fixed downward on her hands, which were holding on to each other for comfort. 'Yes. Yes, I see,' she said. What made it even worse was that she'd never tried so hard or cared so much about a piece of writing as she did about this one.

'Don't misunderstand me,' said Mr Riseborough, in his silvery, cultured, matter-of-fact voice. 'I could print this article tomorrow and most people wouldn't even notice what was wrong with it. That's because most people are thick. They're impressed by long, fancy words. Never mind the quality, feel the width. But it wouldn't be fair to you, if I were to put this in the paper. It would be rewarding you for something you don't deserve.'

He picked up the pages, gave them a brisk double tap to align them, then stretched back in his chair and silently held out the skimpy sheaf towards her.

Leni rose awkwardly and stretched over the pheasant's head to receive it. But just as her fingertips touched the rejected manuscript, he snatched it away.

'Wait,' he said, raising a hand. 'I have a better idea.'

Mr Riseborough turned the pages on their side and tore them right through the middle, reshuffled the pieces and tore them again. He did this twice more, then tossed the confetti of small squares into the air and laughed as they fluttered down.

'There.' He grinned at her with sudden intimacy, right eyebrow dancing merrily, as if the two of them had just shared a private joke. 'That's gone. Good riddance. Now we can start again.'

Chapter Nine

What Mr Riseborough went on to offer her was so surprising that Leni had trouble taking it in. It seemed that he wanted her to produce a thousand words of writing every week and then bring the piece to him, in person, for critique and evaluation.

'But what . . . what would I write about?'

'You. I want you to write with complete honesty about yourself: your innermost thoughts, observations, reflections, encounters with the people around you. Write from the heart, by way of your mind. Really go for it, don't hold anything back. Show me exactly what it's like to be you, a twenty-four-year-old woman, living right now, in this time, in this place. Give me your unique, unadulterated perspective. Think of it as a kind of learning journal, or a diary.'

'And this wouldn't be for publication in the paper?'

'No, no. It would be an entirely private, confidential arrangement between me and you. I'm not expecting you to do the work for free, of course. It will take time and effort. That's why I'm willing to pay you a hundred pounds for each instalment.' Mr Riseborough looked calmly at her across the broad reaches of his desk.

'But . . . why?' asked Leni. 'Sorry, I'm being really stupid here, but I'm not sure what the point of—'

'The point is this,' interrupted Mr Riseborough. 'You are clearly a writer of talent, but that talent has been criminally warped and squandered. My aim is to help you, first to recover that lost native ability, and then to refine it, through a process of emotional and intellectual honesty. A reprogramming exercise, in essence. But I warn you, these diary entries – if we can call them that – they may not be easy to write. And I won't let you get away with any – how shall I put it? – bullshit. For instance, I don't want another preachy propaganda sheet about this childcare business. I want to read the truth about *you*, pared to the bone, and expressed in precise, powerful, well-chosen words. That's what I'll be expecting.'

Leni shook her head wonderingly, pushing a loose lock of hair out of her eyes. 'Goodness. Thank you . . . I think. It's just – look, the thing is, I'm not sure my life would be interesting enough. To write about, I mean. I don't *do* anything except look after my daughter. And that's important, of course, it's the most important job of all, raising a child. It's just that, sometimes, it can be a bit . . . well, a bit boring.'

A hot clash of cymbals sounded deep in her chest as soon as she spoke the words. She'd just admitted to this complete stranger what she couldn't admit to herself. The reality: that her effortful, performative, Ann-centred days were often rigid with tedium.

'It doesn't matter,' said Mr Riseborough. 'That's the test, you see. A good writer should be able to make any subject compelling. Origami, eel-trapping, astral physics – anything. This is your opportunity to show me what you're truly capable of. And then, when you've made sufficient progress, we might start letting you do some work for us.'

'Writing for *The Sentinel*, you mean?'

Mr Riseborough nodded. 'So, what do you say? Are you willing to accept the challenge?'

Leni paused. Her normal impulse, when she came across the strange and unknown, was to demur, prevaricate, shying away for fear of pain or disappointment. Experience had taught her that. 'Yes, I am,' she said. The words popped out by themselves, leaving her blinking in shock.

'Great,' said Mr Riseborough. He leapt up, strode across the room and swept open the door, then stood there waiting. It was an unmistakable gesture of dismissal. Wrong-footed again, Leni fumbled confusedly with her bag, which had tipped over and become trapped under one leg of the chair, pinned down by her own weight. It took a few inelegant bounces to tug it out. She was pink-cheeked and a little dizzy when she stood up.

The editor gave her an ironic salute as she walked past him at the door. 'This is a rescue mission, Leni,' he said. 'We're going to set you free. See you next Tuesday. Same time, same place.'

Leni returned her visitor's pass to reception and slowly descended the granite steps to the street. Standing on the pavement, she felt trance-like, unreal. People bustled past in the smoky September sunshine, flowing around her as though she was a rock in the middle of a river. She had no idea what to do or where to go. She hadn't thought past her meeting with Mr Riseborough, and now that it was over, she was purposeless.

Home, she supposed. There was no other reason to stay in town.

She crossed the road and walked towards the Chester Street bus stop, to wait for the Number 75, which would take her back to Isthmus Avenue. But once she reached the stop, something made her wander away again, back in the direction of *The Sentinel* offices.

She realised that she didn't want to go home, not yet anyway. The feeling was disorienting. For Leni, home was everything, and without the familiar pull of its orbit she was adrift. There was a blank. What *did* she want to do? After the encounter with Mr Riseborough, her head felt like an old rug which had been seized, shaken and beaten to get the dust out of it.

A new cafe had opened where the Woolworths store used to be. In the absence of any better plan, Leni went inside. There was a long communal trestle table with plug sockets down the middle, and rows of mismatched school chairs painted turquoise and red. Leni slipped into a seat at the end furthest away from the only other customers – two young, bearded men, vaguely simian in appearance, buried deep in their MacBooks. When the waiter appeared, she asked for a hot chocolate. Something sweet, she thought. Something I wouldn't normally order.

She wondered how Ann was getting on at the garden. Her precious little girl! Leni felt her breasts tingle and fill with milk, as they often did when she thought of Ann. The bond between them was so deep, it was a real, physical part of her. She hoped that Theo would be able to manage the bottles of expressed breast milk she'd packed in the cool bag, together with Ann's lunch. Yes, of course he would. Theo was so capable, much more than Leni, really.

And there was no need to worry about the ex-offenders. Everything was totally supervised, Theo had reassured her, and actually they were quite a decent bunch of guys, more victims of circumstance than hard-core criminals. There weren't any murderers or paedophiles among them, were they? She'd had to ask.

But Theo said definitely not, and she knew she could believe him.

Leni suspected that Theo intended the child-free day as some kind of respite for her, maybe even a small consolation prize for agreeing to Patti's extended stay. Though he knew better than to put it that way, because Leni would adamantly deny that time away from Ann, on her own, was something she would ever crave or consider a treat.

And yet here she was, alone and unencumbered. No responsibilities, no sticky little hands in her hair. For the first time since Ann was born, she had hours and hours all to herself.

While she was waiting for the hot chocolate to arrive, Leni pulled her phone out of her bag. She considered texting Theo but then decided against it. She was nowhere near ready to explain what had happened with Mr Riseborough. Instead, she opened her Gmail account, which was one of several places where she'd carefully saved a copy of her article. She needed to read it again in the light of what he'd said. Was it really just poorly written propaganda?

As she re-read, Leni didn't think it was as bad as all that. But recalling the editor's sceptical expression, she felt embarrassed about the eager, undeniably evangelical tone of the piece. She'd been so keen to sound grown-up and well-informed – not hopelessly young and clueless – that she'd overdone the weighty, academic-sounding jargon. That part was true.

An echo of the shame she'd felt in Mr Riseborough's office shuddered through her, but this time it caught fire and flamed into righteous anger.

These weird remedial lessons he proposed – why

exactly had she agreed to them? What did he think she was, some kind of special needs case?

The unbelievable arrogance of the man.

And the bossy, dictatorial way he'd spoken to her. Bombarding her with insults masquerading as compliments, and compliments hiding behind insults, until she didn't know which way was up.

And then actually ripping up her work, destroying it, right in front of her? What kind of person behaves like that?

The waiter arrived with the cup of hot chocolate. It had a pool of proper cream, not the squirty stuff, floating on top. Leni put down her phone and took a sip. Oh, delicious. The contrast between the thick warm chocolate and the coolness of the cream was wonderful.

It had been years and years since she'd tasted hot chocolate. Saturday morning swimming lessons – goodness, yes, that must be the last time. Shivering with damp, chlorinated hair by the drinks machine, the thin stream of brown liquid draining into the cardboard cup, and then that first quick gulp, scalding, but comforting too, because it meant that swimming, with all its floundering, eye-stinging terror, was over for another week.

This luscious drink was nothing like the machine-made kind, but it had a similar effect on her mood. By the time she finished it, using a teaspoon to scoop up the last chocolaty dregs from the bottom of the cup, she was determined to make the most of her one day of freedom.

Chapter Ten

After a dreamy hour spent in the second-hand bookshop on South Street – the luxury of being able to linger over the shelves, browsing without interruption – Leni decided to take herself out for lunch. She went to Koko's, a popular Vietnamese restaurant near City Hall, where she and Theo – joined, of course, by Ann – had celebrated their second anniversary in the spring.

Koko's was busy, as usual, but the waitress was kind and found a spot for her at the bar, setting a bamboo place mat and bringing a carafe of iced water. Leni preferred sitting there, facing away from everyone else – it made her feel less conspicuously solitary. It would have been nice if she had someone to eat with. Never mind, she thought, I'm perfectly capable of enjoying my own company.

When Ann was born, she'd become quite close to a couple of the younger women in the mother and baby group at the Ormonde Road library, but then they'd gone back to work after their maternity leave and Leni had lost touch with them. Now her only friends were Facebook friends, living elsewhere, immersed in their far-flung, free-wheeling lives. Cara McCullough was working for a PR company in London, and Leni was familiar with every aspect of Cara's feverishly Instagrammed world. Although she suspected that the minutely documented parade of images – launches, openings, riverboat parties – was largely curated, an elaborate show designed to impress, it didn't stop Leni struggling sometimes with quite painful pangs of envy. It was ridiculous of her. Despite the dreadful thing she'd said to Mr Riseborough about her life being boring – oh, Ann, I'm sorry! – Leni knew that she was incredibly lucky to be so blessed.

After a lunch of prawn bao buns and jasmine tea, she was ready to head for home, maybe for a nice snooze on the bed. Besides, Ted would need to be let out for a pee, there was only so long that his ancient bladder could hold out. Goodness, yes – it was five past two, the poor old boy would be bursting. Better get a move on.

But when she came out of the restaurant, she stopped short. There, parked on the double yellow lines, was a DeLorean.

Leni was thrilled. She loved DeLoreans. It was nothing to do with the souped-up, flux-capacitator nonsense of the *Back to the Future* films. She just thought they were incredibly sexy – low and sinister and alluring, everything a sports car should be. She'd been amazed when she discovered that they'd been made right here in Belfast, years ago, during the Troubles. The only one that Leni had seen before was in a museum.

This DeLorean was empty, no sign of its owner. It looked like a squat steel spaceship, poised for a zip around the stars. She ran a hand along its flank, expecting cold metal, but the car was warm from the sun. She imagined opening the gull-wing door, sliding in and bombing off to another existence, fully encased and powerful in her stainless steel Exocet missile.

She stroked the DeLorean once more before she walked away. When she took a peek behind her, she was almost surprised to see the car still parked there on the double yellows, defying the law. Part of her thought it might have disappeared.

By the time she reached the bus stop, it had started to rain, but in less than a minute the Number 75 arrived, so she didn't get very wet. As the bus chugged past *The Sentinel* offices, she looked up at Mr Riseborough's turret, blurred by jerkily descending raindrops. She remembered him tearing her article in half, and found herself smiling. Suddenly it all seemed richly absurd.

Certainly, he was a very odd man, no doubt about it. But although he'd scorned her writing, he'd seen great promise as well – 'raw natural talent', was that what he said? She wished she could recall the exact words he'd used, so she could commit them to memory. He must have meant it, because he was taking such a personal interest in helping her improve – and he was even going to pay her.

She had Mr Riseborough to thank, too, for today's unexpected holiday. It would never have happened if it wasn't for him.

~

'Well? Any news?' asked Theo, struggling through the door with Ann and her enormous denim changing bag in his arms. It was exactly 6.00 p.m., the time he'd said they would be home. Normally, Leni welcomed Theo's total predictability, but today she felt a prickle of unfair irritation. Both he and Ann looked damp, bright-eyed and exhausted, and Ann's neat topknot had obviously come down and been re-tied in a loose, lopsided sprout above her right ear. Ann reached instantly for Leni, both arms stuck out straight and tiny fingers semaphoring urgently, bottom lip trembling a little from the intensity of the long, unfamiliar day.

'Hello, my Baba.' Leni held her daughter close, breathing in Ann's sweet, rainy smell. Her breasts purred in satisfaction, heavy and content. She had a fleeting impulse to lie down on the floor like an animal and let Ann climb on to her chest to suckle. 'I'll give her a quick feed before dinner,' she told Theo. 'It'll be another ten minutes before it's ready. I made that spinach and cheese thing you like. The Nigella one.'

Theo looked at her questioningly as he pulled off his muddy boots, standing on one foot at a time, and dropping them into the willow basket that Leni had provided for that exact purpose. 'So, what did Mr Riseborough say? Did he agree to publish your article?'

'No. He didn't.' Leni gave a regretful half-shrug. Ann, balanced squarely on her hip, kicked both legs energetically to dislodge her own wellies, and they fell on the tiled floor with a double bump.

'Aw no, Len. Seriously? The man must be mad. That was a fantastic piece of writing, even I could see that. And you worked so hard on it.'

'I know, I know.'

'To be honest, when I didn't hear from you today, I wondered if it hadn't gone well. I mean, I thought you'd text or call or something if—'

'Yeah, sorry. I just didn't feel able to—'

'No, no, don't worry, I didn't mean you should have got in touch – it's fine, you deserve a bit of time to yourself. I'm just so disappointed for you.'

'Thanks, T.'

'Though at least we don't have to worry about the money – that's some comfort,' said Theo. 'You know. What with Patti coming. I mean, it would have been far worse if we were desperate for the cash, right?'

'Well, that's the thing actually. I *am* going to be earning money,' Leni announced, a little defiantly.

'What? How come? I thought you said—'

'Mr Riseborough made me a special offer. I'm going to write an article every week and I'll get paid £100 for each one.'

'Leni! That's wonderful news!' Theo threw his arms around her and Ann. 'I'm so proud of you,' he said, mouth muffled in Leni's hair. 'My God, writing for *The Sentinel* every week! Remember you said it wasn't possible? But I knew it, I knew you could do it.'

Ann reached up and patted his cheek. 'Dada, my Dada,' she crooned happily, her equilibrium restored.

'We've got to celebrate, Len,' Theo said. 'It's a special occasion, we should go out and do something. Hey, listen, do you fancy going to Koko's for dinner? You can put the spinach thing in the freezer, can't you?'

Leni disentangled herself from the family hug. 'Hang on a minute. It's not exactly the way you think, T.'

It was a sort of training scheme, she explained to Theo, which was being offered because she wasn't a qualified journalist. Pride, or some other instinct, made her leave out the worst parts of Mr Riseborough's criticism. She described how she'd be paid for one practice article every week, as a kind of maintenance allowance, while she was undergoing the training. Then, once she had reached her targets, she could start contributing to the paper. It might take a little while, she said, since media work was very different from writing essays at university. Leni was conscious of trying to make it all sound formal, measured and predictable, not – as she half-suspected – sudden, spontaneous and highly irregular.

'Right, no, I get it,' said Theo, nodding enthusiastically. 'But it's a great opportunity, Len. And the editor wouldn't have suggested enrolling you for this training scheme if he didn't think you were well worth it.'

Theo, naturally enough, seemed to assume that it wasn't Mr Riseborough who would be delivering the training and Leni, still acting on unexamined instinct, did not correct him.

In the kitchen, the oven timer went off with a clear, cheerful 'ding!' The house was filled with the wholesome scent of baked breadcrumbs.

'Let's eat here tonight,' said Leni. 'Just the three of us, at home together. Honestly, I'd like that better than anything else.'

It was Theo's night for the futon. Leni was lying beside Ann, drifting on the blurred edge of consciousness, when her phone buzzed on the bedside table. She picked it up blearily: *23.37*. A text message, from an unknown number: *Thank you for today.*

Leni stared at the words. It must be a mistake, she thought. Then she tapped back: *Who is this?*

Beside her, Ann snuffled in her sleep, a small wet sound. Leni glanced across at her. She hoped Ann hadn't caught a cold from getting damp at the garden.

The phone buzzed again: *RR.*

Leni sat up, wide awake. Her first reaction was to turn the lamp on, as though that would make sense of things, but she switched it off again immediately – sudden light or noise could disturb Ann, who was otherwise a sound sleeper. With the same idea in mind, Leni flicked the side switch on her phone to silent and waited, sitting tense in the dark. A new message arrived:

You really made a difference. Helping you took me out of myself.

Leni was wondering how to reply to that when another one appeared:

I've been having a difficult time recently. I lost my dog.

Her lips parted in sympathy. She typed back:

I'm very sorry to hear that. I love my own dog very much, so I know how hard it must be.

After that there was a pause, and then:

I am badly in need of a friend. Could you be my friend?

Leni breathed in sharply. She hesitated. The seconds slipped by. But it seemed that there could be only one response. She tapped it out:

Yes.

After that, she waited for over half an hour for another message, but nothing more came.

Chapter Eleven

Roddy was parked in his car opposite Leni's house on Isthmus Avenue. It was just after 11.00 p.m. Almost fourteen hours since she'd walked into his office at *The Sentinel.*

It hadn't been difficult to find out her address, just a case of buzzing Pam and casually asking her to forward him Leni Moffett's contact details. And then, later, the short drive along the Ormonde Road to her home.

All day she had been in his head. He felt saturated by her presence. Those startled grey-green eyes, flicking up at him from unplumbed depths, like a mermaid's tail. Delicately chapped lips, a tiny rip or tear in one corner, carmine-red, where blood had recently flowed and been stanched. Around the pale nostrils a smattering of pink, a rabbity rim of dampness. Paper-white face and paper-white fingers. Her hair, her hair, her hair . . .

Not beautiful, no. You couldn't call her that. Too tall. A tendency to hunch over. Awful clothes: clumping great boots and a dun-coloured shapeless dress. She seemed itchy, fidgety, uncomfortable in her own skin.

It didn't matter. Her flaws were exquisite – they made her more fully herself: a rare creature passing unseen through the world. But Roddy recognised her. Roddy saw.

He looked up again at the red-brick terrace, silent in a row of silent houses. At 10.00 p.m., shortly after he'd arrived, the lights had gone off downstairs, behind the curtained bay window, only to come on again, a few minutes later, at the right-hand first floor window – the one with a child's wooden mobile hanging from the top of the frame. The shade was down but he saw a man's shadow pass across it, reaching up as though to pull off a T-shirt or sweater. Her husband, Theo? Must be. At the window on the left, the shade was half-down and the room was dark. At 10.32 p.m., the light in the right-hand window went out. There had been no discernible movement in the house since then.

That photograph she'd sent him, attached to her original email – straight away, he'd sensed there could be some kind of connection between them. She was laughing in the snapshot, but she could just as well have been crying. Roddy could almost smell her dissatisfaction, buried just below the cheerful surface, simply from examining that flat digital image. Lost girl; brittle; breakable. He strongly suspected she needed rescuing, someone to take charge of her. And then when she walked into his office this morning, he'd known it.

To be sure of her full attention, he'd had to hurt her. That was an old tactic, familiar to Roddy, and it almost always worked: the stimulating stroke of the cane, applied exactly at the most sensitive point – in this case, the girl's writing ability. In fact, the article she brought him was technically impressive, far beyond the semi-literate standard of most *Sentinel* hacks. A bit overblown in style, yes, though nowhere near as badly as he'd made it out to be – the faults were minor, easily corrected.

He had no interest whatsoever in the subject matter, of course, which seemed to him to be a manifesto for spoiling infants. What Roddy simply wanted to do, in the first instance, was to give the young woman a sharp emotional shock. He had to take something away from her – her pride – and then present her with a way of getting it back. It was while he was tearing Leni's article to pieces, quite literally – yes, that was an inspired extra touch of cruelty, he thought, with a flicker of a grin – that the idea of commissioning her to write weekly diary entries came to him.

The plan was ideal: a means of getting privileged access to her life, her thoughts, her relationships, under the guise of nurturing her writing skills. No, no, not the guise. He really meant it. He would do his absolute best to help her with her writing, just as he'd help her with everything else, once she was safely under his charge. In saving her, he would save himself. Everybody wins.

That husband of hers, the blessed Theo, what about him? Sappy milk-and-water type. Too pretty: more a girl than a man. Roddy had his suspicions that Leni wasn't entirely happy there, despite her fervent praise for him – or rather, precisely *because* of that fervent praise.

Admittedly, it was pure recklessness to offer her a hundred pounds per instalment. He would have to pay that in cash out of his own pocket. Hopefully the girl was too naive to realise. He'd have to find a way of getting her on the freelance rota, sooner rather than later, but without arousing any suspicions. Yesterday, Roddy had received an ominous message from Mitch Wallace, wanting to discuss some anomalies in the editorial expenses account, which Jackie Shields-Maguire had highlighted at their last meeting – the one Roddy had inadvertently missed, when he'd hared off to Millisle after that motorbike. He really was going to have to start keeping more regular hours at the office, if only to keep Jackie in check.

Ah, forget the office, forget Mitch and Jackie. He

summoned up an image of Leni, bare-legged, in the shortest possible brown velvet skirt, kneeling in front of the stone fireplace at Honolulu. She was looking over her shoulder to meet his watching gaze from the shadows. Yes, that was good, he liked that. He had her bend forward, raw elbows resting on the rough granite, the fall of russet hair dangerously close to the fire, as the rising skirt became a proscenium arch for her pale exposed thighs. Perhaps there was a slight heat rash, the merest flush, across the tops of the thighs – was there? Yes – yes, there was.

The fantasy excited him. He was fifty-seven years old, but he felt as young and infatuated as a teenager. Steady, he warned himself, don't rush ahead, this will take time; you've got to give it time.

The car was steaming up. Roddy leaned over and wiped a circle in the passenger-side window so he could see the house again. He opened the glove compartment, took out his leather hipflask and swallowed a burning throatful of whiskey. Then he slipped a small pair of silver scissors from the inside pocket of his jacket and began very deliberately to trim his nails. It was a regular habit of his, these DIY manicures, which he'd taken up to curb a vulgar tendency to bite the nails instead. The scissors came from the Judge's old shaving kit, and the worn blades, still sharp, were curved like little scimitars. Roddy always carried them with him. Like whittling wood, they calmed his mind, gave his hands something to do – particularly useful when he was stuck in traffic, coming into town in the mornings, the dull weight of the day ahead of him. The black-carpeted footwell of his car was littered with thin white crescents.

He looked at his watch: *23.22*, said the illuminated figures.

For the last few hours, merely sharing her proximity, being close to Leni's home, had been enough to content Roddy. He knew he should leave soon. He was stiff from slouching low in the driver's seat, his feet were cold and far away at Honolulu, Terence would be waiting, hungry and whimpering and pacing the floor. But when Roddy turned the key in the ignition and the dashboard lit up red, the prospect of driving away alone, empty-handed, filled him with despair. The desire to make contact with Leni was overwhelming.

He had her mobile number. She was probably asleep, but what would be wrong with leaving a text message for her to read in the morning? Maybe now was the time to show her his vulnerable side.

Roddy sent his stealthy text into the sleeping house, not expecting to get a reply. But within moments, her response lit up the phone in his hand. She wanted to know who it was. He told her. Immediately, in the upstairs window with the half-pulled blind, a light flashed on and off again. A sign – no, more than that – a signal!

But no reply came back. He sent another text. Still nothing. Roddy felt desperate. He could not tolerate being ignored. He craved relief from his loneliness and need.

As soon as he told her that Terence was lost, with the clear implication that he was dead, he regretted it. Tempting fate and all that. But it worked – it worked beautifully. Now he had her sympathy.

Should he risk a further push? Ask her for something more?

Leni's response to his final question chanted in

Roddy's heart the whole way back to Honolulu. *Yes.* Yes . . . yes . . . yes. A world of promise in that one sweet word.

He drove fast, the seatbelt unbuckled, taking frequent swigs from the leather flask propped between his thighs. Music now, there must be music, he needed a soundtrack for this mad euphoria he was feeling. He grabbed his favourite CD of sixties girl bands, shoved it into the slot of the player and fast-forwarded rapidly through the tracks. Ha, yes – 'Egyptian Shumba' by The Tammys. Those crazy jungle yelps, rising to an orgasmic shriek of girlish joy. Perfect!

Hammering out the syncopated beats on the steering wheel, screaming in falsetto along with The Tammys, Roddy powered through the night.

Chapter Twelve

Leni slept fitfully that night, waking up every hour. She felt as if she'd been drinking too much coffee, though all she'd had was her usual cup of green tea with a spoonful of honey before bed. Even when she managed to drift off, she was in that semi-adrenalised state which keeps a prankster part of the brain awake and causing trouble. Twice, she woke with a sickening jump as the bed seemed to tip sharply, sliding her down the slippery sheets to oblivion.

It was Mr Riseborough's weird messages, of course, that were disturbing her. Towards dawn, she fell into a deeper sleep. She had a horribly vivid nightmare in which Ted had escaped because she hadn't shut the back door properly. She found him frozen to death in the middle of a snowy field, and when she fell to her knees beside him, digging the snow away with frostbitten hands, she discovered it wasn't Ted at all, it was Ann's little body lying there. Leni surfaced from the dream-horror on a rising wail of noise to find Ann sitting up beside her in bed, howling, bubbles of snot erupting from both nostrils and one cheek blazing red. So she had caught a cold at the garden after all.

After Theo left for work, Leni and Ann had an awful morning together. The freedoms of yesterday – books, food, the mystery DeLorean – might never have happened. Ann couldn't feed properly because her nose was blocked, so she kept snatching her head roughly away from Leni's nipple, which was both painful and infuriating, especially since Ann had teeth now. Still suffering the afterburn of the nightmare, Leni felt guilty for being impatient, but she couldn't lose the irritation either, in fact, the guilt seemed to increase it.

Rooting aggressively at the breast in her pink all-in-one sleepsuit, short blonde eyelashes spiky with tears, Ann resembled a cross little piglet. Her flailing hands had spread sticky, clear mucus everywhere. Leni gave up, strapped herself back into her nursing bra, wiped Ann's face and hands with a damp cloth and inserted her into the highchair, a little less gently than usual, so that she could get on with preparing breakfast. But the porridge soon ended up on the floor, the plastic dish tipped over by Ann's fretful, imperious spoon. The clotted remains dripped from the highchair tray onto Ted's black head as he licked up the mess. Leni swore under her breath and fetched the mop.

Waiting at the sink for the bucket to fill with soapy water, she gazed out the window at the honeysuckle vine. It seemed to be dropping its leaves very early. It was only September, normally they didn't fall until well into the autumn. Maybe the vine needed re-potted or fed? Yet another thing needing her attention.

The water from the tap was barely warm: the decrepit bloody boiler again. She must remember to put on the immersion heater later for Ann's bath.

What did he mean, 'Will you be my friend'?

Why would someone like Mr Riseborough want her as a friend? What could she possibly have to offer him?

If Ann hadn't woken up with a cold, Leni had planned to visit Magill this morning. Magill owned a hardware and fancy goods shop on the Ormonde Road, close to Leni's house. Amid the vintage clothes stores and the

Scandinavian-style cafes serving single-origin coffee and avocado toast, Magill's shop was a wonderful anomaly. It looked as if it had violently burst open and spread its contents over the pavement. Hard-bristle yard brushes jostled in metal crates on either side of the door, surrounded by rolls of chicken wire, plastic boxes filled with cut-price bottles of bleach and a wide selection of swing-top bins. Hanging from hooks on the red-and-white striped canopy over the entrance were coal scuttles and storm lanterns and enamel teapots of every possible size.

The shop itself was dim and narrow, smelling strongly of Jeyes fluid and beeswax furniture polish, and the shelves were densely stacked with various items of household importance, ranged according to purpose: cooking, gardening, car maintenance. Small cardboard boxes, labelled in marker pen, held slot-headed brass screws, chrome bolts, mixed fuses. Under the counter, there were illicit light bulbs for sale, if you knew to ask for them – the old-fashioned incandescent kind, so much warmer and softer than the flat, cold glare of environmentally-friendly bulbs. Magill himself lived in the flat upstairs, above the shop.

Both Leni and Ann loved going there. Occasionally Leni bought some little thing – corn-on-the-cob skewers, say, or a retractable measuring tape – but mainly she came to chat with Magill, who took a gentle, flattering interest in the day-to-day minutiae of her life.

She suspected that many of Magill's other customers came here for exactly the same reason – that bright-eyed, sympathetic quality of attentiveness, and the feeling that he had all the time in the world to talk to you. How he made enough money to live on, considering how much time he spent chatting to people, Leni had no idea. 'Estd. 1968', it said on the sign, originally put up by Magill's late father, who had also been called Magill. Surname or Christian name? Nobody seemed to know, and Magill wasn't saying. He rarely talked about himself.

Leni had a particular reason for visiting Magill today. She was planning to write about him in her diary for Mr Riseborough. To Leni, Magill seemed like the living embodiment of his own shop: eccentric and homely, naturally idiosyncratic, full of hidden riches. He was ageless, or at least of indeterminate age. He had a whooping laugh like a rooster which would erupt suddenly and surprisingly from the back of his throat. His sandpapery skin was almost the same shade as his dust-coloured hair, which he wore in a high, whipped-up quiff.

Maybe they could still go to the shop, if she wrapped Ann up really well. Some fresh air might do her good; might do them both good.

'Hey Annie,' she said. 'Want to go see Magill?'

Ann beamed blearily through a film of porridge, tears and snot. It was her first smile of the day. 'Magoo,' she cried. 'See Magoo!'

When they arrived, Magill was on a stepladder outside, hanging a brass fireguard from the shop's canopy. He was in his usual gear: denim jacket, denim jeans, a checked shirt and a thin white leather tie. In front of his large ears, a pair of unfashionably long sideburns were squared off at jaw-level. The tip of his tongue poked sideways through his lips, as it always did when he was concentrating. Leni put the brake on the buggy and stood beside Magill's drainpipe legs, waiting politely for him to finish.

Magill glanced down, and when he saw Leni and Ann,

his eyes creased up instantly into bright blue triangles, like chips of coloured glass. 'Well, look who's here,' he said. 'It's Snow White and Rose Red.' That was what Magill called them; he liked to make up his own names for people. 'And poor wee Rosie's got the cold, I can see. Come on inside, girls.'

He backed down the ladder and Leni followed him gratefully into the shop, pushing Ann in the buggy. It was like being taken under a warm wing.

'Wheel the pram in there, Snow, in front of the Superser,' said Magill, pointing to a bulky gas heater sitting on the floor behind the counter. 'It'll only take me a second to get her lit.' After much fruitless clicking of the starter button, there was a gassy belch and one of the heating bars slowly flushed orange. Magill squatted beside Ann, his huge face close to hers. 'Now, little queen. Not feeling so good today?'

Ann shook her head and turned away, bashfully smiling into the furry trim of her hood, as though she'd found a precious secret in there.

'Well, let's see if there's anything we can find to make you feel a bit better.'

Ann peeped out from the shelter of her hood and watched Magill intently as he scanned the shelves. 'A-ha. How about this?' He lifted down a china figurine of a rosy-cheeked boy, with hair like curls of melted chocolate. The boy was dressed as a waiter, in bow tie and tails, and he was clasping a small hourglass. Magill showed Ann how the hourglass rotated to allow the sand to flow from one chamber to the other. 'And when it's finished, that means your boiled egg is ready, and you can have your tea.'

Ann reached out eagerly for the figurine.

'Magill, no, it's too delicate – she'll break it,' warned Leni.

'Oh no, she won't break it,' he said. And sure enough, Ann took it with great care, turning the hourglass with one tiny exploratory finger and watching, fascinated, as the sand slowly trickled through. Leni smiled at her daughter. It was so much easier to enjoy her when they were in Magill's company.

'I've got something to show you, too,' said Magill to Leni. 'Recent acquisition. Come this way.'

'A new cutting for the Mary Jo museum?' asked Leni as she followed him. She kept a watchful eye over her shoulder on Ann, who was still absorbed by the spinning hourglass.

The entire rear wall of Magill's shop was a shrine to Mary Jo Kopechne, a young American woman who died on a summer night in 1969, near Chappaquiddick Island, on Martha's Vineyard. Mary Jo had been the passenger in a car driven by Senator Ted Kennedy. Nobody knew exactly what happened, but Kennedy ended up crashing off the end of a bridge and the car plunged into the water. He managed to break free and escape, swimming to the surface. But he left Mary Jo behind, and by the time the wreck was discovered, next day, poor Mary Jo was dead.

Magill had pinned every single newspaper or magazine article he could find about the Chappaquiddick incident to the corkboard at the back of the shop. Some clippings were crispy with age, but a few were more recent; every so often the case would return to the news, because it was still an unsolved mystery, though most people had forgotten it by now. Several of the photographs on the board were duplicates: the same black-and-white image of Kennedy's Oldsmobile being dragged from the water – its windscreen cracked, roof stoved in like a battered hat – appeared at least ten times.

'Poor girl,' Magill would say, sorrowfully shaking his head. 'Can you believe it? Kennedy saved himself and left her trapped there underwater, certain to die. Went home and had a shower. Said nothing about it for ten hours solid. How that man could live with himself afterwards I do not know.'

Leni wasn't quite sure why Magill was so obsessed with the case. It happened such a long time ago, among unknown people, in a place so different from Belfast that it may as well have been another planet.

She wondered if it was to do with some kind of loss in his own life. Magill had a great tenderness for women, couldn't bear the thought of any of them being hurt or harmed, especially by men – the way his chipped blue eyes darkened, you could see how much it pained him. From the little that he ever spoke of himself, Leni suspected that there had been someone, once, and that she'd been taken from him, perhaps even violently. But that was only guessing: she had no way of knowing for sure, and she would never ask.

'No, not the museum this time,' Magill was saying. 'Something a bit different. Here we are now. Feast your eyes on this fella.'

Standing in a recessed niche, beside a stack of paint cans, was an Egyptian sarcophagus. Magill clapped a friendly hand on its striped blue-and-gold head-dress. 'What do you make of him? Pretty special, hey?'

'Wow,' said Leni. 'Yes, very impressive. But, er, what exactly is it?'

By way of answer, Magill undid a clasp at the side and the entire front section of the Egyptian coffin swung open. 'Drinks cabinet,' he said. 'Bought at auction last week. I call him "Barry".' He gave one of his rooster-ish hoots of laughter. 'Don't suppose you fancy taking the fella on?'

'I wish I could,' said Leni. This was ideal material for the diary. 'Though I don't know what Theo would say about it.' She smiled up at Magill. 'Hey, listen – I've got news too.'

'You're running for president of Ireland.'

'Er, no,' she laughed. 'Not this year. I've got a job – well, sort of. You know *The Sentinel* – the daily newspaper? The editor, Roddy Riseborough, has offered me a place on a kind of trainee scheme. So I'm going to learn how to be a journalist.'

'That's marvellous,' said Magill. 'I didn't know you were a writer, Snow. You're a dark horse. What other talents have you got, hidden away in private?'

'Oh, none really,' said Leni. 'But I've always liked to write. And the good thing is that this scheme is part-time, so I won't be away from Ann too much.'

Her mobile gave a sudden loud buzz-trill from inside the back pocket of her jeans, announcing the arrival of a text message. 'Sorry, hang on, let me just—'. She pulled it out and flipped it open.

'Your darling mother?' asked Magill sympathetically. Leni had explained about her troubles with Patti, having been bombarded by calls from her while visiting the shop one afternoon. But Leni had not yet told him that Patti was coming to stay with her – coming in less than two weeks from now. Telling Magill would make it real, and imminent, and Leni wasn't prepared for that yet.

'No, it's . . . somebody else.'

Leni. I need to see you this week. It can't wait until Tuesday.

'Everything ok, Snow? You jumped a foot in the air when your phone went off.'

Leni snapped it closed and returned it to her pocket. 'Fine, yeah,' she smiled. 'It's nothing. I should probably head on now – better not keep Ann out too long, what with her cold and everything. Thanks for showing me, Barry. Hope you find a good home for him.'

On the way back to Isthmus Avenue, the pavement kept moving up and down as if it was floating on water. Each paving slab seemed to sink beneath her weight and then rise again as she passed over it. It was the strangest sensation, like vertigo – that same dizzy lurch, and the sickish feeling that you were about to fall.

If you couldn't even be sure of the ground under your feet, thought Leni, if something as safe and solid as that could change its nature, then what else could happen? Was it possible that other certainties, the kind you build your life upon, might start to come adrift and slip away too? Her head ballooned at the notion, as if it had been inflated with helium.

No. Stop it. Whatever this nonsense was – fear, fantasy, half-formed wish or dread – it was unthinkable. She didn't get enough sleep last night, and she'd had no breakfast either; no wonder she was feeling a bit off kilter. With determination, Leni curled her toes inside her boots, so that each step became a claw-like grip, and then strode firmly onwards. They were crossing the park now, where Ann would usually demand – and be given – a turn on the swings, but she had fallen asleep in her buggy, hands still clasping the little hourglass. Magill had given it to her as a gift, as they were leaving. Leni paused by the bandstand, took her phone out and sent a reply: *I'm sorry, I don't think I can.*

There. She hoped Mr Riseborough wouldn't be offended, but it was impossible for her to meet him before next Tuesday. Theo had agreed to bring Ann to the garden one morning a week, while she attended her training sessions at *The Sentinel*, and Leni could hardly ask him to take her on another day as well. Even to request it would look odd. And besides, what could be so urgent that Mr Riseborough couldn't wait? He didn't know her; they had only just met. They occupied entirely different worlds. He was a powerful man: he had stature, authority, he was occupied with important matters, directing the complicated operations of a big daily newspaper. And she was . . . well, she was nobody.

By the time she turned into her own street, the pavement had stopped misbehaving. Marta, the nurse who lived next door, was standing outside having an animated conversation with a delivery driver. Marta was Eastern European – Polish or Hungarian: Leni wasn't sure and was always too shy to ask. When she saw Leni coming, she broke off and waved urgently.

'Yes – wait – it's ok, she is here now,' she heard Marta say to the delivery man. Marta had quite a loud voice. 'Leni!' she called. 'This man – he asks me to receive your package because you are not at home. I agree but my God, I didn't know it would be so big, so heavy – look!'

Marta pointed at her small front yard. A wooden crate, about the size and shape of a door, was propped against Marta's fence, which was tilting under the weight. The crate was bound with white tape, on which the words 'FRAGILE: HANDLE WITH CARE' were printed, in red, over and over again.

'Hang on, no, this isn't mine,' protested Leni, turning to the driver. 'I didn't order anything, there must be a mistake.'

'Leni Moffett – 42 Isthmus Avenue?' the man asked in a weary voice.

'Yes, but—'

He held out his iPad and showed her the name and delivery address, which were definitely her own. Marta craned forward to get a glimpse too, her shiny henna bob brushing Leni's cheek. She smelled of bubble-gum and vanilla – her shampoo probably, or it could be the gum she was chewing. Leni had often wondered if they could get to know each other better, maybe even become friends. They were next-door neighbours after all. In fact, what was to stop her asking Marta into the house for a coffee right now?

But before Leni could work up the nerve, Marta said, 'Huh!', shrugged, and went back into her own house with a jangle of brass bracelets.

'I'll need a signature,' said the driver. 'Use your finger, initials will do.'

'Do you have the details of the person who sent this?' asked Leni, as she signed.

'Yup. One sec . . .' He swiped the screen twice. 'Here we are. "One aluminium-backed photo-print, wrapped and crated",' he read. 'And that's the sender's address. Ring any bells?'

Of course it did. Now she thought about it, there was only one person it could have been.

After the delivery man had carried the crate into the house, and left it blocking the stairs, Leni noticed a hairline crack on one of the beautiful blue-and-black patterned tiles in the hall, where the crate had slipped as he'd boosted it over the doorstep. She rushed outside, but the van had gone. On the way back in, she saw that the wheels of Ann's buggy had tracked a long streak of dog shit across the coir welcome mat.

Leni texted Mr Riseborough again:

I will meet you. I will manage it somehow. Where and when?

Chapter Thirteen

Christ alive, she's brought the kid with her, thought Roddy with dismay. It was Friday afternoon and he was standing in the library bar of the 1921 Club, watching Leni, bare-armed, in a negligible shred of a sundress, walk towards him across the vast expanse of deep, maroon-coloured carpet. The carpet was worn with the venerable tread of many male generations past. Their cups, caps, trophies, shields and medals, resting on bands of grey felt, were displayed in a series of glass-fronted cabinets, to inform the uninitiated about their legendary pluck and sporting prowess.

She came to him through sunshine and shadow, the light from the great windows pouring radiance on her copper-coloured hair. He saw the light dying as she passed into the shade of the tall cabinets, then spontaneously reigniting as she emerged and the sun set fire to her head again. She was a flaming beacon, coming to him across the quiet, empty bar. The child – ugh, the child was in some sort of metal-framed contraption on her back, he could see its head poking out the top and bobbing around like a puppet, spoiling the glory of the vision. The first thing he needed to do was to get rid of it.

She arrived in front of him, looking tense, uncertain, very serious. White clavicles, tremulous and eloquent above the frayed drawstring collar of her dress – he must remember that detail for later, when he was back at home. The monkey peeking over her shoulder regarded him with frank suspicion, a fistful of its mother's glorious hair gripped tightly in its hand.

'You're here,' he said.

'Yes. I'm here.'

'Were you able to get in alright?'

Leni nodded. 'I gave my name to the doorman, like you said. He showed me upstairs. I hung my cardigan up in the cloakroom.'

'I didn't expect you to bring your – er, your child. I thought it would just be you.'

Her eyes dropped to the floor, and a stain of pink spread from her neck to her chest, like paint dissolving in water. 'Ann, yes. I'm sorry, I had no choice. There's nobody I could leave her with. Is it . . . forbidden, to bring children in here?'

Roddy had no idea whether it was forbidden or not, but he gave a rueful semi-nod. 'I believe so. They're quite strict about rules and things at the club. They only started admitting women last year.'

Which was, to be perfectly honest, part of the reason he had suggested the club as a place for them to meet. He wanted to see her against the backdrop of this opulent wallpaper, its swirls of dark leaves and fruit, tigers and peacocks preening in the foliage. He wanted to let a young woman in to raise the pile of that dead, flattened carpet as her pale feet passed over it. In fact, Leni's feet were encased in a rather grubby pair of plimsolls. Unfortunate, but never mind – simply bringing her here was enough to lighten the old, stale atmosphere of maleness in the club, so privileged and ponderous. Perhaps because of his two decades in the police, Roddy tended to despise other men. He preferred to think of himself as a lone wolf, separate from the pack.

Another benefit of meeting at the club was that the bar was mostly deserted at this point on a Friday afternoon, after the final lunch guests had departed, leaving the farmyard scent of roast mutton hanging heavy on the air, but before people started drifting in for after-work drinks. The two of them could be reasonably assured of having the place to themselves, other than perhaps a shrivelled nonagenarian with a military tie, muttering and dozing in an armchair by the fire, and there wasn't even one of those around today.

'Oh God, I should go then,' said Leni, raising crimson cheeks. Her eyes were full of unspoken appeal: she seemed to be asking him something urgent, or perhaps she was simply mortified. Either way, it was delicious. A brimming, melting warmth started up deep in the bowl of his pelvis. Funnily enough, it reminded him of how it felt to piss himself as a young boy: the forbidden release, the wonderful free wetness, he had almost forgotten that. But Roddy's bladder, like everything else about him, was well under control.

He held up a finger. 'I have a thought. Wait here for one moment.'

He came back with Barbara, the chief waitress in the dining room, bustling stoutly behind him, starched white cuffs folded back over the capable hams of her forearms.

'Ah, the wee dote, look at her. Of course I'll take her off your hands for a bit,' she said to Leni. 'Come on, love, give her here.' The child struggled and clung to the metal frame of her carrier, making whimpering sounds, but Barbara swept her up and whisked her away before Ann – or possibly her mother – could kick up too much of a fuss. Leni called out hushed reassurances as they disappeared through the brass-handled double doors of the bar.

'Now,' said Roddy. 'What will you have? I think I fancy a whiskey and ginger ale. How about you?'

Leni scratched her cheek, darting a distracted glance at the still-swinging doors. 'Oh – no thanks – I don't like whiskey . . . And I don't normally take anything alcoholic, actually – because of feeding Ann, you know—'

She fed the kid herself? Christ, Roddy nearly passed out when he thought about those plump milky pouches, thinly veiled with light cotton, suspended just below the decent limits of his gaze. But he merely smiled. 'Let's have a little champagne then. That never did anybody any harm.'

Soon Leni was chattering and laughing and tossing her hair back, the burdensome child clearly forgotten. She started to tell him a convoluted story about some old rockabilly bloke who owned a hardware shop on the Ormonde Road, but Roddy was barely listening to what she said. Simply being beside her, drinking her in: that was enough for now.

The champagne he'd ordered was a superlative bottle, one of the best the club stocked. It was far more than he could afford and he knew that Leni was entirely unaware of its pedigree, or the exquisitely experienced way it was flirting with their nostrils and taste-buds – a minute ago she'd said it was like 'lovely water' – but he didn't care. The wine had helped create this moment and he was grateful for it, willing to pay anything to keep it going.

'He's probably my only friend,' she said, suddenly serious.

'Who?'

'Magill. The one I've been talking about.'

'Really? That's hard for me to believe,' he said, and winced at his own smarminess. He sounded like an insinuating uncle, fumbling to come up with compliments.

'It's true though. I've been writing about him, actually, for my learning journal. I know we'll discuss it on Tuesday, at your office, but I wondered . . . well, I wondered whether you might take a quick look at what I've done so far? I have it here with me—'

The paper-clipped pages were already out of her bag and in her hand. She bit her lip anxiously as she held them out. 'Only if you don't mind, I mean.'

'Of course.' What else could he say? He put his glasses on and glanced through the typescript, conscious of her eager scrutiny. So she really did care what he thought of her writing. That was good: it meant he was gaining purchase. But go slow, Rodders. Praise her too much and you'll lose your hold – she'll break free. It had happened before, and it could happen again. Give her just a little taste, a morsel to whet her appetite.

'It's better,' he said cautiously, after judging that sufficient time had passed. He'd hardly read a thing, the way her eyes seemed to penetrate the skin of his face was too distracting. The sentences seethed and blurred into one another, only a few disconnected words standing out: 'storm-lantern'; 'chocolate'; 'sarcophagus'; 'Mary Jo'. God knows what the girl was on about. 'Yes, I see some improvement here.'

She seemed disappointed. Her mermaid eyes raised and dropped in that touch-and-go way she had, the brief surface contact, then the flick of the tail as she dived back to her depths. All at once Roddy couldn't bear her to suffer any lack of praise; to suffer any kind of lack at all.

'Actually, I love it,' he declared, and was rewarded with a flash of wide-eyed joy.

'Thank you,' she murmured, fiddling with one of the drawstrings of her dress. He could tell by the secret, pleased curve of her mouth that she was savouring the little triumph privately. But then her expression changed.

'I'm sorry, I just realised – I've been babbling on about myself, when the whole point of coming here was because you needed to see me. Please – tell me what I can do?'

'Nothing,' smiled Roddy. 'Not a single thing. I wanted to spend some time with you, get to know you better. That's all.'

'Oh. Okay. But . . . when you texted me, before, you said you needed a friend. I thought maybe you wanted me to help you with something . . . specific? Not that I'd be much use, necessarily, but I'd be happy to try.'

'Leni, the thing that helps me most is just sitting here talking to you. Truly. You have an incredibly soothing presence. I noticed it when you came into the office. And I'm . . .' here Roddy manufactured the slightest hint of a painful gulp, then cleared his throat briskly. 'Well, for reasons we won't go into, I'm in sore need of some conducive company right now.'

'Of course, yes. I'm so sorry about your – your loss.'

'Thank you. But let's keep talking about you. You're so much more interesting than me. You said you don't have many friends. That seems a shame for somebody your age. You have your family, though, don't you? Your husband, and your daughter?'

She nodded – with a distinct lack of enthusiasm, he noted.

'Yes. There's Theo, and Ann, of course. And soon there will be my mother too.'

'You're expecting a visit from your mother? Well, I'm sure that will be pleasant for you.'

Her answering grin was more of a grimace. 'Not exactly.'

'Oh? What's the problem?'

It all emerged then: old wounds; family differences; lack of money; pressure from the husband; Leni's reluctant capitulation. Roddy listened carefully until she had finished, ensuring that not a trace of the inner glee he was feeling showed itself in his sober, concerned expression.

Now he knew how to proceed. He saw that what she needed was an escape route, and he, Roddy, was the very man to provide it. He signalled discreetly to the waiter to bring another bottle of champagne.

'I don't know why I'm telling you this, it's nothing really,' she said apologetically.

'It's far from nothing,' he said. 'You mustn't play it down, Leni. I don't know your husband, of course. But it seems obvious that he – Theo, you said? – yes, that Theo has allowed financial concerns to override his duty of care to you, as his wife. And that's a very serious thing, in a marriage. It speaks to deeper issues. You – your needs, your wishes, your desires – they should always come first.'

'It's not his fault, exactly. He genuinely doesn't understand how bad my mother can be; he's never seen her at her worst. The stuff she's done in the past – he's only heard about it second-hand, through me, and it doesn't seem to stick. Theo – he has this great respect for women. He puts them on a pedestal, as though they can do no wrong. It's a sort of . . . blind spot he has, I suppose. And it affects how he sees my mother.'

'But what about how he sees you? It's rank hypocrisy for a man to talk of respecting women, and then turn around and ignore the feelings of the woman he shares his life with. He really must be blind, if he can't see how that's bound to hurt you,' said Roddy. He paused for emphasis, gazing at her ardently. 'And I, for one, would hate to see you hurt.'

No. Too much, too soon: his perennial mistake and downfall. She gave him a dazed, blank look, unreadable, and reached for her bag. 'I should go and find Ann,' she said.

She was leaving; she was going to leave. Roddy's anxiety spiked.

'Please . . .' he said. 'Don't go yet.'

'Really. I'd better. Thank you for the drinks – everything —'

As she pushed her chair back, she bumped the table, and the second bottle of champagne, which Roddy had removed from its bucket of ice, ready to top up their glasses, teetered heavily. For a split-second, they both watched it rock, spellbound. As Roddy flung out a hand to catch it, the bottle fell, sending a riptide of foam swirling and spilling across the table and over Leni's lap, soaking her dress and flooding the carpet around her.

The waiter rushed towards them, alerted by Leni's squeal as the cold champagne washed over her, then ran back towards the bar, presumably to grab a cloth. Roddy mopped ineffectually at the spill on the table with his lavender handkerchief, reeling at the thought of the wasted hundreds of pounds he was soaking up. He was aware of Leni standing there motionless in her saturated dress, fists clenched, head bowed. It was only when he heard a choked sob that he realised she was crying, her face contorted like a little girl's, a wrinkled pucker of bright pink above each flaming eyebrow.

'I'm sorry,' she gasped. 'I'm so stupid!'

'Oh darling, no. You're perfect!' He dropped the sodden handkerchief, stepped forward and gathered her into his arms. A sort of convulsion seemed to pass through her body, and he tightened his grip on her in response. She held on to him as though she was drowning.

Roddy knew that she couldn't see his smile of triumph, because it was hidden behind her back.

~

Something happened today.
Yes. I know.
Did you feel it too? When we touched each other?
Yes.
It was incredible. Kapow! Instant connection!
That has never happened to me before.
Me neither.
What should we do now?
I don't know. What can we do?
I don't know.
It's really difficult.
Yes. But I'm sure of one thing.
What?
I'm falling in love with you, Leni.

Chapter Fourteen

Leni was upstairs in the bedroom, humming to herself as she got ready to go to work. It was mid-afternoon, late October. The clocks would go back tomorrow, making the days even shorter and colder, but Leni didn't mind. She'd grown to love the darkness.

Besides, the house was tropically warm, now that Patti had paid for a high-powered new boiler to be installed, shortly after she arrived last month. Sometimes it was even a bit too warm, and they had to open a window. But obviously it was a relief finally to have a functioning heating system.

Leni paused for a moment and listened. Her mother and Ann were down in the kitchen, preparing some kind of 'surprise'. At first, she could detect no sounds at all, which was slightly ominous, but then she heard Ann's high-pitched giggle ring out, so everything must be going alright.

The truth was that Leni wouldn't be able to do this work if it wasn't for Patti. The learning journal stage was over – Mr Riseborough had said that her progress was remarkably fast – and now she was doing two sub-editing shifts a week at *The Sentinel*, on Tuesdays and Fridays, from 5.00 p.m. until 10.00 p.m. Patti had volunteered to babysit Ann during the gap between Leni leaving and Theo returning home from the garden. 'It's so important for you to have a career, darling,' she'd said. 'Children grow up and leave you – you need to have something of your own.' That seemed a bit rich coming from Patti, given that she was the one who had abandoned her infant daughter and decamped to Berlin. But Leni had accepted her mother's offer. What other choice did she have?

The work itself wasn't exactly onerous: mainly proofreading copy and checking captions. No writing yet; Mr Riseborough said that would come later, in the next stage of her training. Martin Sharkey, the chief sub-editor, was her line manager. He often seemed vaguely surprised when Leni arrived at his desk at the start of each shift, ready to be briefed on her duties for the evening, and sometimes she had the impression that he didn't really know what to tell her. But she was glad to be earning a small official wage; no more cash in hand. The bundle of banknotes, stuffed in a used envelope, had felt rather tawdry somehow. Now her nice clean payments went directly to her bank account, and she received a monthly remittance slip in the post – all above board.

At Mr Riseborough's discreet suggestion, she'd gone out and bought herself new clothes, proper work clothes, paying for them with the rarely used family credit card. Business attire, wasn't that what it was called? Close-cut satin blouses and neat, sweet pencil skirts designed to sit snug on the hips and, best of all, a pair of high, pewter-coloured Mary-Jane shoes with a thin snaky strap and buckle across the arch of her foot – horribly expensive, but impossible to resist. She relished the way they clop-clop-clopped so smartly as she trotted up *The Sentinel's* grand granite staircase, and clip-clip-clipped so resoundingly as she walked across the black-and-white chequered marble floor of the entrance lobby. It was the sound of her new, confident, freshly sculpted life.

Still airily humming, Leni crossed the landing and went into the nursery, shutting the door carefully behind her. She shrugged off her dressing gown, and let it fall to the ground. Her skin was still flushed and damp from the shower. Reaching into the back of the little white wardrobe, she grabbed a lidded plastic storage box containing Ann's tiny outgrown Babygros. Each one had been washed and carefully folded away between layers of tissue paper (she had read somewhere that this was the proper thing to do).

Stashed at the bottom of the box was a small collection of fancy lingerie. It looked shockingly illicit. Leni pulled out a scrap of a bra, consisting of little more than two peachy scallops of naked tulle, and a flimsy pair of knickers to match. Once the knickers were on, she adjusted the tiny satin bows so they sat pertly on either side of her bikini line. Seductive underwear: that was what you wore when you were having an extra-marital affair, wasn't it? You could hardly turn up in your baggy old pants with the frayed elastic.

She replaced the individually wrapped Babygros on top of the lingerie, fitted the lid on the box and put it in its hiding place. Then she slipped her dressing gown back on and returned to the big bedroom.

Because she was so fervently desired, Leni looked at her body in a different way now, almost as though she coveted it herself. The too-small breasts; the postpartum weight of her thighs; even the long, jagged stretchmarks slashed vertically down her stomach, the zip-like scars of her pregnancy, once livid purple, now fading to silver – none of these bothered her anymore. She was made anew. Fresh meaning had been conferred upon her, and every physical thing she did for herself felt like an obeisance to a greater power.

Now even something like putting on a pair of tights

was a kind of sacrament. Previously, if she wore tights at all, she'd yank them on in a clumsy, mindless scramble, rushing onward to the demands of the day. But this afternoon, she sat down on the edge of the bed and drew the tights on slowly, first settling the seam straight below the small knuckles of her toes, then unrolling them upwards, luxuriously, one glass-polished leg at a time: she had shaved her legs in the shower, so smoothly that the long shin bones reflected the light.

What she found so intoxicating was the view of herself that he'd given her.

They hadn't had full sex yet, although they had done almost everything else. She clung to this technical fact – despite knowing it to be logically and morally false – because it kept the guilt at a manageable remove. Not that the guilt was bothering her as much as she had thought it might, back at the start.

When Mr Riseborough seized her in his arms in the 1921 club, barely a month ago, a miracle had happened: every ounce of shame was instantly obliterated from the world. Never had she felt such an overpowering sense of connection. There was nothing safe or tender about it. The jolt of electricity was brutal, it kicked her alive, it demanded immediate satisfaction. She was tear-stained, streaming with spilt champagne, but she had wanted to take him inside her right there and then. Afterwards, alone with a sleeping Ann in the taxi home, as she mentally prepared the first of many lies to Theo, she waited for her conscience to speak up – but for once that shrill, punitive part of her was silent – stunned, perhaps, at what she was about to do.

All the usual rules, she soon discovered, were suspended, swept aside by the absolute burning necessity of this thing between her and Mr Riseborough. She would have said she'd lost her senses, if it were not for the certainty that she had – for the very first time – *found* them. There seemed to be a constant whistling, bubbling, tripping sound in her head, as though life itself had been tuned to a higher pitch.

Their time to meet was after Leni's twice-weekly shifts at *The Sentinel*. Although she finished work at 10.00 p.m., she'd told Theo that her shift ended at midnight. Mr Riseborough would be ready, parked in the private underground garage nearby, engine running. She'd tap in the code he'd given her to open the street door, and clatter down the lino stairs. He drove an old beaten-up Jeep Cherokee, not at all the sort of car she would have imagined him owning. Inside the Jeep it was warm and dark, and it smelt foreign, male.

Last Friday night, they had driven to Tullynether woods, high on a hill above the lough. The car park was deserted apart from one other car, parked well under the trees, its windows blanked out by thick condensation. Mr Riseborough turned off the engine. She couldn't see his face but she felt his gaze turn on her, and she heard him breathing; heard herself breathing. As her eyes became accustomed to the darkness, his pale shirt – tie-less, open at the neck – emerged from the gloom like an apparition.

'Shall we get into the back seat?' he'd asked softly.

The memory made Leni feel hot all over. She walked across to her dressing table and picked up a tall black glass bottle of perfume. Uncapping it, she applied two lavish squirts to her collarbones and one to each wrist, then rubbed her wrists together and replaced the lid. The new ritual.

Although she'd told Theo that she'd bought the

perfume herself, it was actually a gift from Mr Riseborough. A very special fragrance, he'd said, created in Paris in the last year of the war. It had been Marlene Dietrich's signature scent (Leni didn't like to ask who Marlene Dietrich was, for fear of looking stupid), and his mother had loved it too. Leni never normally wore perfume, she found it too sickly-sweet and cloying, but this scent was like nothing she'd ever smelt before: it was sensuous, powerful, and very grown-up.

Watching herself provocatively in the three-way mirror, she pulled open the waistband of her tights and pushed the perfume bottle down inside the skimpy net of her pants. She felt it cool and glassy hard against her. Then she sat down at the dressing table, straddling her legs wide to accommodate the bottle, and began to put on her make-up.

At Tullynether, they had clambered into the back of the Jeep one at a time, squeezing through the gap between the front seats. Leni went first, conscious of the swell of her bottom passing close beneath his face as she wriggled past him, then he slipped in beside her, slim and agile as an eel. He didn't seem old to her anymore. He had the pure body of a boy, only harder, steelier, more dense. His chest was hairless. She told him, shyly, that she thought he was beautiful, too, but he didn't seem to like being admired – it was as if compliments sank inside him without trace, instead of landing and spreading warmth, as they did with other people.

'We're like a pair of teenagers,' she murmured a few minutes later, coming up for air. 'Kissing in the back seat of the car.'

'You make me feel like a teenager,' he said, as he unbuttoned the tiny, padded buttons of her blouse. His hands were animals: quick, definite, feral. 'You make me feel like I'm starting my life all over again.' Low, congested voice, full of heat.

A near full moon was emerging through the black treetops. It was a gusty night, the branches waving and clashing, and for a moment she caught a glimpse of his harsh, suffused face under the moving tracery of shadows. What she saw frightened her, but the fear made her crave him all the more. She had never been wanted like this before, never experienced such fierce adoration.

She always stopped him before they went all the way. (Strange, how the old adolescent euphemisms sprang naturally to mind, as though she really was still fifteen – back in the school cloakrooms, hearing the other girls whisper: 'Did he? . . . Did *she*?') She had to pull back, even when her whole body was crying out for him, because that was the deal she'd made with herself. Denying herself what she wanted most, so that her betrayal – of Theo, of Ann, of the family home in which she'd invested so much – was not complete.

Oh, she knew it was absurd. But Mr Riseborough seemed to accept the situation without complaint – which was strange, given the urgency of his desire for her. Or maybe not so strange. After all, his love for her was total – he told her so constantly – and she knew how much he respected her feelings and wishes. So it was natural, of course, that he wouldn't pressurise her into something she wasn't yet ready for. Yes, it was obvious now – that must be the reason he took her reluctant, whispered 'no's so gracefully. What an extraordinary man he was.

By way of compensation for the lack of full sex, Leni offered him the most lovingly crafted fellatio. While Theo was putting Ann to bed, she locked herself away in the bathroom, the air still thick with clouds of baby powder. She'd sit with her back against the bath, phone switched to private browsing mode, watching pornography clips, and trying to memorise the perfect coordination of hand, lips and tongue. Unlike Theo, Mr Riseborough had no problem with a woman being on her knees.

Last Friday night at Tullynether, when they were finished, he had reached into the front of the Jeep – through half-closed eyes, she saw his slim haunches flit past – and turned on the CD player. Old-time music filled the car. *Sha la la . . . sha la la la . . .* The young women's voices were harsh yet lovely, longing for a love they never found. She lay there floating quietly, listening to the sweet forgotten heartache in the music. It made her think of Magill's poor lost Mary Jo.

'Leni? Let's dance,' said Mr Riseborough.

'*Dance*? Where? You mean here, now?'

'Yes, that's exactly what I mean,' he said. 'What else do we have but here, now? Let's get out and dance together.'

'You're not serious.'

'I really am.'

'I can't believe I'm doing this. It's freezing!' Laughing uncertainly, she began searching for her clothes, but he stopped her.

'No, don't put anything on. Stay as you are. Those other people have gone, there's nobody else here. Come on. Get out of the car and dance with me.'

He opened the door beside him and immediately the buffeting cold rushed in. He jumped out and ran around opening all the other doors, and then he turned the music up as loud as it would go. Leni stepped out barefoot on to dry leaves and twigs. An alien world: bright moonlight blowing around in her hair and scudding over the grass, and the trees roaring and calling to one another from their secret high places. Mr Riseborough took her by the hand and led her to the edge of the wood, where the land fell away steeply, tumbling down through monochrome patchwork fields to the distant silver lough and its islands.

The music was fainter here, tossed by the wind, but it still reached them. *Shama-lama-lama. Hey la-la-la.* Leni stumbled over a tussock, giggling, and he steadied her and held her formally for a moment, in an exaggerated ballroom pose, one icy hand on her waist, the other clasping her own chilly fingers. Then with an ironic, irresistible smile, he began to shimmy and sway, naked thighs twisting low from side to side, and she let herself be moved by him. Awkwardly at first, shivering and self-conscious – but then something in her broke loose and she was dancing too – dancing wildly, wildly, as the sweet dead girls chanted far away in the dark.

'You said you'd set me free,' she'd said, on the way back from Tullynether. She spoke in a low, glad murmur, nursing the wonder of the evening in her heart. She turned to look at him as he drove. Sharp-cut pterodactyl profile; hair springing vigorously from the roots and swept back from the steep, sloping forehead. Melancholy swag of the eyelid; firm hands gripping the wheel. Dear fiend, all hers.

'Remember, the first day we met, in your office? I know you were talking about my writing – needing to lose all the silly affectations, and stuff like that. But you really *have* set me free, in a far more important way. I had this neat, ordered, safe life. It was boring me stiff, though I couldn't admit it. And then knowing my mother was coming to stay made it all a million times worse. Everything was closing in, I was suffocating, and you saw that. You really did rescue me. You showed me how much more there could be, how mind-blowing my life could be, if I dared to take the risk. I'm not fooling myself; I know what we're doing is dangerous. People could get hurt. But I have this certain feeling that as long as I stay in the moment – in the present, I mean, always right here, right now, just like you said, not looking to the past or to the future – I'm protected, and nothing bad can happen. As if we're in this bubble, together, and everyone else is outside. They can't touch us. You know?'

He nodded yes, saying nothing. He was often very quiet, turned in on himself, remote inside his suit, when their time was over and he was taking her to the automated taxi office on the Ormonde Road. From there she'd take a cab home, even though it was only ten minutes' walk to Isthmus Avenue, to avoid arousing suspicion. Not that there seemed to be any question of that – on the nights Leni was working, Theo stayed in the big bed with Ann, and invariably the whole household would be fast asleep when she got in.

Mr Riseborough's silence didn't bother her – it rarely did, so sure did she feel of his love. 'I never was a teenager, you know,' she said, glancing out the window as the sleeping city suburbs rushed by. The clock on the dashboard said 12.22 a.m. 'Granny June was so strict and then when she got ill, I had to look after her, and there was never any time to just . . . I don't know . . . be me, I suppose. I was the steady, responsible one. It was my mother who was the wayward adolescent. That's what Granny always said. So I kind of missed out on that carefree stage. And then I met Theo, and we had Ann so soon afterwards – and there was even less time. Until I met you.' She laughed and turned to him again. 'Honestly, it's like you introduced me to myself.'

'Leni,' he said suddenly. 'Don't go back tonight. Come home with me instead. I want to take you home.'

She couldn't, of course. Not be there in the morning, when everyone got up? Her place on the nursery futon a blank space, empty, when Ann charged in to wake her? No, it was impossible, unthinkable. The bubble that held them safe, apart from the world, was strong, but it could not withstand a breach like that.

What Leni couldn't tell Mr Riseborough was that their assignations, and the constant flow of text messages that bound them to one another in between – that these were enough for her; that she didn't need more. 'Ample sufficiency' – another of Granny June's phrases. When Leni was little, her grandmother took her to the carvery lunch at the Slievedore Hotel every Sunday, after Mass. You could eat as much as you wanted of everything, but Granny June said it was important to know when to stop. 'We've had ample sufficiency,' she'd declare, dabbing her lips with a napkin, and suppressing a tiny burp. Leni too was replete, contented, after her time with Mr Riseborough, feeding off it for two or three days, until Tuesday or Friday came around and the longing would rise again, insatiable and inevitable, and she'd find herself doing crazy things like pushing perfume bottles into her pants and using them to make herself come. Oh, quickly, quickly – banish the thought of what Granny June would have said to that!

A second revelation, which she knew must also remain unspoken, was that life at home had never been better. The 'Seven B's' of attachment parenting, the mantra to which she'd clung, faded in importance; she found it wasn't needed any more. Twice-weekly shots of Mr Riseborough's psychoactive love made her into the mother she had always hoped she would be: cheerful, capable, unfazed by chaos, supremely patient, ever ready to play and feed and wipe and console.

Ann was turning two on Sunday, growing up fast. They were having a small family party to celebrate the occasion, and Leni was planning to make a special birthday cake – immaculate white icing, with Ann's name picked out in tiny gold stars, and two perfect golden candles in the middle.

As for Theo – well, Theo just seemed relieved, and unquestioningly grateful that he had a happy, well-run household to come back to every evening. He still hadn't managed to find a new DJ gig, but neither of them had mentioned it.

Leni completed her make-up with a coat of clear lip gloss. There – all ready. Nothing incriminating left lying about. The perfume bottle was safely back in its place on the dressing table.

As she opened the bedroom door, she heard Ann calling her from below. 'Mama? Mama? Come see!'

'Coming, Baba!' She smoothed her skirt and skipped briskly downstairs.

Chapter Fifteen

The kitchen looked as though a glitter bomb had been detonated. Everything sparkled. Even Ted, who came forward to greet Leni with a slow tail-wag, had a faint dusting across his nose, and his short black eyelashes glistened as he blinked. The table was the epicentre of the chaos, piled with discarded tubes, crumpled foil, stray lids and upended tubs. In the middle of it all was a cake which had clearly been decorated by Ann: it was covered with deep and erratic splodges of pink icing into which a tiny, forceful finger had pushed, one by one, chocolate hearts, sugar flowers and star-shaped sweets. The cake was thickly dredged with glitter and crowned by two pink and white candles, each set at a drunken angle.

'Surprise, Mama! We make my birfday cake!' shouted Ann, manically jumping up and down. 'Surprise, surprise, surprise!'

Patti was perched on the edge of the kitchen bench, a cigarette tucked in the corner of her mouth. She grinned at Leni through the fall of her razor-cut fringe.

'Don't worry, darling,' said Patti, the cigarette bouncing on her lower lip. 'I'm not actually smoking this. I just like the feeling of having it there. I promise you I won't light it until I go out to the back yard.'

Sitting at the table, in front of a half-drunk cup of coffee, was Marta from next door. She smiled at Leni and waggled her fingers in greeting.

Leni placed a calming hand on her daughter's head. It was the only part of Ann that wasn't covered with icing or glitter, and she didn't want her work clothes to get messed up.

'It's a gorgeous cake, Baba. Hush now, well done. You and Granny P did a great job,' she said.

Ann gradually subsided from jumping and shouting to bouncing and giggling.

'Hi, Marta, it's nice to see you.'

'Hi, hello, Leni,' said Marta, 'I hope it's okay for me, being here?'

'Of course! You're more than welcome.'

'I met Patti outside,' said Marta. 'She was talking to my cat, Tims, with young Ann here, and she says, "Come in for coffee – go on, we're going to make a birthday cake together, you must join, it will be so jolly." And I say, "Yes, why not? It's my free afternoon" – and so here I sit.'

Leni smiled. 'That's great. I'm going to work soon, but please stay as long as you like. I'm sure Patti and Ann will keep you entertained.'

'Oh they will, this crazy pair, you should see them play with the cake paint, making it squirt up high, and flinging the spangles! The laughs! Leni, you're so lucky, you have a real fun mum, you know – not like a granny at all.'

'I know,' said Leni. 'She really is something else.'

~

For the first few days after her mother moved in, Leni was brittle with nerves. For some reason the muscles of her face wouldn't work properly: expressions seemed to freeze and get stuck, smiles solidified and went on for far too long, until she'd notice the lag and hastily reassemble her features.

She was hyper-aware of Patti's presence in the house, tracking her mentally wherever she went. The house itself gleamed; Leni had spent hours washing, scrubbing and polishing. Not for Patti's benefit – her mother's natural condition was squalor; she was completely indifferent to cleanliness and order – but for her own. In order to survive, Leni felt she had to present a shining, impregnable front, as a bulwark against Patti's depredations; a way of keeping control of what was hers. She had to say: 'I am what you are not.'

Ahead of Patti's arrival, she had even made a short, bullet-pointed list entitled, 'Private Topics: not for discussion with my mother,' which she'd printed out and given to Theo. (When dealing with Theo, she knew it was often better to spell things out quite literally.) Items on the list included:

> No talk about parenting Ann, including her diet, clothes, bedtimes, physical and mental development
>
> No talk about our relationship
>
> No talk about our finances
>
> No talk about my work at *The Sentinel*

'I'm just going to tell her I got a part-time sub-editing job at *The Sentinel*, nothing more than that,' she told Theo. 'Don't give her any details, even if she starts asking, ok? Just keep away from the topic completely. Otherwise she'll be constantly interrogating me about it. You know what she's like.' Leni, of course, had her own particular reasons for avoiding too much scrutiny of the time she spent at the newspaper office.

She would have liked to tell Mr Riseborough how tense she felt, but she had developed a superstitious fear that even to mention Patti's name to him was a sort of jinx – like invoking a bad fairy – so she only ever referred to her briefly, in passing, as 'my mother'.

But then, from the moment Patti walked through the door, she was at her most marvellous. She was gracious; she was grateful; she seemed to radiate an exciting kind of heat – perhaps a fraction combustible – but so wonderfully warm, it invited you to come closer to bask in it. There was no mention of any of her health concerns, not a single complaint about anything – and no probing questions either.

The attic room? Such a precious spot, and what an amazing view over the rooftops – Patti *adored* the feeling of being up high. No, no, the stairs wouldn't be a problem, they would keep her fit, and she wanted to be as fit as possible to enjoy Ann's company – she needed to be able to keep up with her grandchild!

The neighbourhood? My God, what a transformation, the darling little shops and delis! So like Notting Hill, but better, far better, because the people here were friendly and kind and polite, they took the time to say good morning and ask how you were.

Ann was immediately smitten, and followed her grandmother around everywhere. 'My ragamuffin', Patti called her, often shortened to 'Rags', or 'Muffin', or some other variation. 'Come see, Miss Muff,' she'd say, swinging Ann up in her arms and taking her over to the window. It gave Leni a shock to see the two pairs of peacock-blue eyes together, Patti's and Ann's – they looked almost identical. 'Look, there's that naughty cat, Tims, trying to catch the birdies again. He won't get them, because he's blind, he can't see a thing. But look at him jump! Whoops, there he goes, tumbling down, paws in the air. What a silly kitty, eh, Muff?'

As well as paying for the replacement of the boiler, Patti went to the most expensive children's shop in town and bought Ann an entire wardrobe of new clothes. The sale of the flat in London had gone through, she said – 'so lucky it was in my name, not in Conrad's' - so she wasn't short of cash. And, she declared, she liked nothing better than spending it on the people who meant most to her – her family.

Naturally all of this only made Leni mistrust Patti more.

Then one day her mother completely disarmed her by admiring the way she'd decorated the stairs – how she'd painted the inlaid parts of the white spindles on the bannister the palest shade of blue, to pick up the deeper blue of the tiled floor below. Leni never expected Patti to notice something as subtle as that. The surprising surge of pleasure – no, it was stronger and sharper than pleasure, it was more like vindication, a sense of winning, for once getting something absolutely right – caused by her mother's praise put her even further on her guard for a while. It reminded her too forcibly of her desperate childhood attempts to win Patti's love and attention. But, like a stretch of fine summer weather, Patti's good humour lasted. It looked as if it might even be permanent.

Leni found herself wondering if she had been too harsh in judging her mother. Could it possibly be that Theo was right? He'd said from the very start that if Leni gave Patti what she wanted, by letting her come to stay, Patti would be content.

Or maybe it was because her mother had done the unthinkable and given up drinking. A fresh start, she'd said, announcing her decision shortly after she arrived. Maybe those pickled oceans of white rum had been the real problem, all along.

Not that things were perfect, of course. Her mother had unsavoury habits – like leaving the bathroom door open when she was using the toilet, and squashing lipstick-printed cigarette butts into Leni's pretty zinc window-boxes. She left smears from the black kohl she used to circle her eyes all over the white towels, and the towels themselves were frequently dumped, wet and stained, on the landing floor. And while Leni hadn't dared go anywhere near Patti's room, at the top of the house, she could imagine what state it was in, even though most of her mother's possessions – furniture, books, clothes and so on – were in a rented self-storage unit near the docks.

Food was a bit of a problem too. Patti referred to herself as 'an experimental cook': she liked to mix ingredients with strong, pronounced flavours together, and she expected Leni and Theo to relish her creations as much as she did. This wasn't too much of a difficulty for Theo, who was raised to appreciate whatever was set in front of him, but Leni struggled.

It was as if food could never have enough bite to satisfy Patti. When she was out in public, she even carried a mini bottle of Naga chilli sauce around in her handbag, so that she could add a few blistering drops to whatever she ate. One of her favourite concoctions was something she called 'Lunch Dish' which, despite the name, she loved to eat at any time. She'd adapted the recipe from a 1980s cookbook, and it involved avocados which had been deliberately allowed to become murky, dark and over-ripe ('The only way they taste of anything,' declared Patti, busily lining up the avocados on the top of the radiator to soften). The mess of grey-flecked green was mashed together with hard-boiled eggs, chopped scallions, a liberal dousing of vinegar and several cloves of crushed raw garlic, and served on toast with Gentleman's Relish – otherwise known as Patum Peperium, a reeking salty mulch of anchovies and spices which was another of her mother's culinary essentials. Uncertain of maintaining a guaranteed supply in Belfast, Patti had brought twenty porcelain pots of the stuff with her from Harrods, and they sat like little black pucks in the cupboard alongside Leni's loose-leaf teas and herbal infusions. 'Patti-pepper', Ann soon started calling it, and she loved licking scraps of it from the tip of Patti's none-too-clean finger, as Leni bit back her disapproval.

Compared to what she had been dreading, however, these were minor matters.

~

'You know what? This girl is a real star,' declared Patti, swinging Ann up to sit beside her on the glitter-strewn kitchen bench. It made Leni feel uncomfortable to see Ann perched there – what if she fell? – but she was trying to trust her mother more, so she said nothing.

'It was such a joy to watch her work on that cake,' said Patti. 'The masterful way she uses colour! Her instincts are so true, so definite, so completely uninhibited. I've never witnessed anything like it. Leni, I really do believe we have a budding artist here.'

Marta clapped her hands together. 'Just like grandma! For did you not say, Patti, that you make art yourself?'

'Ah, that was a long time ago, Marta. Practically another lifetime. The world has changed and left me behind. But once, yes, once I was an artist. You could say that I made my mark.'

'And now you have handed your gift on to Ann,' said Marta. 'It is a very special thing to see.'

They heard the latch of the front door click and then Theo walked into the room, bringing a waft of the outdoors with him: damp soil, burnt leaves.

'Wow,' he said, when he saw the state of the kitchen. 'Some serious business going on here. Hi, Patti. Oh, hi, Marta – how are you?'

'You're back very early,' said Leni, as he leaned over to say hello and kiss her forehead.

'Yeah, the last group left at three and Gavin said he'd close up. There's not much going on at this time of year, so I thought I'd head for home,' he said, taking off his coat. He walked over to Ann and tousled her hair. 'Hello, sticky girl. Bath time's going to be fun tonight.'

Leni didn't like Theo seeing her all dressed up for work: it made her nervous. What if he could read the truth in the sheen of her tights, the height of her heels, the explicit scent of her perfume? The buttons of her shirt began glowing red-hot. Surely they were starting to smoulder? But Theo didn't seem to notice anything. He sat down at the end of the table next to Marta, picked up a stray chocolate heart and ate it. 'Hmm. Not bad.'

'Hey, Puppy,' said Patti, turning to Theo with a sly sideways grin. The cigarette had disappeared from the corner of her mouth as soon as he'd walked in the door. 'Check out the new trainers I bought today.'

Puppy – that was her nickname for Theo, though she also called him 'T', Leni's own name for him. Patti stretched out her left leg and held her little foot right under Theo's nose, barely an inch from his face, tilting her ankle back and forth.

When it came to men, Patti had always behaved as though she was 16 years old and irresistible. Now aged 59, she still had undiminished confidence in her own power. It wasn't entirely delusional. Leni had witnessed Patti flexing her charms only the night before, when Mack from across the street knocked on the door to complain – again – that the Moffetts had taken the parking space outside his house, where Mack liked to park his motorbike. Mack was large, grim and rather scary. But it was almost impossible to get parked on Isthmus Avenue, and you had to squeeze in wherever was available. Patti answered the door when he had rung. By the time Leni came to see who it was, her mother was already in charge. Mack was laughing – actually laughing – at whatever Patti had just said, and his dour cheeks were flushed with pleasure. It occurred to Leni that Patti's power wasn't so much in making men desire her, as in making them feel desirable – if and when she chose to do so.

'What do you think, T?' asked Patti. 'Cute shoes, aren't they?'

'They look great, Patti. They suit you,' smiled Theo.

'Grab a hold and feel the softness of that suede.'

Theo cupped the heel of the silver trainer and gave it a tentative stroke with his thumb. 'Oh yeah, that's really nice. Sort of velvety texture, isn't it?'

Patti smirked, full of mischief. 'Give it a kiss,' she said.

'What?' said Theo.

'Kiss my new shoe.'

Theo looked up at her, perplexed. He twiddled the end of his ponytail.

'Umm . . .'

'Go on. Give it a little kiss. Just on the toe there. I dare you!'

There was a perceptible shift in the atmosphere in the room: a little frisson of excitement. Everyone was waiting to see what Theo would do. Glancing awkwardly across at Leni, he bent his lips briefly to the tip of Patti's shoe. Marta cheered. Blinking and blushing, and looking both embarrassed and rather pleased with himself, Theo sat back in his chair. Ann slithered down from her perch at Patti's side, climbed on to his knee and rewarded him with three smacking kisses on the cheek. '*Good* boy, Daddy!'

'You're a brave man, T,' grinned Patti. 'Many wouldn't have risked it. Now, can I pour you a coffee? There's plenty left in the pot. Marta, would you take another?'

'I'd better go now or I'll be late for work,' said Leni.

Patti gave her a regal wave. 'Of course, of course. Off you go, my darling, and don't worry about a thing. I made extra Lunch Dish earlier, so that's dinner all sorted. And I can help T with Ann in the bath. You enjoy your evening's work, you deserve it.'

'Want to take the car, Len?' asked Theo. 'May as well – saves you getting the bus. And it means you won't have to taxi it home later.'

'Thanks Theo, but no, it's okay. I like the usual routine. I'm used to it now.'

As Leni closed the gate, she glanced back at her

house, almost as a stranger might, set apart from the life inside, the lilac front door shut against her. An odd feeling of being dismissed, somehow left out, lingered as she hurried along the street. But by the time she reached the corner it had gone.

Chapter Sixteen

Oh, and there she was – his salvation – standing alone at the Ormonde Road bus stop. It was as if she had suddenly materialised out of the cosmos, like a gift from a merciful god.

Six times around the block he'd driven, since there was nowhere to pull in and park. On each circuit, he scanned the people passing by, fearing that he'd missed her already – yelling curses at the slow traffic lights, blaring the horn at a decrepit old hag perversely inching her way over a zebra crossing, saluting with manic superstition a solitary magpie picking at some rubbish in the gutter. And then finally, he'd been blessed and vindicated on the seventh turn! He could almost start believing in the Almighty, at this rate – or was it his own divine need, the force of his enchanted will, that had called her into being? Anything felt possible.

Leni, hello Leni, it's you, Leni, hello.

Blazing white face and the red roar of her hair as he streaked past the bus stop, braked sharply, then threw the Jeep into reverse against the oncoming traffic, to a fanfare of outraged hoots and beeps. He lowered the window and leaned across.

'Like a lift to work?'

Her answering smile, wry and complicit, reduced his knees to water. He wanted to bury his face in her lap and never lift it again. He wanted to stay there, blissfully immersed in her, sated by joy, devoid of all pain until he left this earth.

She decanted herself into the passenger seat and clicked the strap into its holder, then demurely adjusted the hem of her skirt and glanced up at him from under those flaming brows. The mermaid flick.

How had he ever thought that she wasn't beautiful?

He nudged on his right indicator and shoved his way out into the road again, ignoring a fresh round of aggrieved horns. He had her now, had her and would hold her. Death could wait.

~

'Glad I caught you at the stop,' he said. 'Thought you might have gone already.'

'You were just in time. I'd only been waiting for a couple of minutes, and I could see the bus coming down the road.'

'Ah. Serendipity.'

'Good luck, you mean?'

'More than that. It shows we're meant to be together. The universe is smiling on us,' he added whimsically. How happy he felt!

'That's such a lovely way to put it,' she smiled. 'Were you on your way back from somewhere? I thought you'd be up to your eyes in the office at this point in the day.'

'Had an important meeting out of town,' said Roddy. 'Confidential security source – he can't risk coming into the city. And then I remembered you'd be getting the bus about now, so I thought I'd swing by – just on the off-chance, you know. And there you were.'

In fact, Roddy had been in the middle of a long, tedious briefing from his deputy, Jacqueline, about upcoming feature articles. She was planning to run a piece on something called 'yarn bombing', which seemed to involve middle-aged women vandalising public spaces with insufferably twee bits of knitting, which they draped around lampposts and the like. Personally, he'd rather see an upended bottle of Buckfast in a flowerbed – at least it would be evidence that someone had had some fun. But there was no point telling Jackie that – she'd only go back to the beginning of her spiel and start again, thus doubling the tedium.

Roddy had glanced down at his watch. He realised that Leni would be on her way to work soon. Why not go and intercept her? No sooner had he thought of the delightful plan than he was on his feet, feeling in his pocket for the car keys.

'Apologies, Jackie – just remembered, I need to slip out for a moment. Won't be long.'

Jackie stopped mid-sentence and stared at him incredulously. Her normally iron-clenched jaw hung slack, which he suspected her of doing deliberately, in a kind of pantomime way, to emphasise her disapproval. He longed to deal her a swift flick under that small, reproachful, expensively moisturised chin, so that her mouth closed with a sharp snap. Not hard enough to seriously hurt her, of course. A playful blow really, just with the back of the hand. The pearly crunch of teeth on teeth would be so satisfying, and if she happened to bite the tip of her tongue, well then, all the better.

'Tatty-bye now,' he'd said, lifting his coat from the hatstand.

Now, where had that funny old phrase come from? One of Mummie's? It didn't sound like her. He rummaged briefly in the ragbag swirl of his memory, that jumbled stock of sayings, but nothing came up. Something off the television perhaps. Anyway, it struck exactly the mocking, derisive note he'd been aiming for. Jackie didn't reply.

Beside him in the car, Leni was playing with the pebbles he'd dumped in the Jeep's cup-holder earlier this morning, after finding them in the pocket of his overcoat. Roddy had no use for the cup-holder – a stupid American device. He refused to drink from those takeaway polystyrene coffee cups with a hole in the lid that you had to suck at, like an overgrown infant with its bottle. Roddy preferred tea to coffee anyway. Lapsang souchong for him: a slice of lemon, no sugar and always in a proper china cup – that was his way.

'These are pretty,' said Leni, dropping the pebbles from hand to hand in a slow juggle. They clacked together like billiard balls. 'Where did you get them?'

'On the shore, at home. I picked them up the other day when I was walking Ter— I mean, when I was out for a walk.'

Oh, why had he made her think Terence was dead? He wanted to keep things clean and clear between them, yet here was that ridiculous fib, raising its ugly, troublesome head again. Best just to plough on, hoping she hadn't noticed.

'It was raining, quite heavily, and when the stones get wet, they turn the most amazing colours. You get these wonderful stormy blues and greys, and the white ones – they almost seem to glow. It's like treasure – you just want to snatch it and keep it for yourself. But as soon as they're dry, they're just ordinary stones again. It's the rain, you see, that brings the colour alive.'

'I like this one.' She held up a grey, almost black, pebble, about the size of a quail's egg, with a white fracture running through it like a lightning bolt. 'Hang on, I have an idea.' She popped the stone in her mouth, held it for a moment, then plucked it out. 'There. Look at it now.' The wet stone shone between her finger and thumb.

'That's curiously erotic,' said Roddy.

She giggled. 'You try it.'

'Alright. But I'm driving. You'll have to put in my mouth for me.'

She pushed the pebble between his lips. It was hard and salty, warm from her mouth, with a slightly raised, rippled grain. With his tongue, he rolled it into the corner of his left cheek, behind the line of molars.

'Umm,' he said thickly. 'Feels quite nice actually. Like a gobstopper.'

'Gobstopper?'

'A big boiled sweet. Before your time.'

From nowhere, a grotesque image of 'Chelle, the woman he used to pay to clean Honolulu, popped into his mind. The wet, squelchy, open-mouthed way she chewed gum as she dragged the vacuum cleaner across the floor; how she stopped every so often to add yet another piece to the wad she had already accumulated in her mouth, until it became so vast, sometimes, that it made her cheek protrude like a hamster.

'Chelle had been – probably still was, for all he cared – a part-time beauty therapist, by which she meant she painted women's nails for money. 'Therapist', indeed. 'Chelle practically needed help to cross the road on her own. Funny, he had never actually said her name out loud, but he mentally pronounced it just as she did herself, with the missing first syllable swallowed in his throat. Never 'Michelle', always ''Chelle'. She'd introduced herself with a childish mumble, and a kind of apology for having the presumption to exist at all.

It wasn't long before he'd noticed how her tiny rodent eyes, synthetically rayed with mascara, surveyed him hungrily, hopelessly, as she loaded laundry into the washing machine. The fat droop of her middle-aged thighs, encased in their stone-washed jeans, was pathetic. It was almost a kindness, he told himself, to press against her proffered buttocks – really, the only gentlemanly thing to do. 'Chelle had uttered a small mewl, like a newborn kitten's cry, and dropped to her knees, hands still buried deep in the basket full of Roddy's smalls.

They'd gone on like that for years. Neither of them spoke about it, so it wasn't really a relationship. 'Chelle left orange stains in his bed, from the fake tan she wore, and her fingertips smelled like old smoke. It only stopped when he found a gigantic wodge of chewing gum adhering to the underside of Mummie's teak coffee table in the great room. It was then that the revulsion had finally outweighed the convenience and he'd had to fire her.

'Are you ok?' asked Leni, breaking into his unpleasant reverie. 'You look a bit . . . pained, or something.'

'Me? No, no, I'm fine. Couldn't be better! I was thinking about where we might go later. Maybe we'll take a run up the Antrim coast, towards Cushendun. There's a very secluded car park at one of the glens.' He reached across and clasped her hand, interlinking his fingers with hers. 'Being alone with you in the dark – honestly, Leni, it's what I live for. Remember last week, at Tullynether? Our wild alfresco disco?'

'That was one of the most amazing moments of my

life. I'll never forget it,' she said earnestly. She was rubbing the ball of her thumb over the manicured smoothness of his thumbnail, an endearing little habit of hers.

'Hey,' she said suddenly. 'I've just thought of something! Do you know what I would absolutely love to do tonight?'

'What?' He felt a spasm of uneasiness. She must remember that it was him at the wheel, not her; he had to stay in control. But at the same time, he ached to please her.

'Go to a club. With you.'

'You mean – a *night*club?' Oh, Christ. Roddy nearly choked on the pebble, which he was still nursing in his mouth. He spat it out and it rolled under his seat.

'Yeah! Not for long,' she added quickly. 'Even just for half an hour. I want to dance with you. Properly, I mean, on a dancefloor, with other people.'

'But – you realise we might be seen?'

'Let's take a chance on that.' She laughed. 'I think you must be giving me a taste for risky behaviour. Being with you makes me want to do bad things.'

Well, precisely. Of course he was cultivating her suppressed appetite for lawlessness and rule-breaking, and bending it to his own very particular ends. But he hadn't anticipated that going to some god-awful nightclub would be necessary. Perhaps if he said nothing more about it, she would drop the idea.

They weren't far from *The Sentinel* offices now, bowling along Cormac Street, the traffic into town moving well for once. Up ahead, the lights at the junction with Lady Street changed to red.

'Maybe you'd better let me out somewhere near

here,' said Leni. 'So we're not arriving at the same time. Oh, look! Look over there – it's a DeLorean! See it? In the outside lane, in front of that white van?'

'Oh yes,' nodded Roddy. 'Rare enough specimen, these days.'

'You'll hardly believe this, but I saw one the day I met you. It's got to be the same one. It can't just be a coincidence. Maybe it's serendipity again.'

'You like DeLoreans?' asked Roddy, surprised. Odd interest for a girl.

'I love them,' said Leni. 'If I ever get rich, that's the car I want to drive.'

The lights changed to amber, and the DeLorean shot forward, not waiting for the green. Roddy made an executive decision. Instead of turning left down Lady Street, towards *The Sentinel* offices, he slung the Jeep into the right lane, gunned the engine and sped after the DeLorean.

'What are you *doing*?' cried Leni.

'Having some fun,' he grinned. 'Let's see if we can catch it.'

They flew past the law courts and the wonky old Albert Clock. Up in front, like a silver insect, the DeLorean was weaving its way through the traffic, exploiting gaps and spaces to get ahead.

'This is crazy! You're mad! I'll be late for work!' Her face was blown open with amazement: she looked like a little girl on her first rollercoaster ride.

The DeLorean turned onto Carlisle Street with a flash of its chequerboard tail, neat and sharp as a Scalextric car. The lights changed as they approached, but Roddy lurched the Jeep round on the red, and hurtled up the slip road to the motorway.

'It's getting away!' cried Leni.

'No, no, we won't let it!'

Now the DeLorean was burning up the motorway, a rapidly diminishing dot in the distance, but Roddy remembered that for all their glamour, DeLoreans were tortoise-slow, in sports car terms – lucky to do 100 mph, at a push. He pressed the Jeep's accelerator to the floor. 60, 70 mph – they were gaining on it. Then some asshole in a white BMW – one of those awful swollen people-carriers, ugly and bloated-looking, I mean, Jesus, what had happened to German car design? – swung out into his lane. Roddy tailgated him furiously, flashing his lights, inches from the car's bumper.

'Come on, come on, get out of the way, you fat fuck!' he shouted.

At last, the blimpish BMW moved over, slowly, deliberately taking its time. The road was clear again, and the DeLorean was still – just – in sight. No cops about, thank God. He'd have to call in some serious favours if he was snared on this joyride. He accelerated hard. Seventy . . . eighty . . . ninety mph. And now one hundred! Roddy whooped with delight. Fields, hedges, sheep flew by in a porridge-like blur.

They zipped under a bridge and when they emerged, they were closer – yes, getting much closer to the DeLorean now – he could even see the back of the driver's head. The sports car was out on its own, cruising, no longer racing, just skimming along. What he was actually going to do when they caught it, he hadn't a clue, but never mind – wasn't the real thrill all about the chase? He was showing Leni the kind of wild, spontaneous life he could offer her, if only she'd leave her old, safe, plodding life behind.

But then he looked at her, and what he saw made him hit the brakes, hard.

Leni was frozen – eyes fixed wide, staring straight ahead, knees pulled up to her chin, arms clasped tight around them. One shoe had fallen off. She looked petrified, literally petrified – turned to stone, bone, fossilised wood.

The Jeep juddered and shook as the speedometer plummeted, and a black, oily smell of burning brake-pads filled the air. Ahead of them, the DeLorean surged up a rise in the road and disappeared.

'What is it, Leni, what's wrong?'

She gave the barest shake of her head, hardly more than a quiver.

'Wait . . . wait,' she whispered.

He cut across to the inside lane and pulled onto the hard shoulder, screeching to a stop in a spray of gravel. He hit the hazard warning lights, though what the emergency was, he had no idea. The stationary Jeep stood ticking and cooling, rocked by the slipstreams of passing cars. When he laid his hand on her leg, she flinched, so he took his hand away again. He waited, drumming his fingertips on the steering wheel. Disappointing. Really rather disappointing.

'Sorry,' she said at last, in the smallest possible voice.

'Was it the speed that scared you? Going too fast?'

'Sort of. Maybe. I don't know.'

'Come on, Leni. You must know. You were obviously loving it. What happened?'

'I – it was fun, at first. Exciting. But then – I – I had this sudden memory . . .'

'Yes?' Lord, was he going to have to drag the thing out of her, syllable by syllable?

'Something that happened, ages ago, when I was little – not here, it was in England, on the motorway. But it wasn't a normal memory. It was like I was actually back there, in the car, and it was happening all over again—'

'Strange. What was it that you remembered?'

'There was a swan . . . I saw . . . it couldn't – it got hit, I think, and crash-landed—'

'Leni, I can't hear you when you mumble like that. Speak up. You saw *what*?'

'Oh, it was . . . it was nothing.' She sat up straighter and felt around with her foot for the cast-off shoe. 'Nothing important anyway. Please, let's just forget about it. I'm alright now. Really.'

'Really?'

'Yes,' she nodded, though she still looked all lost and woebegone. 'Can you take me to work, please?'

'Of course. We'll need to go on to the next junction, then we can turn and head back to the city. Don't worry about being late – I'll square it with Martin.'

Since he'd helped Martin Sharkey defend himself against those unfortunate underage allegations a few years ago, his chief sub-editor had proved to be a very good friend to Roddy – more than happy to repay the debt wherever he could. He'd been particularly accommodating about finding a role for Leni in the subs' office. Roddy appreciated that.

Neither of them spoke until they were travelling back towards town, at an unimpeachably sedate fifty mph. Then Roddy said, 'Whatever it was, it's done, you know. The past is over, Leni: it's completely behind you. It can't hurt you anymore. Remember, you're living in the future now. With me.'

Chapter Seventeen

He had no choice but to go to the wretched nightclub, after that nonsense with the DeLorean. He felt he owed it to her, like a treat to make up for a disappointment. And of course it was ghastly. Dank, smelly, loud. A skunky dive called The Kasbah, chosen by Leni because she thought she wasn't likely to bump into anyone she knew there – and there certainly wouldn't be any of Roddy's acquaintances.

The Kasbah occupied the top floor of an old linen warehouse on Font Street, up a narrow, sticky staircase above a tattoo parlour. He had to submit to the indignity of getting his wrist stamped with a blurred image of a cannabis leaf, by a rancid, rattish-looking girl, hunched on a barstool and wearing a grubby fake-fur coat.

Once inside, his eardrums threatened to burst under the jack-hammer assault of the so-called music, and he was periodically dazzled by rolling white spotlights, slicing up and scissoring his retinas. The whole thing was like a Guantánamo interrogation scene, minus the waterboarding – though even that might still transpire, he thought darkly, given the waves of cheap beer sloshing from plastic cups all around them. Accidentally inhaling the local lager would probably be even worse than drinking it, Roddy reckoned.

Leaving Leni sitting at the end of a sleazy-looking sofa – it was low, spreading, fungoid in shape and colour, exactly the sort of furniture you'd see in a micro-budget 1980s porn flick – Roddy made his way through the sweaty, mostly male crowd towards the bar, which was on a raised platform at the back of the club. En route, a rough jolt against his shoulder made him swing round sharply.

'Sorry, mate, sorry,' slobbered a corpulent youth, looming close with bleary eyes, his sparse hair cut so short that pale scalp showed between the gelled and combed grooves on his head. The full pint he was holding slopped between them in perilous proximity to Roddy's favourite sports coat. Roddy extended an arm, gripped the fool by his lardy elbow, and with a discreet but forceful shove sent him spinning off in a different direction, a fat planet on his own gormless odyssey.

Waiting for the two G&Ts he ordered at the bar, Roddy surveyed the unedifying scene below. The girls looked unhealthy, ill-bred and thin – was this what Yolanda, the fashion editor at *The Sentinel*, would call 'heroin chic'? Though perhaps that wasn't 'a thing' anymore. Many of the young men, however, like the one who'd jostled him, were seriously overweight, wobbly guts spilling out from beneath too-short T-shirts. They might be less than half his age, but he was in far better shape than any of these potato-faced mooncalves. The thought gave Roddy a black kind of satisfaction.

When he returned with the drinks, which were mostly ice, and without the benefit of either lemon or lime, Leni was talking to another girl, who was crouched in front of her on the floor. Some sort of nondescript female with short, thick hair – a garrulous and exclaiming type, fairly chunky in her jeans, not wan and drug-ravaged like the others. She kept laughing and smacking Leni roguishly on the knee, and Leni flashed him an awkward glance, apologetic, but she didn't seem especially worried to have been spotted. He lowered himself gingerly onto the sofa, and immediately sank deep into its broken springs.

'Can't believe I haven't seen you since sixth form!' the girl was shrieking, above the harsh din of the music. 'God, this place makes me feel ancient. They don't check ID, so it's full of kids. Babies. I swear, some of them can't be more than fifteen!'

Leni made some smiling response that Roddy couldn't hear, then she caught his eye and inclined her head questioningly towards the dance floor.

He hauled himself up again, holding Leni's drink – his own he'd drained immediately, purely to get rid of the nasty thing – and was aware of the surprised and suddenly speculative gaze of Miss Chunky-Arse following them.

'It's ok,' shouted Leni in his ear. 'She doesn't even know that I'm married.'

Impossible to dance properly to this racket, of course. Ludicrous. He held Leni close and jiggled ineptly, hating his ineptitude. He could feel her wanting to make larger, more expansive movements, to splay out and swing with him, take up more space, but he contained her, tersely, in the tightness of his embrace, imposing a slow, minimal shuffle on them both. Irritation at the indignity of it all bristled up in him.

The song ended in a clatter of broken discords. Roddy needed a break. Pointing to a door bearing the scrawled legend, 'Bogs' – fitting word – he told Leni he would meet her back at the seats. He took a swift, angry piss, holding his breath against the stench of the place, and shoved his way back through the crowd.

The sofa was now occupied by a limp cadre of

teenage stoners, each almost horizontal, communing with their iPhones. No sign of Leni. Maybe she had misunderstood or misheard him. But she wasn't on the dancefloor either – or at the bar, or anywhere in between. In the toilet? She must be, there was nowhere else. Roddy waited beside the entrance to the women's loo, looking up each time the door opened to check if it was Leni coming out. Then a glance of half-amused suspicion from one girl, who turned and said something sardonic to her friends – he caught the curl of her firmly outlined lip – made him realise how appalling he must look, lurking there, furtively peering at the young female clientele.

And yet he didn't want to leave the spot either, because where else could Leni be?

His anxiety was really spiking now. He tried to compensate for both the fluttering panic and the perceived lecherousness by standing up straighter, drawing back his shoulders, adopting a stern, patrician expression. But that was worse, because it reminded him of his father, and for a sick moment he felt he actually was the Judge – the old soldier resurrected and fantastically transposed to a guard post outside the women's toilet of a filthy Belfast nightclub.

No, this was unbearable, he couldn't stand it any longer. He set off on another frantic loop of bar, dancefloor, seating area, and that's when he saw her, at last, standing in the appointed place beside the sofa, obviously scanning the heads of the crowd for him. He strode up to her and grabbed her arm roughly.

'Let's go,' he said, without waiting for a reply, and began walking her towards the exit. Inside he felt close to tears of rage, tears of relief.

He rushed her down the stairs, still keeping his grip,

binding them together as tightly as if they were in a fast three-legged race. 'Where were you?' he muttered furiously.

'What? I was just – I went to the loo and I met Shona Bryce again, that girl from school – it was hard to get away, she was going on about various people from our year, she's organising a reunion next summer. And then when I went back to the seats, you weren't there so I went to the bar to see if . . . Look, what's happened, why are you so angry with me?'

Now they were standing on the pavement facing each other, and the adult, rational part of Roddy knew that this was the point at which he should calm down and apologise for his rudeness, as well as for the unjustifiably rough treatment he'd given her. But something infantile and destructive in him was stronger, and so he gave in to the awful luxury of letting it rip.

'It's all about you, isn't it?' he sneered. 'Everything always has to be about what suits you, and I'm just expected to go along with it. Pick you up at this time, drop you off at that time, because God forbid that anything would interfere with your precious fucking home life with fucking Moominpapa!'

'With – with *who*?' she stammered.

People passing by on the street were looking at them, but he didn't care. 'Oh, the blessed Theo, the perfect sainted father of your child! Got to get back to Theo at the witching hour, so he doesn't wake up and wonder where his wife is, and what she's getting up to on the back seat of a stranger's car. Not actual sex, of course, because Leni's such a good girl, she would never allow a man who wasn't her husband to *fuck* her.'

Leni looked stunned, as though she'd been slapped in

the face. But he had too much to say to consider stopping. 'Yes, we've got to keep Theo happy at all costs, even though he's a passive, cringing, sex-averse little neuter-boy, one of these pathetic male feminists – probably sits down to piss! He's all about respect for the ladies, because basically he is one himself.' Now Roddy adopted a high, mincing tone, 'No, no, Leni, don't give me head, it's morally abhorrent to me! Keep back, stay away – you are the mother of my child, you must remain pure!'

Leni stared at him. 'I should never have told you that,' she said quietly.

'And as for *you* – what sort of perverse, masochistic game are you playing? Setting yourself up as some throwback 1950s housewife, when you're barely out of college and everybody else your age is breaking loose, off seeing the world, snorting coke on a beach in Thailand. What did you do? You put yourself under house arrest. You built this cosy, soft-furnishings prison with matching crockery, and No-Balls Moominpapa as chief jailer, and just to keep yourself really tied down you pop out a kid. And then, as if that wasn't bad enough, you invite dear old granny to stay – because Theo, despite all his precious moral principles, really fancies getting his paws on his mother-in-law's cash.'

'Wait, no, it's not like that! You've twisted what I said—'

But Roddy still wasn't done. 'You tell me you're so *free* now, after I came along and rescued you – but you're just as bound up in your sweet little domestic life as ever. Don't think I don't see that! And the biggest fucking joke of all is that I'm the one who's making it possible. I provide the attention and the excitement and the freedom – all the things that were missing before. *You* can enjoy the solid home comforts, the family meals, and the games, and the kid, and the dog, because now you have this secret life as well. The balance between the two is just perfect. Bingo! You get everything you want! Lucky Leni! But what do I get? What's in it for *me*?'

His voice, which had been rising to a sort of bellowing shriek, cracked and broke on the last word. And now here came the tears, spilling over uncontrollably – oh God, what an awful bore! Hard, spiky sobs dredged themselves up from some unknown place within, tearing his heart to ribbons as they fought their way out of him. He needed to hide his ugly blubbering face and so he turned and flung himself against the wall behind him, pressing his forehead into the rough brick. Part of him was disconnected, quietly observing himself as he stood there vomiting up his old grief like any other street drunk.

After a while, really quite a long while – so long that he began to fear that she'd walked away – he felt a gentle, tentative hand arrive on his shoulder and settle there.

'I'm sorry,' she murmured. 'I'm sorry. You're right.'

They walked hand in hand back to Roddy's car. Everything was soft and calm and reborn between them. Nothing keeping them apart now. He confessed, quite easily, about the little miscommunication about Terence, and was quickly forgiven. He did not confess the reason that he'd held back from full sex – had been quite willing, in fact, to accept her last-moment gasped refusals – because there was no need. Miraculously, the fear that had fuelled it was gone.

In the past, with other women he'd loved, Roddy found that his desire for them mysteriously withered as soon as he felt certain that they belonged to him, that he'd captured them – won them, in fact. By a weird coincidence this often happened once things got serious sexually. All the aching and longing disappeared, or rather it turned into a deadweight on his back, and he'd be seized with an overpowering need to throw it off and to flee.

Worshipping Leni as he did, he'd been haunted by dread that the same thing would happen with her. But now he knew, with a new, glorious certainty – a soul-certainty, such as he'd never experienced before – that Leni was different. It was the touch of her hand on his shoulder that did it: just as simple as that. It sealed the symbiosis between them. This was Love, and she was The One, come to him at last, after a lifetime of whittling alone in the firelight. There was nothing to fear. He asked her to go to Honolulu with him – now, this moment, tonight. She knew what it meant. And this time she said yes.

Chapter Eighteen

Ann's second birthday celebration began shortly after dawn on Sunday, when she ripped the shiny paper from Patti's personal gift – a white electric ride-on car with lights, horn, and its own USB port and speakers. Ann barely glanced at any other presents after that, including the toy wooden workbench with hand-painted screwdrivers and spanners that Leni and Theo had chosen for her.

Later, Theo's family arrived – Bill and Dorothy and the other Moffetts. Nobody was coming from Leni's side of the family, since apart from her mother, Leni only had Great-Aunt Caroline, Granny June's sister, and she was too frail to travel from her home in Rostrevor. Theo's older brother, Mike, brought his sons, aged five, eight and ten. The boys clustered in a shy, brown-eyed bunch, watchful and silent, staying close to Mike, until Patti suggested a party game. Now the whole house resounded to shrieks and yells and the beat of hammering feet as the boys charged through the rooms, led by Patti, with Ann tucked under her arm, orchestrating some manic version of hide-and-seek. Even Theo joined in, thumping joyously up the stairs with a most un-Theo-like battle-cry.

Downstairs in the kitchen Leni, or somebody resembling Leni, was preparing the birthday tea. A tray of sausage rolls was cooling on the rack, and Ann and Patti's garish birthday cake sat waiting on a flower-sprigged Cath Kidston plate. There were supposed to be three trays of sausage rolls, but she'd burnt the first two, totally incinerated them, which set off the smoke alarm, and then, while she was trying to silence the alarm by wafting it with the tea towel, she'd knocked over and broken a glass jug waiting to be filled with homemade lemonade.

There was no fresh mint for the lemonade either. Even at this time of year, Leni could normally count on harvesting a few leaves from the sheltered corner of the backyard where she grew her herbs, but when she went out to pick some, she found that several of the terracotta pots had blown over and broken, and the mint plant was just a neglected bundle of twiggy stems. Leni decided to forget the homemade lemonade. She grabbed one of Patti's two-litre bottles of Diet Coke and upended it into a plastic jug. The kids would like that better anyway.

Since 4.30 a.m. on Saturday morning, when she came back from Honolulu with Mr Riseborough – or Roddy, as she really must call him, now that everything had changed, Roddy, Roddy, Roddy, but the name wouldn't stick, it seemed too casual, too impersonal, ironically enough – she had been beside herself.

Plausible excuses, in case anyone was awake – yes, that was the first thing she needed. As her cold fingers turned the front door key as slowly as possible in the stiff, early-morning lock, Leni prayed that old Ted wouldn't hear her and bark. She rehearsed a number of elaborate explanations for the ungodly hour at which she was returning: a late-night print crisis at *The Sentinel* – some kind of technical failure resulting in chaos, missing copy, the urgent need for all hands on deck. But the house was quiet as she crept up the stairs to the nursery, shoes in hand.

Sleep was impossible, of course. Her whole body was vibrating with the intensity of the past twelve hours.

What Mr Riseborough – Roddy – had said outside the club was painful, but she saw almost immediately that it was true. She had been monstrously self-centred in thinking that she could have both him and her home life: so perfectly complementary for her, but so selfish and unfair to him. The time had come to choose which man she wanted, and quite frankly the choice was obvious. She could not live without Roddy, and so that was that.

Roddy had been very understanding when she explained that leaving Theo, breaking up their home, couldn't happen while her mother was staying with them. It was impossible to deal with such a huge change while she was there in the house, and he accepted the point, agreeing to wait a little longer. Her mother would be leaving as soon as she found a place for herself, and after she left Leni would tell Theo that their marriage was over.

So the imaginary bubble which Leni had counted on to hold her suspended, always in the here-and-now, had vanished with a pop, and she was forced to grapple with a new, complicated reality, telescoping vertiginously into the future.

Half-formed, unanswerable questions assailed her.

Theo, what would he—?

And Ann, oh God, her poor little Ann, how would she—?

And *where*, where on earth would they—?

Not Honolulu, surely. Please, no, not there. The house had reared up out of the night island like something from a nightmare, rain hissing on the pebbles of the beach, the sea close by, whispering, watching. Roddy ran ahead, scooping snails from the path, slinging them in long, loping arcs into the wet bushes. Inside it was cold as a meat-locker, with a strong smell of burnt turf. The dog – alive, not dead, and oh, how she pitied Roddy for that desperate little lie! – whined and scraped behind a distant door. In his haste, Roddy didn't turn on the lights, and she felt rather than saw a vast empty space yawn above her before she tumbled down with him onto musty animal softness, and disappeared.

After it was over – and it was over quite quickly – Roddy disentangled himself and moved off into the darkness. There was a click and the room lit up.

Leni's eyes widened.

The walls were papered with golden palm trees, rising to the distant ceiling. Where the gilt of the palms had flaked off, there were great drifts of grey-and-black mould.

Strange metal tools hung from the lower parts of the walls – no, wait, they weren't tools. They were weapons. Leni saw axes, cutlasses, swords. There was a malevolent looking thing, like a pair of giant pliers, and another one that resembled garden shears. A circle of long tapered knives was arranged around a studded metal shield, so that the shield was like the sun, and the knives were sunbeams radiating out from it.

Leni realised that her head was resting on the shallow hearth of the fireplace. Gazing up, she smelt as much as saw the soot-blackened underside of the mantelpiece, and the high stone-built chimney breast towering above. Beneath her body was a sheepskin rug, grey and gritty, giving off a barnyard reek that mingled with the turf smoke. She gripped a tuft of wool in each hand and sat up.

Across a clutter of chrome-framed chairs and smoked-glass tables she saw Roddy standing beside a brass flamingo, almost as tall as himself. From the beak of the bird hung a white tasselled lamp, the shade partly torn from its rim.

'Leni, say hello to Honolulu,' said Roddy. He made it sound as if the house was a person. 'I can't believe you're finally here. I've waited so long.'

He came back over, clasped both her hands and swung her to her feet. 'Alley-oop! Way-hey and up she rises, earl-aye in the morning. Which it is. Very early.' He consulted his watch. '1.46 a.m., to be precise.'

'Those things on the wall . . .' said Leni, laughing a little nervously. 'What exactly are they?'

'Oh, they belonged to the Judge. My father. He collected primitive weaponry. He put that stuff up after Mummie died. She would never have allowed it while she was alive – spoiling the décor. I suppose I've got so used to it that I don't really notice it anymore. But there are some very rare and interesting specimens here. Extremely valuable, actually. Several of them are supposed to be cursed, heebie-jeebie voodoo nonsense, you know – but I can never remember which ones have the hex.'

Dodging a bar-cart full of grimy gold-rimmed cocktail glasses, Roddy reached up and unhooked a black device with three long metal claws that curved into sharp points at the ends. He blew the dust off it and slipped it on to his right hand. 'Come over here and I'll show you how this one works . . . It's quite simple really,' he said, stepping behind Leni. 'You just creep up on your victim like this, softly, softly, don't let them hear you . . . And then, *voilà*!'

He lunged over her right shoulder and in a swift, brutal movement pretended to rake the weapon across her neck. 'Jugular instantly severed. It's a throat-cutter.

Burmese, I think, or maybe Indian. Not sure of the date. Don't look so horrified! Come on, we're just playing. Leni! You must know I would never harm you.'

'No, I know. I know! It's just . . . creepy. Thinking of what that thing has done. How many people it's murdered.'

'Hmm. Morbid thought. Let's put it back.' He reached up and returned the weapon to its place beside the sunburst of knives.

'Roddy?' Trying his name for the first time, now that they were proper lovers.

'Yes, my Leni?'

'Your mother – was it her, then, who decorated the place like this? With the palm trees and everything?'

'Oh yes, it's all Mummie – apart from the weaponry. She wanted it to be like Hawaii, you see, and so she called it Honolulu. Bit of a joke, you know. Mummie was a great joker. This was where she had her famous bohemian parties in the seventies. I wish you could have seen what the house looked like then. All rather faded and dusty now. I really should engage the services of a cleaner again.'

'When did she pass away?'

'Mummie? Oh, many, many years back. I was sixteen when it happened. Very sudden. Ovarian cancer. Mercifully swift, I suppose. She was here, and then . . . she was gone.'

'I'm sorry. You were so young.'

'Don't be. It's a long time ago. She's buried here, on the island, so in a way it's as if she never really left.'

Chapter Nineteen

On Monday, Leni, Patti and Ann went for lunch at Happy Sunshine, the vegan cafe on the Ormonde Road. Ann was in a vile mood, tearful and volatile, exhausted after yesterday's birthday excitement. Leni knew it was asking for trouble to bring her somewhere public, like a busy café, but she needed to get out of the house or her head was going to explode.

Patti ordered a plate of sweet potato fries and a double espresso. Leni asked for a child's portion of the fries too, and a babycino, realising that Ann would demand whatever Patti was having. When the food arrived, Patti took the usual travel bottle of extra-hot chilli sauce out of her handbag and sprinkled it liberally over her meal. Ann watched suspiciously. She studied her own little dish of bright orange chips then eyed Patti's plate again.

'Annie want Granny P chips,' she whined.

'No, no, no, Granny's chips are burny, bad for Annie,' Leni explained to Ann, blowing on her fingers to illustrate. 'Ach, ach, too hot, not nice!'

'Annie want Granny P chips,' Ann insisted, on a querulous, rising note. Leni sighed. She could see where this was going, and she was in no state to handle it.

'Annie want Granny P chips!' wailed Ann, sudden and loud as a fire alarm. Other customers turned to look. Leni felt the mingled sympathy and irritation in their glances.

She picked up a pink plastic pot of chia seeds from the table and jiggled it temptingly in front of Ann.

'Hey, Baba, look! What about these funny little things? Want some of them?' She shook a few on to Ann's portion of fries, but Ann batted the pot away with a howl of anguish and rage, and the seeds flew everywhere.

'NO! ANNIE WANT GRANNY P CHIPS!' she shrieked, puce and rigid, tears shooting out like projectile missiles. Leni bent down to search for the pink pot on the floor. The world was turning too quickly. She wished she could crawl under the table and stay there, holding on to its sure, solid legs until the spinning stopped.

'Leni, let me deal with this, darling,' said Patti soothingly. She lifted Ann out of her highchair and set her on her knee. 'Now look, Miss Muff, Granny P is going to give you some of her special sauce, but only a tiny bit, because it's very, very strong, ok?'

'Mama, no, even a sniff of that stuff would blow her head off,' exclaimed Leni. 'And besides, I've just told her she isn't allowed it. We need some consistency here.'

'Watch and learn, darling, it's all going to be fine,' said Patti. 'You have to be smart when you're dealing with children. Always keep a step ahead.'

Taking parenting advice from her mother did not sit well with Leni, but she let it go. Arguing the point would take far too much effort.

Patti lifted the black-and-red bottle, with its cartoon skull and crossbones on the label, removed the cap and, while covertly sealing the opening with the tip of her finger, pretended to shake a few drips on to Ann's sweet potato fries. Instantly, Ann stopped howling. Leni, grateful for the reprieve, said nothing.

The waitress, a friendly young woman with bright purple hair, arrived with Leni's noodle salad. 'You must have the magic touch,' she smiled at Patti, nodding toward Ann, who lay in Patti's arms, sucking a chip. Ann stared up at the waitress angelically, blinking through tear-thorned lashes.

'I feel sorry for little kids,' said Patti, after the waitress had gone. 'It's so tough on them, they never get to taste the good stuff. All the bland pap and crap they're forced to eat. I remember when you used to visit us in England, Leni, you'd beg and beg to try some of my rum. Sometimes I'd let it wet your lips – a baby sip, no more – and you loved it. No harm in a small amount like that.'

'What age was I then?' asked Leni, trying to roll the slippery grey noodles round her fork. She remembered those moments, enough to recall that it wasn't the taste of the rum that she had loved – noxious stuff, with its spicy turpentine stink, even when sweetened with coke – but rather the brief, nestled feeling of closeness with her mother.

'No idea,' said Patti. 'Maybe eight or so?'

After lunch, they set off for Magill's shop. Leni said she needed to buy a new yard brush, which wasn't exactly true – the real reason she wanted to go was that she felt an almost overwhelming need for Magill's benign, calming presence. On the way, they passed the long double windows of an upmarket estate agent, one side of which was filled with pictures of tempting rental properties. Leni slowed her pace and gazed at the photographs, hoping Patti would take the hint. If only her mother would find a flat or a house and move out, so that Leni could get the dreaded showdown with Theo over, make some practical arrangements and begin her new life, rather than being stuck in this queasy limbo. But

Patti, absorbed in chattering with Ann, didn't seem to notice the estate agent's display.

As they crossed the road to Magill's side, Leni tipped the buggy back to lift it on to the kerb, an automatic manoeuvre which she'd done thousands of times. But this time she tripped over one of the back wheels and fell forward onto the buggy, and her sudden weight must have dislodged the folding mechanism, because the whole thing collapsed in on itself, half on the kerb, half in the gutter, with Ann crushed inside.

Leni scrambled to her feet and dragged the buggy on to the pavement, away from the traffic. She forced the frame open and clicked the lock back into place, and squatted down to check on Ann. Ann's mouth was a miniature 'o' of surprise, but she wasn't crying and she didn't seem to be hurt.

'It's ok, Baba,' Leni said. 'Just a tumble, like Tims the cat. Oops-a-daisy! All done now.'

Patti was staring at Leni through her black over-sized sunglasses.

'Darling. Are you alright? You seem a little . . . *frazzled*, these last couple of days.'

She knows, thought Leni instantly. She knows what I've been up to.

Patti's attic window flashed into her brain – had the blind been raised when she stole home in the early hours of Saturday morning? Were those huge unblinking blue eyes awake?

'I'm fine, Mama. Maybe a bit tired after the party yesterday.' Leni concentrated on adjusting Ann's safety-straps, making sure they hadn't come loose in the fall.

'Well, what a wonderful day it was, all thanks to you,' smiled Patti. 'You're such a perfectionist, Leni, but you must take care not to overdo, you know? Always remember to take time for yourself, especially now that you have me here to help you.'

Her mother patted her absently on the head and strolled on a few paces, then stopped to look in the window of a record shop. Mirrored in the reflection, Patti's giant sunglasses loomed still larger, shrinking the proportions of her already tiny face and body. It gave her an alien, insect-like appearance, somehow not quite human.

Nothing was wrong, Leni tried to reassure herself. She was just being paranoid. This was an old, irrational fear – the cringing belief that her mother could see into her mind. How could Patti know about her and Roddy? She didn't know who he was, had never even heard Leni mention his name.

When they arrived at Magill's, Patti was instantly entranced. 'Look at all the tacky little knick-knacks, and bits and bobs, and what-have-yous! Oh Leni, what a goldmine – I didn't think places like this existed anymore. Pure kitsch, just what I love. It's hilarious! I mean, look at this.' She held up a plastic windmill with yellow sails, attached to a little jointed man, in black cap and red waistcoat, wielding a wood-axe over a block. 'How does it work, I wonder?'

Magill appeared behind Patti, wiping his hands on his jeans. 'It's called a whirligig. It works like this, whenever the wind blows.' He spun the sails of the windmill, and the obedient little man began to chop away at nothing on his block.

'I'll take it,' said Patti. She turned to Leni. 'Wouldn't it be wonderful if we had a garden to put it in, darling? You're always saying you wish you had a proper garden for Ann, not just a back yard. Well, who knows? Maybe one day.'

'Hi, Magill,' said Leni. 'This is my mother, Patti. Mama, this is Magill.'

'At your service, Madam,' said Magill, performing a low, elaborate bow. He gave Ann a wink. 'How's my little red Rosie today?' he asked her.

'Ah Magill, yes, so lovely to meet you,' trilled Patti. 'Now, could you bring me a shopping basket? I can see I'm going to have some fun in here. I want to buy *ab-so-lute-ly* everything.' She descended with a cry of rapture upon a small, gilt-framed picture of two playful kittens, tangled in wool, and the words, 'Home Sweet Home' engraved above. 'Oh, and by the way, her name's Ann, not Rosie,' she said to Magill, over her shoulder. 'But don't worry, you can't possibly remember the name of everyone who comes into your shop, can you?'

Magill ended up obediently following Patti around the shelves, holding the basket while she loaded it with items, while Leni went outside with Ann to choose a new outdoor brush. When they came back in, Magill was still waiting patiently behind Patti, who was debating aloud whether to choose a set of novelty Irish coffee glasses or a crinoline doll designed to cover up toilet roll.

Leni caught Magill's eye. 'Sorry about this,' she mouthed, pointing apologetically at Patti.

Magill grinned and gave a philosophical shrug. At least he would make a fortune in till-takings today, thought Leni, because of Patti's spending spree. But she didn't get a chance to talk to him, or even just to feel the ease of his presence, until they were standing at the checkout desk. And then Magill seemed rather stiff, constrained, not his usual effortlessly talkative self.

'That will be fifty-eight pounds and 64p please,' he said.

'Oh, and I'll pay for Leni's brush as well,' said Patti. 'Can you add that on?'

Magill laboriously typed the figures into the ancient cash register, tongue caught between his teeth, while Patti rolled her eyes with humorous impatience at Leni. She began to drum her fingertips on the countertop.

'Sixty-one sixty-three,' pronounced Magill. 'Make it sixty-one sixty. I'll let you off the three pence. Special discount by the management.'

'Ok. I'm assuming you don't take cards?' asked Patti.

Magill shook his head. 'I'm afraid not.'

Patti slapped three English twenty-pound notes on the counter, then began poking in the zipped compartment of her purse for change.

Magill turned to Leni. 'Haven't seen you for ages, Snow. I suppose you've been busy at *The Sentinel*. How's Roddy Riseborough treating you? I heard the other day that he can be a hard boss to work for. Bit of a temper on him. Made me wonder about you.'

Oh! Don't blush, don't . . .

'Really?' said Leni. 'I don't know. I hardly ever see, er, Mr Riseborough. He's the over-all editor of *The Sentinel*, but my boss is a guy called Martin Sharkey, he's the chief sub-editor, I report to him. Seems ok, pretty quiet. He doesn't pay me much attention, to be honest, but I suppose that's better than a boss who's always looking over your shoulder . . .'

She was babbling, words spilling out at random. She could feel her cheeks blazing. Magill nodded, apparently oblivious to her agitation.

Patti hadn't looked up, thank God – she was still

sorting out coins – but her busy fingers had slowed to a mechanical pace and she seemed to be listening intently. Finally she found the correct change. She dumped the coins on top of the notes in a rough scatter of silver and coppers.

'Let's go home now, darling,' she said to Leni, laying a suddenly trembling hand on her arm. 'I'm not feeling very well. I think it's a migraine coming on. It must have been those horrible, sweet chips I had for lunch. Sugary things always set me off.'

Chapter Twenty

The unfettered roar of his old chainsaw, the blue cloud of petrol smoke, the way the blades sliced effortlessly through the living wood, spraying a confetti storm of sap-scented chips: all these things gave Roddy joy.

He'd decided to take Monday off work to tackle the garden, especially the willow trees that were encroaching on the back of the house, blocking the morning light. All through the summer, they'd been extending their territory, throwing out long whip-like branches, building up their girth – you could practically see them advancing, like a stealth army. Autumn was the time to mount a counteroffensive, show them who was in charge around here.

And of course, since Friday night Roddy had a hundred new reasons to set about bringing Honolulu back to its old glory. The willow trees were just the beginning. He would get the Judge's weapons cleaned and properly valued, then flog them off at auction. Nasty old stuff – not at all the sort of thing Leni would want hanging around in her home. No doubt he'd get a sizeable return on the sale, and he could use that to start sprucing the place up. Get the goldleaf on the great room wallpaper restored, for instance. Replace the old Aga too, and perhaps even put in a new kitchen. Leni liked cooking; he knew that. Maybe she could make him a beef bourguignon, say, or a pork stroganoff, garnished with those little triangles of fried toast, one corner of each dipped in parsley. His mouth watered. He missed the extravagant dishes of his youth.

For a moment, the gurning face of the child intruded unpleasantly on his dreams, but Roddy flicked it away, like a balled-up snot-rag. Nothing was going to spoil his mood. The kid could live with Devoted Dad. No need to have it stationed here at Honolulu.

Roddy had allowed himself a slow, meditative start to the day. He kept the flame on low under the Moka, so that the coffee stayed hot and fragrant, getting ever more syrupy the longer he left it. On *Woman's Hour*, one of his favourite radio programmes, Jenni Murray was talking about domestic slavery with some ethnic playwright or other, and then there was a conversation about how to make taramasalata. Wonderful fruity voices, ah yes. Let them yabber away.

Roddy tilted his chair back and propped his feet up on the table. His dressing gown parted and the morning sunlight, refracted through the window's thick bulletproof glass – another carry over from the Judge's reign – fell kindly on his shins. Unseasonably warm for the last day of October. Hallowe'en tonight, he thought, mentally inserting the proper apostrophe. The Feast of the Dead. Another old Irish custom bastardised to ruin by America. At least there was no risk of trick-or-treaters out here on the island.

The sky was a gentle milky blue, barely a breath of wind ruffling the treetops. He noticed a lone yellow birch leaf which seemed to be slowly rotating in mid-air just outside the window. How peculiar. Spooky, almost. But then he saw that the leaf was actually suspended from a long strand of spiderweb, so fine as to be almost invisible, and grinned. He sat contentedly, sipping his coffee and watching the leaf spin.

Leni had shown him how to take and send pictures on his phone, so he texted her a close-up shot of Terence wolfing his breakfast, snout deep in the trough. The mobile network was unreliable at Honolulu – the signal came and went – and he had to keep pressing the send button. Then he realised that he'd sent her the same picture five times. Oh well, no matter. After that, he fired off a block of fifty 'x's, finishing with a purple unicorn with hearts for eyes. Leni had demonstrated the use of emojis too, which he was too blithe and love-sated to treat with scorn, as the old Roddy would have done.

God, he really was happy. Silly-minded and happy. He wriggled his sunny toes and sighed with pleasure. Perhaps a bath first, then a final cup of coffee, before starting work in the garden.

It had been close to midday by the time Roddy went looking for the chainsaw. He really must clear out the boathouse, it was crammed to the rafters with useless junk. After a great deal of excavation, he found the chainsaw lodged behind the mildewed corpse of a garden swing – one of those fringed and canopied 1970s affairs, like a rocking sofa, covered in brown-and-orange flowers. Roddy dimly remembered it in its heyday. The exposed springs were now a mass of salty rust.

He'd found the petrol tank much more quickly, because it was nearer the front of the boathouse. He had filled the tank up on the forecourt of the petrol station in Ardpatrick last summer, when he'd taken a notion to mow the side lawn. It was a huge, heavy, cumbersome thing, which had originally been used to store petrol for the outboard motor on Mummie's boat. 'Carron Marine

Fuels', it said on the side. The attendant at the petrol station had come running out in a flap when he'd seen Roddy pumping 30 litres of unleaded into the tank – may as well fill her right up to the brim, he'd thought – which was sitting in the open boot of the Jeep.

'Sir, sir, sir, stop! You can't do that, it's illegal!'

'Well, I've done it now. What do you want me to do, pour it all out again?'

In the end, though, he'd never got round to mowing the lawn: something distracted him, and he forgot about it.

Now, he managed to decant a little of the petrol from the old tank into a tin watering can, so that he could pour it more accurately into the fuel chamber of the chainsaw, itself a fairly elderly piece of equipment. Roddy was dubious. Could petrol go off, like milk? But it was fine – when he yanked the starter cord, the saw fired into life with an exultant clatter.

For the last hour-and-a-half he had been slashing through the willows, severing their limbs, showing no mercy. The saw was weighty in his hands, and it was hot, sweaty labour, but Roddy relished it. Better than whittling, any day. Willow-wood was white and soft, the saw melted sweetly through even the thickest branches, and it gave off a sharp green smell, prickling the still air and keeping him invigorated for his task. He used the saw to dismember the branches into shorter pieces, then piled these on the side lawn. He could burn them later.

While he was cutting the willow, Roddy had kept Terence shut in the house, for the dog's own safety, and now that the chainsaw was silent, he could hear him crying and scrabbling, begging to be let out. Roddy crossed the lawn and opened the back door. Terence barrelled into the sunshine, tiny bat ears bouncing, and immediately dashed over to investigate the stack of cut wood. Roddy continued into the kitchen, where Radio 4 was still blaring away. He took a can of Guinness from the fridge and pressed the cold tin to his cheek and throat. He noticed that his fingernails were rimed with muck. Good. He didn't have the same urge to trim them anymore. It seemed a bloodless, spineless sort of activity. Effeminate, really. What did a man like him need with a manicure?

Pleased with the thought, Roddy popped the tab of his beer and strolled back out into the garden, the widget inside the can bumping companionably as he walked. He had a funny king-of-the-castle urge to sit on top of the pile of wood, so he clambered up and lowered himself on to it, wriggling his sit-bones into a gap between the shorn branches.

Terence interpreted this as some sort of game and began charging idiotically round the pile in circles, barking and making flying snaps at the wood. Roddy laughed. He bent to give Terence a friendly cuff each time he careered past, which sent the dog into even wilder circuits. It wasn't particularly comfortable sitting there, twigs jabbing at his rear, and he probably looked like a complete fool, but who cared? There wasn't anyone around to see him.

Out on the lough, a clinker boat with a red sail was crawling across the wide shimmering pathway where the sun touched the water. A heron passed low overhead with heavy wingbeats. It seemed to be making for Roddy's own little pebble beach, and Roddy watched eagerly. He loved to see a heron land: it did so with all the grace of a Russian gymnast – flamboyant wings aloft, legs outstretched, a bounce and then a short running skip, effortlessly controlled. But when the heron heard Terence barking, it hesitated and wheeled off, shoulders hunched in resignation, flapping towards the mainland shore.

Roddy was draining the last few drops in the can when he heard the grumble of a car engine. It sounded as if it was coming along the causeway. He shushed Terence and listened. Yes, there was the drumroll rattle as the car passed over the cattle grid. Christ, who was this, calling uninvited? Roddy never had any visitors. The postman left the mail in the metal box beside the causeway gates, and there had been nobody else for such a long time – until Leni. He didn't count 'Chelle, of course.

An old beige Ford Fiesta appeared from behind the belt of whitethorns and stuttered to a halt on the drive. There was a pause before the door opened. Then a stout wooden walking stick emerged, bayonet-like. The stick was planted in the gravel, and the driver slowly heaved himself out of the car. It was his neighbour, Arthur McQuiston.

Roddy climbed off his perch on the woodpile, waved an arm and began sauntering towards Arthur, Terence at his heels. Stooped and shuffling, leaning heavily on the stick, Arthur started to make his way across the overgrown grass, then gave up and stopped, waiting for Roddy. Above his bald head, a cloud of midges danced in the golden afternoon light.

'Arthur, hello, good to see you,' said Roddy, striding up and shaking his hand. He felt the calloused fingers of the other man jump and flutter inside his grasp. Terence, suspicious of the visitor, hung back behind Roddy, growling softly.

'Good to see you too, Mr Riseborough,' said Arthur.

'Grand day. There's some heat in that sun.'

As Arthur spoke, Terence growled louder, exposing the tips of his sharp little teeth, startlingly white against his curled black lips.

'Terence, stop that,' said Roddy, aiming a light kick in the dog's direction. 'Sorry, Arthur, he doesn't know how to behave.'

'Aye. He's some trouble, that lad, isn't he? I recall the night you were chasing him round our place, couple of months ago. Just took off on his own, you said. Looking for foxes in the wood, or some such.'

Roddy almost laughed out loud – he'd clean forgotten that was the last time he'd seen Arthur McQuiston. The misery and shame of that night seemed to belong to a different person entirely. No, not seemed – he really *was* a new person now. No longer the man who peeped through windows, hungry for human connection, hungry for love. He felt sorry for that man, but he was glad he was gone.

'I do apologise for disturbing you like that, Arthur,' he said. 'It won't happen again, I can guarantee it.'

'Aye. It gave our Darlene a quare turn when she caught sight of you. The screech she let out! Like the banshee!' He chuckled wheezily.

Wonderful! Even at the mention of the girl's name, Roddy felt absolutely no guilt at all. But he was starting to feel rather impatient with old Arthur. Had he come up here to talk about trivial events that were over and done with, entirely irrelevant to the present day, or what exactly did he want?

'Is there anything in particular I can help you with, Arthur?' he asked cordially.

'Ah. Well, the thing is, myself and Joan are taking a

wee break. Heading off to Donegal for a few days. Her sister has a place at Bundoran, not too far from the seafront. I'll not be driving much longer, the way I am, so we may as well do it while we have the chance. But Darlene doesn't want to go. Says it'll be bitter cold there at this time of year, and she can't afford to miss any school. Our Darlene's a great girl for the books. She says she'll be fine at home on her own, but she's still young enough to be left alone. Anyhow, the missus says to me, why don't you go up to the big house and ask Mr Riseborough if he'd keep an eye out for the child, while we're away. Didn't see you go past our place in the motor this morning, so I thought you might be about. It wouldn't be much, now – maybe just call by once or twice, if you're willing. And if you could give me your telephone number, so she has it in case of an emergency or anything, that would be appreciated. What do you say?'

'Of course,' said Roddy. 'Absolutely. Always glad to help a neighbour out. You and Joan head off and enjoy yourselves. Darlene will be perfectly safe with me.'

Arthur refused, with grateful thanks, the offer of a can of Guinness. He said he would go and tell Joan the good news. He carefully folded himself and his stick into the car while Roddy ran to the house and scribbled his mobile number on the back of an old receipt, then jogged back to give it to him.

The best thing, Roddy realised afterwards, as he was putting the chainsaw and the fuel tank away in the boat house, was that every word he had said to Arthur was true.

Chapter Twenty-One

When they got back to Isthmus Avenue after shopping at Magill's, Patti went straight up to her bedroom in the attic and stayed there all afternoon with the door shut. At 6.30 p.m., Leni knocked tentatively.

'Mama? I made you some soup. Can I come in?'

No reply. Leni opened the door a crack.

She heard a faint moan from inside the room. 'Mama?'

Patti was in a tight foetal curl in the centre of the unmade bed, arms clamped around a pillow. She was still wearing what she had on earlier: a creased black linen catsuit and a pair of red high-top Converse trainers with the laces untied. Leni had to suppress a gasp when she saw the trashed state of Patti's room. It was far worse than she had imagined.

The floor was almost invisible beneath piles of cast-off clothes, shoes, crumpled tissues, tossed-aside magazines, brown plastic bottles of prescription pills, blue glass bottles of homeopathic supplements. The bag of spoils from Magill's shop had been slung into one corner, the contents half-spilled, so that the little wood-chopping man on the whirligig was raising his axe against the crocheted skirts of the toilet-roll doll. The big package that had been delivered ahead of Patti's arrival, well over a month ago, was propped against the chimney breast – the only place in the room it could fit upright, because of the low sloping ceiling. The outer wooden casing had been removed but whatever was inside remained wrapped in cardboard.

On the windowsill, beside a beautiful lemon-coloured artificial orchid, its petals delicately spotted with pink, which Leni had placed there when she was getting the room ready for her mother, was a dish containing the sodden remains of some Coco Pops. The swollen grains of puffed rice were leached of their original chocolate colour, and a cluster of lipstick-crushed cigarette butts floated on the surface of the brown milk.

As Leni entered, Patti raised herself on one elbow, eyes bleared with black kohl, her short white hair standing on end, then sank back with a moan.

Trying to keep the brimming bowl of soup from slopping on to the tray, Leni picked her way gingerly through the detritus. Her shoe crunched on something that sounded like glass. She sat down on the edge of Patti's bed, avoiding an unpleasant-looking stain. The mingled smells of smoke, unwashed clothes and some kind of sweet, decaying odour that she couldn't identify – like forgotten cream left to rot at the back of the fridge – pressed around her in the airless little room.

'How are you feeling?' Leni asked.

'Horrific,' muttered Patti weakly. Up close, Leni observed the strong lines of her mother's face, her hawkish nose, the oily, pliable skin. Patti let out a long, plaintive, wet-sounding belch, which seem to echo from the very depths of her intestines.

'Could you try some of this soup?' asked Leni, setting the tray on the bed. 'It's very light, just the broth from a poached chicken, and a few vegetables and herbs Theo brought home from the garden. It might settle your stomach.'

'I – I don't know if I can manage it, darling . . .'

'I can help you, if you prop yourself up a bit.'

Shakily, Patti clung on to Leni's arm and hoisted herself round so her back was against the headboard. Leni popped a pillow in behind her.

'There, that's better,' said Leni, settling the tray on Patti's lap. But Patti didn't take the spoon. Her eyes were closed and her mouth was slightly open, like a baby bird.

Oh God, she wants me to feed her, thought Leni.

She dipped the spoon in the hot broth, blew on it, and held it to her mother's lips. Patti sucked the liquid in greedily, eyes still shut, then held her mouth open for more.

'Good?' asked Leni.

Patti nodded. 'Keep going,' she said. 'It's helping.'

Leni ladled in nine more spoonfuls before Patti opened her eyes again. She fixed Leni with a long blue baleful stare.

'I don't like that Magill,' she said.

'Magill? Ah no, Mama, he's nice.'

'He's a weirdo. All that stuff about the dead Kennedy girl. And the way he talked to Ann, so chummy-chummy, but did you notice he got her name wrong? I wouldn't trust him anywhere near her.'

'No, no, that's his nickname for Ann. He calls us Snow White and Rose Red – Snow and Rosie. It's just a bit of fun, nothing to worry about.'

'He seems to know an awful lot about *you*, doesn't he? More than I do. All about your job and everything. Your boss.'

Leni's eyeballs skittered down nervously into the half-empty soup-bowl, as though they could somehow submerge themselves there, safely beyond scrutiny, but there was no escape from Patti's gaze. She seemed to be boring into Leni's mind with one single, all-seeing cyclops eye.

'Magill's my friend, Mama,' Leni said. 'I like to chat with him sometimes, that's all.' She picked up the corner of the sheet and folded it in on itself, then folded it again.

'Why did you never tell me that your—' began Patti, but suddenly she broke off. Her lips stretched taut over her teeth, which had clenched tightly, in an awful kind of jack-o'-lantern grin. The tray tilted, the bowl slid sideways and Leni snatched it away just in time, as Patti collapsed on to the bed and lay there groaning.

Leni jumped up. She was really worried. 'Mama, I'm going to call the doctor. This is serious – it's got to be more than just a migraine, if it's making you feel that bad.'

'No . . . no . . . wait,' Patti gasped. 'I have to – I'm going to be—' She rolled to the side of the bed, retched twice and then vomited in a gush over the floor. The regurgitated soup splattered a white silk shirt and the trailing wire of a phone charger.

Patti flopped on to her back and let out a long whistling sigh. 'Better now,' she said.

Leni hovered uncertainly. 'I still think I should call the doctor,' she said. 'The local surgery is probably closed by now, so it'd have to be the out-of-hours centre, but they could at least give us some advice. Or Theo or I could run you over there in the car, if the emergency doctor thinks you should be seen.'

'No, darling, no. I'm alright. I've been through this before. If I can make myself sick, the pain goes away.'

Leni was far from reassured. But she knew that it was no use trying to persuade Patti to change her mind, once she'd made it up. She went downstairs and returned with a bucket of hot water, a pair of rubber gloves and a bottle of disinfectant. Patti lay watching as she cleared away the mess. She wiped the vomit off the phone charger, rinsed the cloth, then wrung it out and scrubbed the carpet. She dropped her mother's soiled blouse, dotted with bits of carrot and leek, into a plastic supermarket bag.

'There. That's everything cleaned up. I'll hand-wash this shirt for you tomorrow morning. You should rest now, Mama.'

'Leni, wait, don't rush off. Stay with me a while. Let's have a little chat together, now that I'm feeling better.'

'A chat? What about?'

'Oh, this and that. Anything and everything. Come on. Come sit beside me again. It's so comforting to feel you near me, darling.'

'I'm sorry, Mama, I really can't, I . . . I promised Ann a story before dinner—'

'Ann will be alright; Theo can do the story. I want to show you something. Go over to that chest of drawers under the window and open the bottom drawer. Please, darling. It's important.'

Feeling the old familiar blankness that came over her when she gave in to Patti's demands, Leni obeyed. The drawer yielded to her tug with a stiff squeak. It was full of Patti's underwear, a tangle of bras and knickers, some of which looked even more scanty and provocative than Leni's own secret collection.

'Push all that stuff out of the way,' instructed Patti. 'It's underneath, right at the bottom.'

Leni didn't want to touch her mother's private things, but she did as she was told. There was a large, spiral-bound book beneath the jumble of underwear. A series of watery pink rings marked the faded navy cloth cover, overlapping as though someone had placed and re-placed a wet coffee cup there, long ago.

'Is this what you mean?' she asked, holding the book up.

'Yes, yes, take a look inside,' said Patti, avidly watching from the bed. 'Go on.'

It was a photograph album. Leafing through it, Leni found that every picture it contained was of herself as a child. Beneath each one, someone had written her age at the time, in careful pencil script.

Here was Leni, aged nine, laughing blithely into the camera as she ran down the wide staircase at Mulcaster, the dilapidated Georgian country house in Dorset that her mother and Conrad had rented when they returned from Berlin.

Here she was again, ten years old now, red pigtails flying, careering on her Firefly bicycle through Mulcaster's vast, sun-filled rooms, most of them empty except for shabby sofas of rose velvet and ornate solitary chairs.

Then a black-and-white shot – a picnic lunch in the meadow, Leni making a daisy-chain, Conrad slouched beside her, draining a glass tumbler of wine. In Leni's mind's eye, it was always summer at Mulcaster, because the summer holidays were when she visited Patti.

'Such idyllic, happy times,' said Patti. 'When I'm finding things difficult, I take out this album and it reminds me of how perfect life can be. You were such a wonderful child, Leni. So beautiful, like a living flame darting through the house. My kingfisher girl. Conrad and I just worshipped you.'

Leni looked up. 'Who took these photographs?'

'Me, of course,' said Patti. 'Don't you remember?'

Leni shook her head and returned to the album. She had no recollection of Patti photographing her.

Picnics and ponies and swinging in denim shorts from the lowest branch of the giant cedar tree – this carefree paradise was not her memory of Mulcaster. What she remembered was being homesick for Granny June's austere love, the strict routines and observance of good manners, each day marked out by the precise pointed hands of her grandmother's gold wristwatch. Mulcaster was the very opposite.

The nights were cold in that elegant, ruined shell of a house, even in July and August, so the heating was often left on overnight, ancient water clanking through the pipes and spluttering, sloshing and moaning inside the cast iron radiators. In bed, Leni would listen to the clunks and gulps, lying small, still and silent, a lonely little pilchard in her tin, far away from the firelit drawing room with the record player where Patti and Conrad drank and sang and smoked until dawn.

A sort of empty, aching nothingness was what she associated with those summer visits – punctuated with stabs of terror when the deadly, shark-like look, which was the sure precursor of a rage, flitted across her mother's features.

From out of the past came a blast of hot fish, as a plate of burnt turbot in caper sauce, flung by Patti, flew past Leni's ear and crashed against the red wall of the Mulcaster dining room, just above Conrad's head. Conrad, stone-faced, got up and left, and Patti grabbed the bread knife and slashed the crimson brocade where the plate had smashed to wet, saucy threads.

Yes, that had happened.

But the gentle ponies, their soft, insistent noses, searching her palm for chunks of bitten-off apple: they had been real too.

Maybe the loneliness and fear and homesickness Leni remembered were not the main part of the story, but only a small part of it. Maybe that small part had spread like an ink stain, saturating her memory of those childhood summers and obliterating all the good times.

Was that a possibility?

The little girl in the photographs certainly seemed to be enjoying herself. And these images were visual evidence – proof in a way – that there had been joy. Leni's kind, indulgent mother loved her so much that she let her ride her bicycle in the house. What child wouldn't be happy with such freedom?

'All those pictures were taken with my father's Leica M3,' said Patti. 'My first camera. It's still the best. That big bright viewfinder, it just opens your eye up to the world. It made me feel like Daddy was with me, showing me the way, you know?'

Leni nodded. She closed the album and set it gently on top of the chest of drawers. 'Thank you for showing me this, Mama. It's very special.' She picked up the bucket and the bag with the soiled shirt inside. 'I'm glad you're feeling better. Hopefully you'll get a good night's sleep. I'm going to take this stuff downstairs now and let you—'

'Daddy adored me, you know,' interrupted Patti. 'Did I ever tell you that? I was everything to him, and my mother never forgave me for it. I was only six when he died. Just six years old when all the love was taken away. And Mother spent the rest of her life trying to freeze me out and punish me because she knew I was his favourite.'

Patti spoke as though the people she was talking about had no connection with Leni – the grandfather she had never met, the grandmother who raised her. Typical Patti: she only saw things from her own perspective, nobody else's. And Leni was very familiar with this particular lament. But tonight, perhaps for the first time, Leni allowed herself a flicker of pity for her mother. If Patti had felt so very unloved by her own mother, Granny June, then no wonder she found it difficult to show love to Leni. A new picture of Patti swam into focus: not someone scary, domineering and self-centred, but someone frightened, lonely and desperate for love. A whole other person, hiding in plain sight.

'Go on, Mama,' said Leni. 'I'm listening,'

Patti looked delighted. How easy it was to please her, really, Leni found herself thinking.

'Well, Daddy's camera – that was my first inspiration. But then, when I went to art college, I discovered my muse. Leni Riefenstahl. There was never such a reviled, misunderstood woman as Riefenstahl. "Hitler's girl", they called her. The Führer's filmmaker. Queen of Nazi propaganda. But I soon worked out that Riefenstahl was no Nazi. God, no. She was a feminist pioneer! The innovation, the technique, the courage, the imagination – no woman had made art like this, ever, in the entire history of the world.'

Leni nodded patiently. She had heard it all before. She was tired, and she really wanted to go downstairs. But she made herself stay a little longer, for the sake of her mother's feelings.

At least Patti had stopped probing her so suspiciously about her job. Better to listen to a eulogy to Leni Riefenstahl than have Patti ferreting out information about Leni's relationship with her boss. No chance of that now, thank God. Patti was well away, transported, in full flow on the subject of her muse. It was incredible to think she'd been writhing in pain half an hour ago.

'I'll never forget the first time I saw *Olympia*, Riefenstahl's film about the 1936 Berlin Olympics,' she was saying. 'Those diving sequences – the bodies of the divers, black against the sun – oh, exquisite. Beauty: *that's* what Riefenstahl was in love with; *that* was her guiding force. Beauty alone. Nothing else mattered. She didn't care about politics and propaganda, she was above all that. "If an artist dedicates himself totally to his work, he cannot think politically" – that's what she said. It was Leni Riefenstahl who made me into an artist. So of course, when my beautiful baby girl was born, such a wonderful surprise, I knew straight away the name I would give to her.'

Leni shifted from foot to foot. The metal handle of the bucket was cutting into her fingers. 'I know, Mama. Thank you. But now I really must—'

'Wait!' said Patti. 'I'm not finished yet. There's more you need to hear. Things you don't know.' She paused, staring down at the bedclothes as if seeking answers there. She gripped the sides of her nose in a pincer movement and exhaled a long, slow breath.

Before Patti could continue, the door crashed open and there stood Ann, giggling and alight with mischief.

'Ann!' exclaimed Leni. 'What are you doing up here? You're not allowed to go up Granny P's steep stairs, you know that.' She must have left the safety gate at the bottom of the stairs open when she went to get the cleaning things. Stupid – but at least it allowed her a reasonable escape. 'Come on, Baba, let's get you down again. Granny P's not feeling well, she needs to sleep. Mama, I'll bring you up a cup of tea after dinner and we can talk then, ok?'

Patti waved a curt hand of dismissal and looked away. 'Yeah. Whatever.'

Chapter Twenty-Two

Once dinner was over, Leni felt so exhausted that she sank on to the sofa and lay there, staring into space, while Theo bathed Ann and put her to bed. When Theo came back to the living room and saw how wiped out she was, he offered to make Patti's tea and take it up to her, and Leni gratefully agreed. Shortly afterward, she crawled up to bed, not even bothering to brush her teeth.

The nursery futon was where Leni slept every night now. It began after she started working at *The Sentinel* – she didn't want to risk disturbing Ann by coming in late. Theo and Ann seemed to enjoy sharing the big bed, and the pattern had stuck. Besides, there was no actual need for Leni and Ann to sleep together anymore: Ann was less and less interested in breastfeeding, and Leni's milk had started to dry up. The 'Seven Bs' of attachment parenting seemed to belong to another life.

Hours later, she was woken by a choking sensation. It felt as if something heavy was sitting on her chest, restricting her breathing. She flung the covers away: the room was swelteringly hot. Theo must have put the heat on earlier and forgotten to turn it off again.

2.01 a.m., said her phone. A text had come in from Roddy at 23.37 and another at 1.04. Nothing requiring an immediate answer, just sweet words of love. She smiled, returned her phone to its place under the pillow and rolled over, wafting the covers to generate some coolness.

Somebody was standing at the foot of the bed, watching her.

Leni sat up with a strangled half-yell and switched on the light.

'Shh, shh, darling,' said Patti. She was still dressed in her black catsuit and trainers. 'It's only me. Nothing to be scared of.'

'God, Mama, what's wrong? Are you feeling sick again?'

'No, I feel perfectly well now. But I can't sleep. You didn't come back to see me. You said you would.'

'I know. But I was so tired. I needed to get an early night.'

'There's something else I have to show you. It's urgent, darling, or I wouldn't disturb you like this.'

'Now? Mama, it's after two in the morning! And I have to sleep, I have work tomorrow – today. You should be resting too.'

'Leni, I cannot rest until I do this. You must come. I'll wait here all night if I have to.'

'Mama . . .'

'Come.'

A faint smell of vomit from earlier lingered in Patti's room. 'What is it you want me to see?' asked Leni. 'Please, let's make this quick.'

'Bear with me, darling. I need to set the scene first, so you'll be able to understand what I'm about to show you. Now, remember I was telling you about your namesake earlier?'

Leni could scarcely believe that she was standing in her mother's bedroom, in the middle of the night, listening to Patti deliver a lecture about Leni Riefenstahl's aesthetics – yet that was exactly what was happening.

'So I took Riefenstahl's ideas and I applied them to my own practice,' Patti said, making no attempt to lower her voice; she sounded as though she was giving a gallery talk. Leni closed the door so that Theo and Ann wouldn't be disturbed.

'I applied them to the photographs I was taking in my own time and place: the streets of Belfast, the Troubles. I realised that it didn't matter how frightening or horrifying the subject might seem to be, there will still be beauty, if you look for it. It was just a case of choosing to see differently. I began to visit the aftermath of bomb explosions, and to photograph what I saw, always with this idea in mind. A destroyed hotel, every window shattered by the blast – yes, but look how the white net curtains billow out through the empty window frames and flutter so freely in the sunlight! Or a blackened gap in a row of brick buildings, where a jeweller's shop had stood – and yet notice the fragments of gold and silver, pearls and precious sapphires, glittering amongst the wreckage! Even in terrible destruction, there is beauty. It's a lesson in hope, one that no amount of violent force can extinguish. That's what Riefenstahl taught me: beauty transcends everything, beauty must always triumph. It's the ultimate redemption. You see?'

Leni felt sick. By now, she had woken up enough to realise where this monologue was going, and where it would inevitably end.

'My photographs never contained people,' said Patti. 'By the time that I arrived on the scene, hours or even days later, the bombsites would be cordoned off, cleaned up. I often had to use a long lens to get the shots I needed. That changed when I was involved in an atrocity myself.'

'Mama, please. I don't want to hear this,' said Leni.

'Leni, you must listen. This is why I came to you tonight, to tell you—'

'But you *have* told me. You've spoken about it so many times in the past.'

Maybe she could deflect her mother by telling it herself, quickly, to get it over with.

'It was August 1992, the car bomb outside the police station in Blackwater Street. You were at the hairdresser's across the road. You weren't hurt because you were out in the back alleyway having a smoke. You were pregnant with me, but you didn't know it yet. After the bomb went off, you ran back inside and there was nothing left of the shop. You had your camera with you and you photographed what you saw. I know the story. I've seen the photograph. It all happened such a long time ago. Why go over it again now?'

'Because . . . because . . . because that photograph destroyed my life. It was my masterpiece, but it ruined me. You don't know the story, Leni. You haven't heard the ending.'

'Please,' said Leni weakly. 'Please let me go back to bed.'

'Let's look at the picture together, darling,' said Patti. 'My own irreplaceable artist's proof. I keep it close to me, always. It will help you understand.'

Patti waded through the mess of the room and hoisted the big cardboard package in both arms, then struggled back with it and let it fall with a heavy bounce on to the bed. Leni was at the door, her hand on the knob.

'I'm sorry Mama, I just can't,' she whispered.

Her mother seized her by the wrist and pulled her back towards the bed. 'You must. Now help me.'

Patti dug her nails into the top left-hand corner of the package and tore a long diagonal rip through the cardboard. Leni tugged ineffectually at the bubble-wrap underneath. At last the photograph was exposed. 'There,' breathed Patti.

It was the whiteness of the two women's bodies that Leni remembered, although she hadn't seen the image for many years. The force of the blast had blown their clothes right off. They lay on smoking rubble at right angles to one another. Their faces were obscured, turned away from the camera, but their arms were outstretched so that their fingertips, miraculously intact, were almost touching. Beneath a torn piece of blue sky, and perfectly encircled by a frame of jagged brickwork, they shone like marble sculptures.

'You only see the beauty,' said Patti. 'That's what Riefenstahl said. And she was right, wasn't she?'

'I don't know. I don't like to look.'

'Oh, but you do, Leni. Everyone likes to look. At one time, "Two Women" was the most famous, most looked at, most talked about photograph in the world. It made me. Awards, interviews, magazine spreads; exhibitions in Berlin and Budapest and New York. I was even on the cover of Italian *Vogue*, can you believe that? Me, Patti Barbour. I became *known*, I was celebrated – fully established and recognised as an important artist. Oh, I had my detractors, of course. No gallery in Ireland or England would show my work. And that preaching little moralist, Susan Sontag, she said I was a fascist, a beauty freak – the new Leni Riefenstahl. Ha! Little did she know that she could give me no greater compliment!'

'But then . . . why did you say that it ruined you?'

Patti stared down at the photograph on the bed for a

long time before she replied. 'I met a man', she said. 'Here in Belfast. It was two years after I'd presented "Two Women" at the Basel Art Fair. I was at the very pinnacle of my career. This man – he told me that he knew something about me. He said – he said – he dared to say that I had moved the bodies.'

'Moved the bodies? I don't understand.'

'Shifted them, after the explosion, so that they were lying like that, reaching out towards each other. But I didn't, Leni. That was exactly the way I found them, I promise you. I'm not a bad person. I would *never* drag dead bodies about. Though other photographers certainly did, in the past. Did you know that? Felice Beato, in 1858 – he rearranged human bones in an Indian palace courtyard, four months after a massacre happened there. Or Alexander Gardner at Gettysburg – what about him? He took the corpse of a Confederate sharpshooter from the battlefield and placed it in the ruins of a house, just to make a better composition. I don't blame Gardner. The soldier was dead, wasn't he? He was beyond anybody's help. But it's not something I could ever do myself.'

'And the man . . . this man you met?'

'He threatened me with exposure. He said he would tell the world that I was a fake, and worse than a fake. He was going to ruin my career, my livelihood, everything. And it *would* have ruined it, you see, because my work was already so controversial. If people thought that I had actually *interfered with* . . . No. Impossible. I'd be done for.

'My instinct was to run, Leni. It was self-protection. It crucified me to leave you behind, of course. You were so young. But I had no choice, no alternative, I had to get away. I needed to go to somebody who would understand. Immediately I thought of Conrad Weiss. I'd met him when he bought the first edition of "Two Women" in Basel. I flew to him in Berlin, arrived in a state of near-collapse, and he took me in. He and his wife Hedda had a flat in Charlottenburg, near the Bröhan Museum. I holed up there, waiting for the sky to fall.'

Patti paused dramatically. 'Well, it never did. Nothing happened. But ever since, that evil threat has been hanging over me. The fear – it never goes away. It's like a permanent disability. It wrecked my health. It poisoned my art, completely killed it. I – I never had another show.'

'It's alright, Mama. Don't get upset. I understand. I just don't know why you're telling me all this now.'

'In case you ever heard anything. Here in Belfast. Stories, rumours – I don't know. It's such a small place. Lies get about. I'm finished now as an artist. I don't care about my public reputation. All that matters to me is that my family knows I'm a good, caring, trustworthy person. My family – that's my whole future. You and Theo and Ann are all I have left.'

'This man, though, I don't see how he could harm you now – how he could prove anything—'

'He said he saw me do it.'

'He *saw* you move those bodies?'

'No, no, he didn't see me – don't you understand, Leni, that was the lie! He made up this terrible falsehood because he wanted power over me. He wanted to take what was mine away from me. And I can't let that happen ever again.'

Patti stood there trembling like a terrified child. It was shocking to see her mother so lost and vulnerable, stripped of all her power. Impossible, in that moment, not to feel compassion for her. Leni reached out a hand and touched her gently on the arm.

'Don't worry, Mama. That's all in the past. You're safe now, here with me.'

Chapter Twenty-Three

In the Dublin hotel where Roddy and Leni were staying for the night, everything was white. Roddy had let Leni pick their accommodation, and this place, The Court, a revamped townhouse near the canal, was what she had chosen. She liked the idea of white walls, white bed linen, white carpet, everything pale and simple and airy. Minimal, and kind of sexy, she'd said, doing that flick of the eyes he'd seen so many times now.

But the problem with white – which Leni, with her domestic fixations, should certainly have known – is that it doesn't stay white for long. The pristine look disappears almost immediately. And that was what had happened to this gimmicky hotel. The owners had obviously tried to disguise it with lots of drapes and dim-burning candles, but Roddy noticed that the nap of the carpet in the lobby was distinctly yellowish, like the fur of an old, zoo-bound polar bear, and there were black scuff marks on the walls near the lift, where suitcases must have banged and scraped the paintwork. In their room, which faced onto a bleak courtyard occupied mainly by bins, there were grimy fingerprints on the blinds. The effect was seedy, not sexy.

Not a cheap place to stay either, not by any means.

But he resolved not to say any of this to Leni, who had immediately gone into the bathroom to do things to her face.

They were in Dublin because Roddy had been summoned – rather peremptorily, he must say – to a meeting with the Wallace brothers. Normally Mitch came up to him in Belfast to do his strutting overstuffed sausage act. But this was to be on the brothers' own turf, at the NewsWest offices on Harcourt Street, and it would be a two header – unusually, Sean, the older and more recalcitrant of the pair, would be present too. That was all Roddy knew: he had not been forwarded a copy of the agenda. Well, it all had a funny look to it, he could see that, but his confidence was riding at an all-time high, and he was certain that he could assuage whatever difficulties the Wallaces were planning to lay before him.

His first thought, actually, when he opened the email from Mitch, was that this was the ideal opportunity for a night away with Leni. It was so easy – she could simply tell Moominpapa that she was being sent on a two-day training course at NewsWest HQ. Why hadn't he thought of such an excellent plan before? And that was exactly what she did, no bother at all.

He'd booked a day off work himself, and Arthur McQuiston had agreed to take Terence for the night, in return for Roddy's temporary guardianship of Darlene, which had gone swimmingly. Nice bright girl, actually. Sweet-looking, in her little denim jacket. She wanted to be a journalist, funnily enough – kept asking him for advice. He'd taken her to Ardpatrick on the Saturday afternoon and bought her a takeaway pizza from Giuseppe's, and the girl was starry-eyed with gratitude. It had been surprisingly enjoyable, playing dad for a day.

And now here they were – Roddy and Leni – in Dublin, with the delicious luxury of extended time together, hours and hours without interruption stretching out before them.

His meeting at NewsWest was not until 10.30 a.m.

the next day. Leni had come down today on the early train, and he had followed on the mid-morning express – not really necessary, but somehow, he liked the romantic idea of arriving separately – and they met outside the Clare Street entrance to the National Gallery. After a quick lunch in a nearby cafe, they walked to the hotel. Leni was excited, raving on about some multi-instrumentalist busker she'd heard on Grafton Street earlier. Roddy tried to sound interested, but he felt weary all of a sudden – heavy and somehow depleted. What he really wanted to do was lie down and blot everything out with sleep for a while. There were probably some chemical additives in that foul wine he'd had on the train, he thought, sulphites or the like, which were affecting his energy levels.

Roddy now pulled the plastic beaded cord on the blind to shut out the view of the courtyard dumpsters, and made a short tour of the room, critically inspecting the mini-bar and checking the tea-making facilities. Were there complimentary biscuits in that square white tin? No, just teabags. He threw four small, ridged plastic pods of UHT creamer into the bin, where they obviously belonged. On the wall was a piece of tortured-looking wood plastered with streaks of gold paint. He removed this 'artwork', mentally applying the ironic inverted commas, and put it behind the trouser press, where it couldn't pollute his immediate environment.

There. Now he could rest. He kicked off his shoes and lay down on the bed, crossing his ankles. He sat up again and pulled off his socks too, balled them and tossed them on the floor, then flopped down once more. The only sound was the constant high drone of the bathroom fan. Through the half-open door, he could see Leni's reflection in the mirror. She was scratching frantically at her face. The skin was raised and inflamed, blotchy looking. As he watched, one of her busy nails actually drew blood. The bright red bead swelled rapidly then trickled down her cheek. Leni frowned, tore a piece of tissue from the wall-mounted dispenser, and pressed it to the little wound.

'Leni, that's fucking disgusting,' Roddy spat out suddenly. 'Stupid ugly cow.'

Christ Almighty, where had that come from?

She emerged from the bathroom smiling eagerly, still with the scrap of tissue held to her cheek. 'What did you say? Sorry, that fan is like a jumbo jet taking off.'

'Nothing, darling – I . . . I . . . was just wondering what you were up to in there.'

Her face looked awful, all puffy and pink. But there was no excuse for what he'd said. Thank God she hadn't heard him.

'Oh, it's just my rosacea,' she said. 'It's flared up for some reason – which is funny, because it hasn't been bad for ages. Gets so maddeningly itchy, it's hard to leave it alone. I've got some cortisone cream, that should calm it down. I'll put it on now. Won't be long.' She blew him a kiss – no hand, just a fleeting pout of the lips – and retreated into the bathroom again. She closed the door behind her this time.

Roddy didn't want to sleep any more. He put on his glasses and consulted the room service menu, then picked up the white phone and called reception. The woman who had checked them in answered – he recognised her voice: a thick, foreign-sounding murmur, although he couldn't place the accent. Turkish, possibly. Rather nice.

'This is Mr Riseborough, Room 38. I'd like to order

two club sandwiches and a bottle of champagne, please.' They had finished lunch barely an hour ago but that flaccid sliver of asparagus quiche at the cafe had done nothing to satisfy his appetite. Besides, Roddy liked ordering room service. The familiar ritual helped him get his bearings when he was somewhere new. He only ever ate club sandwiches when he was in hotels.

'Certainly, sir. I will send this to you very shortly.'

'Are they served with crisps, or chips?'

'I'm sorry, sir?'

'The club sandwiches.'

'I'm not sure, sir. I would have to communicate with the kitchen. Would you like to wait while I confirm?'

'Yes, please,' said Roddy.

Lilith, her name was, it had said so on the name badge over her heart. As a lifelong connoisseur of women, Roddy prided himself on noting and remembering little details like that. It was a kind of automatic inventory. Lilith was wide, billowing, with a considerable acreage of brown leathery chest showing above the neckline of her tunic. When she'd passed him the key of Room 38, he was momentarily swathed in her scent. It reminded him, nostalgically, of geranium leaves: the smell of the long-gone greenhouse at Honolulu – blood, fish and bonemeal; the woody, jointed stems of the plants reaching up into the light. Lilith was about fifty, Roddy reckoned. As she'd bent over the desk to check his credit card details, he noticed that the tips of her oil-black straight hair were scarlet, as though dipped in red gloss paint.

'Hello, sir?' She was back.

'Yes?

'It is crisps.'

'That's fine, Lilith.'

With satisfaction, he sensed the slight jar of surprise, at the use of her name, resonate down the line.

'Thank you, sir,' she said. 'It will be ready in about ten minutes.'

'Oh, and Lilith? Have the order delivered to reception, will you? I'll come down and pick it up myself.'

'You want it to go to reception, sir? But then it is no longer room service, though we must charge it at the same rate.'

'Well, that's what I want, Lilith. Can you do that for me?'

'Okay, sir. As you wish.'

A few moments after he replaced the receiver, Leni came out of the bathroom, releasing the high shriek of the fan again. When she closed the door, the noise dwindled and finally died. In the silence that followed, she unzipped her skirt and stepped out of it, smiling bashfully at him, then removed her blouse. It was like watching an overgrown schoolgirl undress – she looked so gawky and young. She stumbled as she peeled off her tights, hopping about in an ungainly way to recover her balance. Her matching bra and knickers turned out to be a rather loud shade of mauve. Not Roddy's favourite colour, to be perfectly honest.

She climbed on to the bed beside him, nuzzling up close. She must have put make-up over the sore parts of her face, though the skin still looked a little warm and corrugated.

'My lover,' she whispered, her breath tickling against his ear. 'My love.' She began to unbutton his shirt.

For once, Roddy had no idea what to do.

The ecstatic urge to erase every millimetre of space between them was gone. His hand lay limp on her thigh, congealing there. He patted her, once, twice, and pulled her awkwardly against him. No, he felt nothing except a dull throb of absence. Something vital seemed to have been fatally mislaid. But that was impossible, impossible! Roddy released her, swung his legs off the bed and stood up, breathing quick and shallow, smoothing out his shirt. Leni looked surprised.

'What's wrong?' she asked.

He forced a smile. 'Back in a moment. I ordered some food and wine. Just going to nip down and get it from reception.'

'But won't they bring it up? I thought—'

'Two ticks. I'll be back before you know it.'

And then he was padding urgently along the sad polar bear carpet of the corridor, raking and tugging at his hair so hard that his eyes slanted upwards.

'Get a fucking grip, Rodders,' he muttered to himself.

A middle-aged couple were having trouble opening the door of Room 34. They were the effortfully young type you tended to encounter in hotels like this: he was sporting an unforgiveable grey mullet and a mustard-coloured waistcoat, while she was in jeans so shredded they were just a web of frayed denim.

'No, Jake, you have to wait until the green light flashes,' Roddy heard the woman say. They turned to look at him as he passed, their twin stares blandly registering his rumpled hair and half-open shirt, and then dropping simultaneously to his naked feet. Roddy strode on, chin held high. No dignity, people like that. No ability to act their own age.

When he reached the lift, he pressed the call button, then sank on to a white rattan chair to wait. On a low table beside him was a life size marble head of Buddha.

White too, of course, like everything else in this godforsaken dump. Roddy lifted the head on to its lap and stared at the smug, jowly face with its serenely closed eyelids. The lift arrived with a melodious chime and the doors slid open. It was empty. The mirrored interior, bright as an operating theatre, showed Roddy his own haunted features.

He wanted, suddenly and very badly, to use the Buddha's head to smash up the lift. Why not? A few hard cracks with that marble forehead would be enough to do it. The crash, the shatter, the sharp falling shards: God, it would feel so good! It might even buy him a little temporary peace. *And how very fucking Zen that would be*, he thought, with a bitter grin.

The urge was intense, but Roddy controlled it. He replaced the ornament carefully on the table, entered the lift and pressed the button marked 'G'. Perhaps a few moments in Lilith's greenhouse-scented presence would bring him back to himself.

As the doors opened, he glimpsed a tray with a bottle, two glasses, an ice bucket and two snowy napkin-covered mounds waiting on the high counter of the reception desk, beside a jar of white lilies. Ah good, this was more like it. Roddy walked forward briskly, but the anticipatory smile died on his lips.

Behind the counter, a ginger pube of a youth was hunched over the desk, breathing adenoidally. He was ticking a series of items off a list with a green biro pen. A sprinkle of lily pollen fell onto the page, perhaps dislodged by the waft of Roddy's abrupt arrival. The pollen was exactly the same burning shade as the youth's hair.

'Where's Lilith?' demanded Roddy.

Ginger looked up. 'Sorry, sir. Lilith is on her break. Can I be of any assistance to you?'

Roddy's jaw tightened. 'No. This is my order, this stuff here on the tray. Room 38. Put it on the bill.'

'Certainly, sir. Have a good day, sir.'

Roddy lifted the tray and headed back towards the lift. Wait, no, the stairs would be better: three floors, it would take longer. He trudged heavily up the first flight. His mind reeled and spun, searching for words, sayings, bits of film dialogue, Bible verse – anything at all to distract him from the present moment. Scraps of song by The Shangri-Las, The Marvelettes and The Shirelles echoed through his brain and died away. But as he plodded upwards, a distinct phrase came out of nowhere, and attached itself to the slow, leaden march of his feet:

'You do not do.'

'You do not do.'

What the hell? You do not do . . . what? Ridiculous, meaningless, it wasn't even a whole sentence. There was probably another line afterwards that made it make sense, but he could not for the life of him think what it was.

Some sort of miserable poetry maybe – ghastly Sylvia Plath or the like?

He thought of Jeannie McAlindon, in the sixth form at Ashgrove: she would read suicidally dark poems aloud to him while they lay on her bed together, taking turns to touch one another. She had a birthmark that looked like a flattened raisin, right at the base of her spine, just above her tender coccyx. After they broke up, she went to Cambridge to study classics.

'You do not do.'

Well, here he was, back at the room again. Using the

corner of the tray, he gave a cheerful bump on the door. 'Room service, Madam!' he called out in a loud, happy voice.

'You do not do.'

~

It was Lilith who helped Roddy through the rest of the afternoon and all of that night. Not the real Lilith, from reception, whom he might never see again, but her dream sister – a depraved, voracious and very willing handmaiden. Once summoned, she sashayed into his mind: big, brown and completely bare, apart from a delicate band of snaggle-toothed cowrie-shells around each wide ankle. He sucked on the scarlet tips of her hair and buried his face deep in each of her hot furry armpits, where, he discovered, the intoxicating geranium-scent was at its strongest. Her tongue was purple, like a plum, and very wide and dexterous. There was so much flesh to disappear into, so many dark, comforting places in Lilith for him to hide.

He did not feel disloyal, because he was doing this for Leni, doing it for both of them. By then, he had worked out what had gone wrong. Well, of course: it was just a temporary glitch caused by performance pressure. So obvious, once he thought of it. Their times together before were always snatched, rushed, and so it was natural that when they finally had all the time they wanted – when he finally reached the coveted prize of hours alone to fully explore and enjoy her – that nerves would get the better of him. It wasn't that he didn't want Leni – no, the disturbance happened precisely because he wanted her *so much*. A form of stage-fright, really. In the old days, bridegrooms on their wedding night would suffer the same affliction. And if he needed a little passing assistance from phantoms like Lilith, in order to give Leni the love she deserved, who was it hurting?

They were up before eight the next morning because of Roddy's meeting with the Wallaces. Leni seemed to enjoy the continental breakfast buffet. She helped herself to ham, cheese and a slice of orange melon. Roddy knocked back two espressos and a banana. Sitting opposite her, he noticed her glowing skin, barely a trace of yesterday's rash showing. She looked enviably peaceful and dreamy, as she cut the melon into small chunks with the side of her fork. Suddenly he felt like snarling something hateful at her again, but he crushed the impulse down fast, before any words had a chance to escape. This date with Mitch and Sean was clearly getting to him more than it should.

Instead he said, 'You look blooming today.'

She leaned across the table and whispered, with a bubble of laughter, 'I know why.'

~

Rather than have Leni hanging around the NewsWest offices waiting for him, which could lead to awkward questions, he arranged to meet her at Connolly Station at 11.30 a.m., as in order to catch the midday express to Belfast. That should give him plenty of time. His usual meetings with Mitch rarely exceeded half an hour, and even with Sean there too, he didn't imagine that this mysterious business would take more than an hour at most.

But it was two minutes to noon before Roddy came

charging into the station. He grabbed Leni from her lookout post beside the ticket barrier and rushed her along the full length of the platform, before pushing her ahead of him into a first-class carriage.

'Wait – no – my ticket is for second class—' panted Leni.

'Fuck it. I'm upgrading you. Get in!'

It hadn't gone well with the Wallaces. Behind his back, Jacqueline Shields-Maguire had apparently highlighted 'concerns' with them about Roddy's editorship of *The Sentinel*. The bitch royale had presented the Wallaces with a dossier, a treacherous log, detailing his erratic timekeeping, departures in the middle of meetings, and numerous unanswered emails. No formal complaint had been made, and no investigation process had been activated – or at least, 'not at this stage,' intoned Sean, blandly issuing the threat – but they were going to need some very specific, very concrete reassurances, fully evidenced, that Roddy was taking steps to remedy his behaviour.

Of course, he didn't tell Leni any of this. Instead, as the train lurched out of the grotty backyards of Dublin and picked up speed, heading north along the coast, he told her he was offering her a weekly column in the *Style* section of *The Sentinel*, starting next month, with her own photo byline.

Leni's face flew open. 'You're not serious!'

Roddy stretched his legs out into the aisle, making a deliberate show of relaxation. 'You should know by now that I never say anything I don't mean.'

'But isn't Jacqueline in charge of *Style*, will it be ok with her?'

'Leni. Who's the boss?'

'You, Roddy. Always you.'

Chapter Twenty-Four

It was after she returned from Dublin that Leni started spending time with the fridge. Especially in the evenings, when the others were in the living room and the kitchen was dark and empty, apart from Ted snoring away in his bed under the table.

What she liked to do was stand at the open door and list the contents, reciting them silently in her head. First everything in the main compartment, then the salad drawers, and finally the racks on the door. It wasn't because she was hungry. It was more a sort of meditation. The fridge was a small, predictable world, coolly lit and self-contained. It reminded her of the doll's house she'd had as a child. When she used to lift off the green pitched roof, and peer inside, she had the feeling she was looking into lives that were safe and quiet and orderly. With the doll's house, she could be certain that nothing would have changed while she was away.

Sunflower and pumpkin seed bread. Greek yoghurt. Damson jam, the Bonne Maman one with the red and white fake-gingham lid.

An oval blue dish of homemade ratatouille, left over from dinner, covered with tin foil. Three quarters of a chorizo sausage, the salami kind that came in a horseshoe shape, the stapled end still dangling on its twisted cord like an old-fashioned phone left off the hook.

Eggs: free-range, organic, with authentic streaks of hen dirt, from the Saturday farmers' market in town.

Watercress; pears; an opened net of mandarin oranges. 'Man-doros', Ann called them.

Milk; apple juice; Theo's ginger kombucha.

An extra-large bottle of hot sauce, the bright green nozzle sticky with clotted drips.

Leni looked at the hot sauce bottle for a while, examining the tiny Chinese lettering on the label, then slowly closed the door of the fridge. She knelt down on the floor beside the table and pulled back one of the chairs so she could crawl in next to Ted. He gave her a sleepy, two-beat wag as she rubbed the sweet spot under his collar, at the top of his chest.

'Old Teddy boy. How's my lovely old Ted?' she murmured. When he was younger, scratching him there made him cycle his left back leg with manic ecstasy. Now that he was doped up on heart medication, he accepted the caress with nothing more than a grateful snuffling sigh. The daily dose of pills made him lethargic, but it was the only thing keeping him alive.

Leni pulled her mobile from its usual place in the back pocket of her jeans. No, still nothing. She bent over and pressed her face into the warm crevice behind Ted's clustered paws, inhaling his distinctive musty scent, comforting in its familiarity.

It was silly to be worried. Roddy had warned her that he wouldn't be in touch as much as usual this week, because of some serious problems at work he had to sort out. He didn't say what the problems were, but she guessed they had something to do with the meeting in Dublin.

He'd cancelled their assignation last night for the same reason, and at very short notice – it had been 9.50 p.m., and she had already visited the women's loo to touch up the concealer on her face when his text came in, full of 'sorry darlings, and accompanied by a herd of heart-eyed unicorns. He was working late, couldn't get away – he wouldn't do this if it wasn't absolutely essential. A thousand apologies. Leni wrestled with the impulse to go and knock boldly on his door. Stalk in and straddle him in his chair. But that would be reckless, especially when they had both been so careful to keep their relationship secret at work. No, the risk was too great. And anyway, he wouldn't like to see her behaving like that. He'd disapprove.

Without Roddy, she'd been at a loss what to do for the next two hours. She could have gone home, of course, but then questions would be asked, which would require answers, and what could she say? It was so tiring and demoralising, continually coming up with plausible sounding lies.

She'd imagined arriving home unexpectedly, walking in on Theo and Patti all cosy together in the living room – Theo strumming on his guitar, Patti lounging like a teenager with her legs over the end of the sofa, joining in with her rough, low warble when Theo played a song she knew, Ann tucked away upstairs in bed. Leni felt that she would be a kind of interloper, breaking up their contented evening.

Absurd, of course. Her own suppressed guilt talking, no doubt. But it was true that Patti and Theo seemed especially close since Leni's trip to Dublin. Theo had taken the day off work – that alone was unheard of – and they'd gone to the zoo with Ann. Although it was mid-November, the weather was perfect for an outing; it had been the warmest, driest autumn since records began, no rain for weeks on end. Climate change, said Theo, pessimistically. He thought it was sinister to see the leaves turn gold and fall when it felt more like spring.

Patti had come back from the zoo with fifty-four photographs on her new iPhone: Ann squatting on the grass with the prairie dogs; Ann watching the sea lions being fed; Ann, Theo and Patti making silly faces beside the monkey enclosure. Later, Theo had taught Patti how to set up her own Instagram account and she uploaded every shot. When Leni returned from Dublin the next day, her mother insisted on logging into Instagram on Leni's laptop so that they could admire each picture together, one by one. 'I never knew how brilliant social media could be!' exclaimed Patti.

Last night, after Roddy had called off their usual Tuesday assignation, Leni had left *The Sentinel* offices and walked to the 24-hour Sainsbury's on Dunway Link, where she spent a long time drifting among the empty aisles. She bought a bottle of pine and mint ecological toilet cleaner which was on special offer. Then she'd gone to the taxi depot opposite the bus station in Glenminchin Street and sat in the grim little waiting room, waiting to be murdered. Well, not quite. But it was a lonely enough spot to be hanging about late at night. The only things in the vandal-proof room were a freephone to call the taxi company and the grey plastic bench on which Leni was sitting.

The airport bus had pulled up at the stop outside and a group of sunburnt young women got off, clearly just back from a holiday somewhere hot. They bundled into the waiting room with their flashy suitcases and bags of duty free, ignoring Leni, and one of them ordered two taxis on the free phone. After they were picked up and taken away, Leni was left alone again. She swung her feet back and forth. She checked her phone in case Roddy had changed his mind and couldn't bear to go a night without seeing her. Once, surreptitiously, she opened the bottle of toilet cleaner in order to sniff its bright, astringent smell, before replacing the childproof lid again. Finally, at ten to midnight, she'd called her own taxi and gone home.

Now, under the kitchen table, Ted rolled over and stiffly extended his right leg, which meant he wanted Leni to tickle his belly. She started to pull the mobile from her pocket again then shoved it back in with a sharp tut. Stop it. This was getting obsessive. Nothing was wrong, she knew that.

What she should really be doing, instead of mooching about so pointlessly, was working up ideas for her new column in *The Sentinel*. She needed to be ready once the time came. Such an incredible gift that Roddy had given her, completely out of the blue like that, on the train home from Dublin. Unfortunately, Jacqueline Shields-Maguire had not been pleased with the new developments.

'I hope you know what you're doing,' she'd said, when Leni called by her desk to say hello.

'Well, I haven't done anything like this before,' said Leni nervously. 'It's a massive step up but I'll do my best, I promise. And of course I'll take whatever guidance you give me – you know, editorial advice, or whatever you think I need . . .'

Jacqueline's lips retracted into a thin salmon-coloured line. 'That's not what I meant.'

Well, Jacqueline was known to be touchy. Probably she was irritated because Leni had been imposed on her without any discussion or negotiation, as a *fait accompli* by the editor. That was understandable, but it didn't make the situation any easier.

The inadmissible truth was that Leni didn't really want the column. It was ungrateful of her – perverse, even. She should have been excited and terrified and bursting with anticipation. And yet she wasn't. She didn't care about writing any more or getting published in the paper. All she cared about was her relationship with Roddy. Nothing else mattered.

Ted was asleep again, paws twitching, far off in his own private dreamland, where he was young again, and could run with the wind. A burst of laughter came from the living room, with Ann's high-pitched giggle the top note. Marta from next door was there again tonight. At Patti's invitation, she had joined them for dinner and stayed on for coffee by the fire. Marta was Patti's greatest fan, endlessly appreciative of her jokes and advice and general thoughts on life. She was like an ever reliable, one-woman audience, always ready to applaud.

Leni knew it was unsociable to be skulking in the kitchen, but she also knew that if she joined the others in the living room, Patti would want her to get her laptop out to show Marta the zoo pictures – 'The images have so much more impact on the larger screen, don't you think?' – and then she and Theo would be expected to supply a background chorus of 'oohs' and 'aahs' while Marta enthused. Theo would play his part gladly, of course, but Leni didn't feel able to summon up the necessary energy this evening.

At least there had been no more dreadful confidences or confessions from Patti, no more forced midnight viewings of her 'masterpiece'. Leni hated the thought of that awful thing up in the attic, but she was relieved that

Patti did not want to return to the subject. It belonged to the past, and Leni's overriding concern was with the present, and the immediate uncertainties of the future.

Knowing that her mother hadn't just run off to Berlin on a whim, all those years ago, but had fled out of genuine fear, did make a difference, however. She felt she understood Patti better now.

Having her mother around – with the exception of that one hallucinatory night – was nowhere near the endurance test she had feared. It was even fun at times. Patti had a way of livening up any situation, however dull or humdrum. She was extremely generous, too, constantly buying gifts. Leni was bombarded with perfume, flowers, shoes, candles, silk pyjamas. A couple of days ago, it was a new floor-length trench coat in the softest black leather, which must have cost a fortune, and was really more Patti's style than Leni's – but you couldn't mistake her genuine wish to please.

And this morning, while Leni was plaiting and twisting Ann's hair into the usual two short, horn-like braids that Ann currently demanded, Patti had announced that she might just have found herself a new house. Yes, a real house, not a flat – and it looked wonderful, ideal in every respect. Exactly what she had been looking for: size; location; everything. It even had its own walled garden. But Patti didn't want to say anything more until she was absolutely sure she'd got it. Houses were such slippery, headstrong things, so hard to pin down. You couldn't take your eye off them for a second, or they would escape. But, fingers crossed, she had found something perfect.

So in a month or two, or maybe even less, depending on the rental agreement, Patti would be gone – moved into her own place. And then, after that . . . after that . . .

Leni scrambled out from under the table, fighting a rising sense of panic. She opened the fridge and looked inside.

Ratatouille; pears; apple juice.

Chorizo; eggs; jam.

Milk – there wasn't enough milk. She needed it for Ann's porridge with honey in the morning. Here was something, at least, that could be easily sorted.

Leni grabbed a coat from the cupboard under the stairs and popped her head around the living room door. 'Hey, just going out to get some milk from the garage, we're a bit short. T, are the car keys about? They weren't on the hook in the hall.'

'Leni! Come in, darling, join us!' exclaimed Patti. 'Where have you been hiding? We've been talking so much about you.'

Patti was sitting on the floor and Ann was peering over her shoulder, chubby arms locked around Patti's neck. The old photograph album lay in front of them on the rug. It was open at the page showing ten-year-old Leni feeding apples to the ponies in the Mulcaster paddock.

'Ann wanted to see what her mummy was like when she was a little girl,' said Patti, smiling up at Leni. 'So I popped upstairs and brought this down.'

How young and attractive her mother was looking tonight, thought Leni. Clean and slim and limber as a child. Her hair, freshly washed, fell in a soft curtain across her clear blue eyes – free, for once, of the usual black kohl. The unlit comfort cigarette which used to bounce in a gangsterish way as she talked was nowhere to be seen. But it was her smile that really won you over and made the spell complete. There was so much going on: it was exuberant, playful, almost beseeching, begging you to respond. Its blazing vitality warmed you through to the bone. For the first time since Patti arrived, Leni allowed herself to experience the full radiance of her mother's smile.

'It's Mama!' shouted Ann, pointing at the photograph. 'Mama with horsies. Come see, come see!'

'Soon, Baba, I'll be back soon,' said Leni. 'Mama has to go and get some milk for your podge-with-hun in the morning. Theo – have you got that key?'

Theo detached the car key from the chain on his belt and tossed it to her. 'You were such a cute kid, Len. And Ann looks exactly like you, I never realised how much.'

'Absolutely,' said Marta, nodding so emphatically that her brass bracelets jingled. 'The same, the very same, all over again.'

Chapter Twenty-Five

While Leni was paying for the milk at the garage, she decided to buy a token for the drive through car wash. The Skoda was filthy, covered in a layer of brown grime, and splattered with bird droppings and sticky smears of sap from the fir tree that Theo always parked beneath at the garden.

She posted the green plastic token into the slot. The first pass of water overhead sounded like heavy summer rain drumming on the roof. Next came a creamy slick of suds, blanketing the windscreen. Now the large rotating brushes started, a whirl of blue and yellow. Other brushes came in at the sides, holding the car firmly as they whirred and scrubbed. Leni closed her eyes, leaned back against the headrest and breathed out. Two warm tears leaked from under each lid and spilled down her cheeks.

Almost against her will, and with her eyes still shut, she took the phone out of her back pocket, then blinked them open and looked at the screen. A new message was waiting, and yes – it was from him. Sent ten minutes ago:

I saw this, and it made me think of you x

There was a link attached, and she clicked on it eagerly.

The link took her to a picture of a hairless cat, the sort with pinkish-grey, wrinkled skin and disproportionately large eyes and ears. The words printed underneath read: 'Remember, you are beautiful on the inside, even when you feel ugly on the outside.'

Leni stared straight ahead at the spinning brushes. As if drawn by a magnet, her fingernails flew to her face and began to scratch. Soon she felt the wetness of blood. There was nothing to blot it with except the cuff of her coat, so she used that. Then she remembered that there was a pack of Ann's baby wipes in the glove compartment. The wipe made the raw patch of skin sting bitterly, but there was a sore kind of satisfaction in it – almost a release.

When her face stopped bleeding, she texted him back:

Why? x

The reply came immediately, almost as though he had been waiting for a response, despite being so busy:

Because I know you feel bad about the rash on your face. But you're still beautiful to me x

Leni was confused. She had been so sure that Roddy worshipped her fundamentally, physical flaws and all. Now he seemed to be comparing her to an ugly bald cat. But he had also said she was beautiful. No, that wasn't quite right, he hadn't – he said she was beautiful *to him.* Not to other people – was that the implication? Maybe he was trying to tell her that she was only beautiful on the inside – whatever that meant – and not on the outside. Did he mean he loved her *despite* her ugliness? No, love hadn't been mentioned at all. Oh, what did he mean?

She pulled down the sun visor and slid open the little grey door to expose the mirror. She tilted her chin back and forth, peering at herself in the dim light. The rash wasn't too repulsive, was it? Was it?

Leni snapped the visor shut. She was overreacting ridiculously, seeing insinuations that weren't there. It was just a silly picture of a cat, nothing important. The main thing was that Roddy was thinking of her, and had made time to get in touch.

The wet flailing brushes spun to a halt, retracted, and then a square green signal began flashing at her to go. Leni started the engine again. Before she drove away, she texted Roddy back:

Thanks – I love you xxxxxxxxx

She took the long route home, driving round by the Ormonde Road. Passing Magill's, she was surprised to see the lights on. It was well after eight: why he was down there in the shop and not in the flat upstairs? Leni pulled into an empty parking space and got out of the car.

'Sorry, we're closed!' said the jaunty sign on the door. All the coal scuttles and bins and brushes and bottles of bleach that were normally arranged on the pavement when the shop was open were stacked inside along the narrow aisles, filling the space completely. Right at the back, Leni could see Magill himself, the dusty ducktail of his hair floating about. She knocked on the glass and then, when he didn't hear, she rapped harder. Magill's head bobbed up sharply. Leni raised her hand above the 'closed' sign and waved. Magill looked severe and unsmiling as he manoeuvred his way to the door, but when he saw who it was, he gave a happy hoot, loud enough for Leni to hear. He pushed back the bolts.

'Snow White herself! Are you out wandering the streets alone?'

'No, I was just going by in the car – I was getting milk – and then I saw your lights were on—'

'Well, come in, come in, don't be backwards in coming forwards,' said Magill, shepherding her through. 'I'm spending a little time with Mary Jo tonight, been neglecting her a bit lately. Nice of you to join us. Please excuse this mess, there's nowhere else for it all to go.' He took Leni's hand to help her clamber past a stack of growbags and a bale of netting wire, and Leni hung on tightly until they reached the rear of the shop.

'There we are. Have a seat. Make yourself at home.' He gestured towards a low metal stool in the corner. There were newspaper clippings about the Chappaquiddick incident all over the concrete floor, arranged in neat piles.

'Doing a bit of re-hanging,' said Magill. 'I find that if I keep the museum the same way all the time, I start to forget about poor Mary Jo. She fades away. But if I take everything down and put it up again in a different order, it helps me remember. Makes her real again.' He gazed thoughtfully at Leni, head on one side. 'Would you like a mug of cocoa, Snow? You look cold.'

'Cocoa?' Leni was confused.

'Hot chocolate,' Magill explained. 'We used to call it cocoa. Same thing, pretty much.'

'Oh – yes, hot chocolate would be lovely, actually. If you don't mind making it. I don't want to keep you from what you're doing.'

'No trouble at all. Back in two shakes of a lamb's tail.'

It was the instant kind of hot chocolate, thin and scalding, but Leni accepted it gratefully. She blew on the freckled skin of the surface and took tiny sips as Magill reassembled his display.

'Why do you care about Mary Jo so much?' she asked, after a while.

'Because nobody else did. She was just "The Blonde" – that's what the papers called her.' Magill held up a withered page of newsprint. 'Teddy Escapes, Blonde Drowns', said the headline.

'All anyone was interested in was Ted Kennedy: what was he up to; why did he wait to report the accident; was he guilty; was it a cover-up? And the politics of it too: what it would mean for Teddy; how could he ever be president now? And then right afterwards, there was Apollo 11 – first man on the moon, one giant leap for mankind and all that stuff. Mary Jo, trapped under the water – she was forgotten. Just a dead girl, used by the Kennedys and tossed aside. So I figured that one person, at least, should try to keep her memory alive. And that person happened to be me.'

Leni went on sipping, and Magill went on re-pinning. The silence was soothing.

'Sorry about my mother, by the way, last time we were in,' she said. 'She can be a bit much at times. As I think I've mentioned before.'

'Not your fault, Snow. I thought you seemed on edge that day. Strung out. Face somewhat aflame.'

'Ah – you noticed.'

'Yup. Sure did. I thought to myself, poor Snow is suffering. But I didn't want to mention it in front of your mother, in case that made things worse.' Magill paused and looked at Leni. 'She's not a very nice person, is she?'

'Who, my mother? Oh no, she's just – she's not . . . that's just what she's like.' Leni was amazed that Magill was immune to Patti's charms. Nobody else seemed to be.

Magill bent and picked up a picture of Mary Jo that Leni hadn't noticed before. It wasn't the usual one, the formal photograph from her college yearbook, with the circlet of pearls and the long swan neck. This was a family snapshot of a much younger Mary Jo, carefree and laughing in the arms of her parents, her hair a mass of shining ringlets. Magill smoothed the cutting out and carefully attached two brass drawing pins to the top corners.

'Well, you look after yourself, Snow,' he said quietly. 'You deserve to be happy in your life.'

Leni felt her bottom lip begin to tremble. 'It's not so much my – it's more that I – well, things are complicated, at the moment. I wish I could say—'

'Don't say anything. But I'm always here, should you need a helping hand. Come round any time. If the shop's shut, just ring the street bell for the flat.'

~

When she pulled up outside the house, Theo was standing at the gate, looking uncharacteristically agitated. He ran to the car and yanked open the door.

'Leni!' he exclaimed. 'What took you so long? It's been over an hour since you left, we were getting worried.'

'Shit, T, I'm sorry. I decided to get the car washed, it was filthy, and then I went for a bit of a drive. To dry it off. I didn't realise I was away so long.'

Hiding things from Theo had become second nature now, she thought sadly. She could have told him about visiting Magill, but somehow, she didn't want to. It was too private.

'Did you not have your phone? After it got to an hour, I tried to call you, but it just rang and rang.'

Leni climbed out, then locked the car. She took her mobile out of her pocket and opened it with the screen facing towards her. Four missed calls, all from Theo. No messages. 'God, yeah, I see that. I must have left it on silent.'

'Did you not actually get the milk?'

'Oh! Yes, of course I did.' She unlocked the car again and reached in to lift the carton from the front passenger seat. 'Here it is. Is Ann still up?'

'No, she's had her bath and Patti's putting her to bed: she was knackered. Marta went home half an hour ago.'

'I'll go straight up and say goodnight to her then. Here, could you put this in the fridge?' She handed Theo the cold carton of milk and went into the house ahead of him.

Later that evening, when she was in the nursery changing into her pyjamas, Theo, in boxer shorts and an old grey Joy Division T-shirt, poked his head around the door.

'Hey, can I come in for a bit?'

Leni fastened the last two buttons, right to the top.

'Umm, yeah. Sure, of course. But I was just about to go to bed.'

She pulled the covers back and climbed in. Theo slid in on the other side. He reached across and tousled the top of her head. Leni suppressed the urge to shake him off.

'It's been a while since we've been in bed together. On our own,' he said.

'Yeah. I suppose it has.'

Theo smiled and rolled closer, slipping a hand under her hip. 'Even Patti noticed. She said we need to set aside time to be alone with each other. "To protect the bond," as she put it. You know how Patti talks. But I think she's right.'

When Leni didn't respond, Theo gave her a little

jiggle. 'It's okay, isn't it? Patti being here with us. You seem pretty cool with it now. And she's great with Ann.'

'Yes, it's been mostly okay. Better than I thought it would be. But I guess she won't be here for much longer, now that she's started house hunting.'

Leni could feel Theo's questioning brown eyes on her, tender and intent, but she didn't want to prolong the conversation by telling him that Patti had already found a place to live. Well, Theo probably knew all about it anyway. Patti and Puppy: the best of pals.

Leni gazed at the ceiling, waiting for Theo to go back to his own bed. From far in the distance came a groaning sound, a low mournful keening that came and went, came and went, but never entirely died away.

'What's that noise?' she asked. 'Can you hear it?'

Theo listened. 'That's the shipyard siren. It's a kind of warning signal that goes off when they move the big cranes.'

'I've never noticed it before. It sounds so sad, in the night.'

'Oh, look, you have a text,' said Theo. 'Your phone just lit up.'

Leni's armpits prickled instantly with sweat. Her mobile was charging on the bedside table. She remembered that she'd left it screen upward, fully exposed.

Was this it then? Was this the moment when everything came crashing down?

As casually as possible, she stretched out an arm and lifted the phone. Theo crowded in companionably to look.

Sorry. Can't make it on Friday. RR.

There were no heart-eyed unicorns, not even a single x.

'Who's RR?' asked Theo.

'Roddy Riseborough. My boss,' said Leni woodenly. 'I was supposed to be having a meeting with him on Friday. I guess he isn't free.'

Chapter Twenty-Six

The boards of the ancient causeway yelped in protest as Roddy pounded over them. Instinctively, he avoided the gaps where the timber had crumbled away. He could hear the dark sea below, slapping against the stanchions. It would be ages before the sun was up, but he couldn't stand thrashing around in bed any longer. Sleeplessness had infested the room like a stale smell. The tangled sheet became a straitjacket, pinning him down. Eventually Roddy had fought himself free with a roar of frustration that carried him right out of bed and on to his feet. He stood blinking for a moment, then fumbled in the bottom of the closet for his trainers. The singlet and shorts he found in the overflowing wash basket, stiff with dried sweat.

At this hour, the world was made entirely of grey wool. Trees, hills, barns, houses: they all merged together in the granular half-light; secretive and aloof, indifferent to Roddy's presence. When he reached the gate where the causeway joined the mainland, he turned left, towards the series of stone bridges that led to Lisnahee Island. The solitary beat of his feet on the narrow tarmac road echoed through the early morning silence.

He was not thinking about Leni. Not thinking about Leni, and not seeing her. That was the only possible way out of this horror.

He *wanted* to want her. Nobody knew how desperately, how abjectly he wished for that.

But the feeling had gone. And the only chance of

bringing it back was to banish her: from his mind, his home, his car, his life.

It was a radical form of self-denial. He had to grab the scruff of his own neck and show himself the misery of a Leni-less future.

He had to make himself miss her.

Then, perhaps, the love would come flooding back.

If it didn't return – if the unthinkable happened and this emptiness of soul was permanent – there was nothing left for him.

Roddy quickened his pace, huffing clouds of breath into the chill air. To drive away all thoughts, he had to become a perfectly articulated machine of muscle and bone. A hot, hard wheel of motion rolling ever faster along the smooth surface of the road. He was aiming for complete physical exhaustion. It was the only thing that might bring some temporary relief.

He had cancelled Tuesday night at the last moment because, when it came to it, he realised he simply could not face Leni. He told her it was because of problems at work – well, there certainly were, thanks to Jackie's unpardonable intervention with the Wallaces – but what really bothered him was the thought of being trapped alone in the car with Leni. Her sheer choking proximity: the fishy eyes, the inflamed skin, the uncontrollable red hair going everywhere, getting in his mouth when he talked, getting into everything . . . And then, on top of all that, the lover-like performance he'd have to put on – no, God no! Just couldn't do it. By the time he texted her to cancel their usual date, he was already halfway home.

Next day, he'd got caught in a loop of shame and remorse. This was the cruellest part of the huge existential joke being played on him – despite everything, he still wanted so badly to please her, to be her ideal admirer, ha! So he spent most of the morning conference scrolling distractedly through Google images, searching for a sweet animal picture to send her, because he knew she loved those. When he found the hairless cat and its message – a 'meme', was that what the young people called it? – it gave him an antagonistic little jag of satisfaction, which he didn't pause to examine too closely. The very thing for Leni. He'd forward the meme to her right now. She'd be delighted.

On second thought, no – better to save it and send it later. Otherwise he'd get caught up in an endless all day text conversation, and there would be no escape.

Really, there was nothing hurtful about the picture, or indeed the message. He explained the innocence of his intentions when she asked why he'd sent it. He even told her she was beautiful. But somehow it had finished him, telling her that, and he knew he couldn't see her anymore.

Quadriceps screaming, Roddy now sprinted full pelt across the bridge to Lisnahee Island and charged up the grassy hill. There was a ruined monastery at the summit of the hill, fifth century or thereabouts. Roddy vaulted the low dry stone wall of the enclosure, then slowed to a stagger, before collapsing face down on the cool, forgiving grass. For a good ten seconds, breathing in earth, blood thundering in his ears, he was at peace.

It didn't last, of course.

He hauled himself up, spitting out bits of grass. His thigh muscles felt like semi-set concrete.

All that was left of the monastery was the remains of its round tower – a hollow stone stump. It looked as if a giant hand had swooped down from above and snapped the tower off at a ninety-degree angle, right at the base. The circular wall formed a kind of rocky staircase which led to the highest point, about five metres above the ground. Roddy had climbed it many times as a boy.

It had terrified him at first. The broken tower seemed as high as the clouds. A fast scrabble to the top, egged on only by himself, the distant ground tilting sickeningly below him, knees scraped raw by the rough lichen on the stones. What if he fell! But after the first climb, it was easy.

Roddy saw himself again as a boy, arriving at Lisnahee: a slight figure, propping his bike against the enclosure wall and making sure the gate was bolted shut behind him. That was the law of the countryside, his father had told him – you must always close gates, not leave them unsecured for animals to trample through and cause chaos. The wind, coming in northerly off the lough, whipped around his small, dark head as he slid the heavy bolt carefully into place. Roddy wanted to weep for the boy.

How many years now since he'd climbed the round tower? Forty? Forty-five?

On a whim, Roddy decided to climb it again. Maybe the air would be clearer up there.

He picked his way up slowly, feeling for his footing among gaps in the stonework. No headlong scramble these days. It was steeper than he remembered too. At the top, he found a certain smooth broad stone to sit on. Strange to think of that stone being here, all this time. Centuries before him, centuries after. Inanimate, unchanging.

Enviable, really, when you thought about it.

Ah, God. This was a new low: jealous of a stone. He

groped in the pocket of his shorts for a pack of cigarettes, slightly squashed, and the Judge's gold lighter. Smoking was a disgusting practice that he resorted to only in the most extreme circumstances.

The sun would soon be up. The world was mauve now, not grey, and the outline of the churchyard, where the monks slept in their child-sized graves, was every moment becoming clearer. Roddy sucked hard on the cigarette. From his vantage point, he could see the 'Pit of Uncertain Use', as it was sign-posted: a deep, evil-smelling hole near the edge of the enclosure, secured with a padlocked grille, precisely to keep out boys like Roddy. Nobody knew what the monks had used the pit for.

In the east, just above the horizon, a single pink cloud was drifting alone. The underside was molten gold, lit by the still-hidden sun. As Roddy watched, the cloud stretched and gradually elongated itself across the dawn sky like a lovely scar.

Quite suddenly, he remembered the irresistible sense of yearning he'd felt when Leni came walking towards him that day in the 1921 Club. The entrancing way she moved through those falling bars of shadow and light. He chased after the memory, grasping frantically for the feeling. It seemed so close, barely beyond reach. But the more he strove, the more dried up and empty he felt.

Christ Jesus, it was no good.

And why try anyway? Wasn't he supposed to be *not* thinking about her?

Roddy stubbed out his cigarette on the stone he sat upon, making a smoky hole in the pale green lichen. If he could increase his pace by a further ten per cent on the way back, he might be shattered enough to sleep. Stuff

Jackie, stuff the Wallaces. Going into work was out of the question today.

It was as he was battering past the National Trust car park at Gulladuff Island, about a mile from home, that the refrain started up in his head – the same hateful, mocking, meaningless chant that had afflicted him in Dublin:

'You do not do.'

'You do not do.'

'You do not do.'

'You do not do''

Unbearable. He didn't deserve this. He had done nothing to warrant the torture he was being put through. In no possible sense was any of it his fault.

Chapter Twenty-Seven

It had to be something she had done. He would not cut himself off from her like this for no reason.

After that brief, kiss-less message cancelling Friday night, she had heard nothing from him. All her texts had gone unanswered, and all calls went straight to his voicemail: the terse, thrilling mutter, 'Roddy Riseborough, leave a message'. In work, she had even tried to make an appointment with him through Pam, his PA. But Pam had just raised her drawn-on eyebrows and told her that Mr Riseborough was working from home, and since he hadn't shared his diary, it would be better to wait until he returned to the office.

Everything had been fine until the trip to Dublin. So whatever had gone wrong between them must have happened there. But nothing had happened there, except lots of amazing sex. Roddy had been more ardent and loving than ever before.

It couldn't be her rosacea, she thought, despite that strange cat meme he'd sent her. She'd had bouts of the rash the whole time he'd known her, so it made no sense for him to suddenly find it so off-putting that he couldn't bear to look at her.

Think . . . *Think.*

There's got to be a reason.

Could it be – God, it couldn't be someone else, could it? Somebody he'd met and instantly fallen for in Dublin, just as he had with her? But the only people he'd seen were the two newspaper owners, nobody else.

Unless . . . The receptionist who checked them in at the hotel, an older woman – hadn't Roddy looked at her in a slightly odd way? Sort of . . . appraising. Not polite and impersonal, which would be normal, but as if he was taking special note of her.

Leni hadn't paid much attention to it at the time, but now it seemed to take on a new, louring significance. Her head swam. She felt seasick. What if he – and she . . .

No. Stop. This was madness. Roddy could not possibly have abandoned her, Leni, the declared love of his life, for a person he'd seen once, for less than five minutes. Probably he looked at plenty of women like that. He was a man who appreciated women. He admired and respected them. It didn't mean that he was about to run off with a complete stranger.

She kept circling back to the conviction that it was her own fault – something she'd said or done, without even realising. What, then? What could it be? Leni combed through her memory, searching for the fatal error she felt sure she must have made, but no matter how hard she looked, she couldn't find it.

The withdrawal of Roddy's presence, combined with trying to keep up some sort of normal front at home, left her in a frenzy of suppressed panic. She wanted to flay herself to shreds, leap out of her own skin, do anything to escape this suffocating limbo.

At last she decided to take action.

On Tuesday morning, when Patti was out for a walk with Ann, she called Pam. Leni didn't identify herself, and she spoke a little more deeply than usual to disguise her voice. She asked to be put through to the editor-in-chief and was told, as expected, that Mr Riseborough was working from home at present. 'If you'd like to leave your name and a brief message, I can—'. Leni hung up. She had the confirmation she needed.

Later, at about 7.00 p.m., during her shift at the office, she told Martin Sharkey that she wasn't feeling well. She said she'd been running a temperature all day, and asked permission to go home. Martin was a known hypochondriac, fearful of germs. He reacted exactly as she'd hoped, nodding his agreement – 'Yep, yep, sure thing, on you go!'– as he backed away from her. Leni left *The Sentinel* building and walked to the bus station on Glenminchin Street. From there she took a bus to Ardpatrick, the closest village to Honolulu.

She had been to Roddy's house only once before, on that first night together, and she didn't know the address, or even the exact location. But she remembered passing an illuminated monument to St Patrick, high on a hillside, about five minutes before they arrived, and she thought she could work it out from there. She pinpointed the saint's monument on Google Maps, which informed her that it was located a little more than three miles from Ardpatrick. Not that far. Though she wished she'd thought to bring a pair of trainers, so she could change out of her high heels. Too late now.

The bus dropped her off beside a BP filling station on the edge of the village. It was a clear night, still and, for late November, not very cold. Google Maps directed her to stay on the Slievepatrick Road and head south. The loud, robotic female voice coming from her phone drew the attention of a fat man in paint-smeared overalls, who was filling up his van at the nearest petrol pump. He stared at Leni as she passed by him. Beneath the cold white lights of the forecourt, she saw his half open mouth, and a curl of fairish, greasy hair lolling over his forehead. Leni walked on purposefully, as if she knew exactly where she was going. When she glanced back over her shoulder, the man was still staring after her.

At that point, she was instructed to turn left, along a narrow, unlit road with no pavement, which curved away under a dense cluster of trees. It looked awfully dark, but she steeled herself to do it. Every step she took would bring her closer to Roddy.

She remembered that you were supposed to walk on the right on country roads, facing oncoming traffic – but there was no traffic. Nothing except the fast, tense rhythm of her breath, the marionette beat of her shoes, and the small bobbing pool of light cast by her phone torch on the dusty grey surface of the road. The record-breaking autumn weather was holding, not a drop of rain. Today's *Sentinel* had reported that a hosepipe ban was now in force, unheard of outside summertime, because the reservoir levels were so low.

Once she'd got past the trees, Leni's eyes became more accustomed to the darkness. To her left there was a large sloping field of cabbages, with the moon rising above it. For some reason, the orderly rows of round cabbage heads made her think of soldiers' helmets. Ranks of soldiers planted up to their necks in the ploughed earth, a buried army. Fear prickled her heart, at the strangeness of it all, but she shook it off and forced herself to focus on her own marching feet.

She passed farm gates and the openings of mud-rutted lanes, but there were no houses to be seen. Once, a car tore by, thumping with bass. The headlamps raked her briefly as she pressed herself back into some roadside bushes. An empty beer can, flung from the window, came rattling to a stop beside her. The vast night silence seemed louder than ever once the car had passed.

After climbing steadily upwards, the road took her down past a marshy inlet of the lough, spiked with tall reeds. The ribs of a forgotten rowing boat lay on their side in the shallow water. There had been no more instructions from Google Maps for quite a while now, but Leni kept the app open for reassurance, watching the little blue orb on the screen creep slowly towards its destination.

She came to a house, the first one she'd seen. It was rather grand and Georgian-looking, although it was right on the roadside, with no garden in front, not even a gate. The house stood in darkness; the louvred shutters on each window were padlocked, and she noticed that the fanlight above the front door was cracked in two. Leni hurried by; encountering a deserted, semi-derelict house was worse than seeing no houses at all.

Soon the road began to climb again, more steeply this time, and Leni hoped she might get a glimpse of the St Patrick monument, to help her get her bearings. Surely she couldn't be too far away now?

A moment later, she became aware that something was moving about up ahead, staying low and close to the ground.

Leni froze, heart leaping so high that it almost closed off her windpipe. Heat flooded her body. As she watched, whatever it was emerged from the deep shadow of the hedge and into the pale moonlit road.

A dog. A big one. But just a dog.

She tried to put confidence into her stride as she walked towards it. Coming closer, she saw that the dog seemed to be guarding the ornate gates of a large, modern house, set well back in its own grounds.

Dramatically placed floodlights picked out isolated silver birches in the garden. The downstairs windows of the house glowed behind drawn curtains, and that made Leni feel a little better.

'Ok, pup,' she murmured. 'Nothing to worry about, I'm just walking past your house.' The dog, some kind of shaggy lurcher type, gave a suspicious grumble and trotted towards her. Leni kept striding. She passed the dog and immediately it fell into step close behind her, seeing her off its territory. She did not vary her deliberate, steady pace, and after twenty metres or so, she was aware that the lurcher had dropped back.

But then the dog began to bark. The suddenness of the noise in the still night must have communicated itself directly to the animal part of Leni's own brain because immediately she began to run, clattering along in her high heels, clutching her phone, handbag bouncing ridiculously against her backside. And then something broke loose inside her chest and she began to sob, crying hard like a child, because she felt so unutterably lonely and lost and unloved.

St Patrick, illuminated on his hilltop, eventually showed her the way. She realised that if she kept following the road that skirted the shore, it would bring her to the right place. It had to. She turned off Google Maps because of the speed with which it was draining the battery on her phone. Now she was the blue orb herself, a mute, tight knot of need, focused absolutely on getting to Mr Riseborough. (He had become 'Mr Riseborough' again, not Roddy.) All that mattered was that her need was sated, which it would be by the pure fact of his presence. Whatever happened after that was immaterial.

It was another three-quarters of an hour before she

arrived at the Honolulu causeway. Yes, this was definitely it: there was that odd little cottage, with its row of painted white rocks along the front.

She hesitated, looking across the water at the pitch-dark mass of the island, its closed circle of forbidding trees. No lights at all. She shrank from going into that unknown blackness, allowing herself to be swallowed up by it. But necessity spoke louder than fear, and finally she began to cross the causeway.

The tide was so high tonight that it was nearly flat level with her feet. Little waves, lit by the phone's torch, kept slopping over the sides of the causeway or coming up through the gaps and pooling in the grooved wood. If she could see herself from above, she thought, it would look as if she was walking on water – a woman striding out over a great expanse of sea to the place she needed to be, the person she had to be with.

Once she reached the island, Leni's steps quickened, and she fell into a half-run. Stars reeled overhead, quickly quenched by trees, and, oh! – there it was, the great glass front of Honolulu, staring sightlessly into the night.

Breathless patter over the tarmac. The path; the door; the doorbell. A rich, old-fashioned chime echoing away through the house, and a frenetic series of high-pitched yelps in response: Terence. The wringing urgency of waiting, but the certainty that relief was coming. A moment's wait, that's all, and then he would be here in front of her.

Nobody? Not possible. Ring again.

Wait.

Wait.

Ring once more.

No. There's nobody.

Leni ran back along the path and around the side of the house: she remembered that he parked the Jeep there, where the driveway passed close to his bedroom window. Nothing. There were a couple of tyre-marks on the pitted tarmac – but the space was empty.

He wasn't there.

The realisation came with a sick, sudden plunge of vertigo. Staring at the reeling ground, she became aware of her own aloneness. Small, exposed, abandoned – out here at night on this alien island with its rotten kelpy smell, and the sea whispering unkindly on the shingle, and a multitude of unknown little noises and stirrings coming from the woods. Honolulu itself loomed up like a huge, malign presence. The terrible house still frightened her, but now she knew for certain that she would go anywhere, live anywhere, be anyone, if only it meant being with him.

~

Mr Riseborough's bedroom window was long and narrow, and the sill was very low, no more than knee height above the ground. Leni switched on her phone's torch again. If he wasn't at home, she could at least look at the place where he slept.

The window was bulletproof, she knew that. They all were; it was one of the security measures that had been installed to protect his father, the Judge. 'Even if you held a gun directly against the pane, it wouldn't shatter,' he'd told her. He seemed proud of the fact.

The thick greenish glass absorbed the light of Leni's torch, reducing its brightness. The dim beam darted around the room like a mouse. It picked up a sports bag piled high with crumpled shirts, a half-full bottle of whiskey, and a contraption that looked like an old-fashioned rowing machine. An open hardback book lay face down on the floor. Leni angled the torch so that she could read the cover – *The Behavior of Organisms* by BF Skinner. She'd never heard of it.

When she was here before, Mr Riseborough's bedroom had been as neat and Spartan as a monk's cell. Now the mess was almost as bad as Patti's room. The torch flickered over a tangle of covers on the unmade bed, and for an electric moment Leni thought it was him, in there, asleep. But no, the room was empty.

Hardly knowing what she was doing, she turned away from the house and strayed across the grass towards the sea. Close to the beach there was a low stone building with a humped roof. Beside it stood a flagless flagpole, planted in a circle of concrete. The double doors of the building stood open. They looked as if they had been that way for a long time.

Maybe this was somewhere she could shelter – a place to hide from the scrutiny of the night, while she tried to gather her senses. Maybe she could wait there until Mr Riseborough came back.

There was barely room to step inside. The torch revealed a jumble of rusty paint cans and garden tools. An old-fashioned lawnmower, minus its grass box, hung from two wall-brackets. Most of the space was occupied by a long, bulky shape covered in tarpaulin. Cautiously, Leni lifted the corner to look underneath. It was a boat, the blue paintwork faded and crackled. Its name, painted in red, was still visible: 'Aloha'.

At that moment the torch went out; her phone had finally died. Leni backed out of the building immediately.

There was no way she could stay in there, on her own, in the dark.

The moon was high and far away now; it seemed to be watching her from a great distance, with a single half-closed eye. Gradually she became aware of a soft clinking sound, close by, like loose change being jingled in a pocket. *Ching . . . ching-ching, ching-ching . . . ching.* It was coming from the flagpole, she realised. A strand of the rope which must once have raised and lowered the flag was bouncing against the hollow pole in the light wind. *Ching . . . ching*. The loneliest sound.

It was then that she saw his car. It was parked right on the shore itself, half-hidden by a belt of low trees. Silent, silvered, still, as if enchanted by the faint moonlight, or marooned like a ship run aground. The hide tide was almost touching the wheels.

She ran blindly towards it and crashed through the thicket of trees, barely noticing the brambles that tore at her legs, ripping her tights. Slipping and skidding over the shingle, Leni rushed to the driver's window and pressed her hands to the glass.

The shriek that Mr Riseborough gave was muffled, because it was sealed inside the car – but it was loud and ferocious and sudden enough to make Leni leap back and let out a scream of her own.

'It's me, it's Leni!' she cried.

Slowly he rolled down the top third of the window. She made an instinctive movement towards him, but he raised a hand.

'Stay back.'

She couldn't see his face properly, it was turned away from her, but his chest was heaving, as though he'd been running. She waited for him to speak again, knitting her hands tightly together.

'Why are you spying on me?' he said. His voice was awful, cold and strangled and mean.

'Spying? I'm not spying, I'm— I had to see you. To find out what's going on. I don't understand what's happening.'

'You shouldn't have come here.'

'But there was no other way – you wouldn't answer my calls or texts, and I didn't know what else to do—'

'You shouldn't have come.'

'Can I please get in the car, so we can talk?'

'No.'

'Please! I've come all this way – I got the bus, and then I walked for miles in the dark, and there was a dog, and I – I just can't go on like this. I have to know what I've done wrong. You have to tell me.'

She hadn't really felt the pain of her blistered feet until that moment, but now it was so bad that her legs refused to hold her up anymore. She let go of her bag and sank down on to the stones.

He seemed to soften, fractionally, because his voice was a little less harsh.

'I need some time to myself. It's not possible for me to explain why. You'll just have to take my word for it.'

'It's not me, then?'

'No. It's not you.'

'So we'll be together again? After you've had this time?' At once Leni was up off her knees, heedless of pain, eager with hope.

No response.

'Do you know – is it possible? I'm just wondering how long you might need?'

No response.

'Sorry, I – I don't mean to push you. I can wait. I'm good at waiting. As long as I know that we'll definitely, that you'll definitely . . . But yes, it's okay. I'll wait for you. I'll be there, ready, whenever you are.'

Face still averted, Mr Riseborough said it was time for her to go. He posted a crumpled fan of notes through the window – money to pay for a taxi. He would drive back to the house and call one for her.

No, he did not want her to come up to the house with him to wait.

No, he would not tell her why he was sitting out here alone on the beach.

She was to walk to the causeway gate – right now – and stay there until the taxi arrived.

The cab came after about twenty-five minutes. She saw the yellow light on top crawling along the road around the shore, searching for the pickup spot. The driver pulled in when she stepped out from the gateway and raised her arm.

'This for you, pet? Riseborough the name?'

Leni shook her head and nodded at the same time. She was freezing by then. Even when she was huddled in the back seat of the stuffy taxi, she could not manage to get warm. Luckily the driver wasn't the chatty kind. She couldn't have spoken a word.

~

When she got back to Isthmus Avenue, the light was on in the kitchen. Patti and Theo were sitting together at the table, which was covered by official looking documents and headed letters of various kinds.

'Leni! We didn't expect you home so soon,' said Theo, jumping up in surprise. 'It's only half eleven.'

Leni was surprised herself: it wasn't even midnight, but it felt as though a whole day and night had passed since she'd left the house this afternoon. Theo's hand reached towards the papers on the table, as if to scoop them up but Patti, smiling, raised a finger and he stopped.

'What's happening here?' asked Leni, finding her voice.

'Wait, what happened to your *legs*?' asked Theo.

Leni looked down. She'd forgotten her wet, muddy, bramble-torn knees.

'Oh . . . I fell.'

'Oh no, poor Len, that's awful. Take your tights off. I'll get some Savlon from the bathroom. Back in a sec. Stay there, don't move.' Theo seemed strangely flustered.

'Sit down, darling,' said Patti, kindly. 'You look absolutely exhausted. We're doing some business, as you can see. I was planning to tell you all about it in the morning, but here you are, and there's no time like the present.'

Theo came back with a box of plasters, a roll of cotton wool and a tube of antiseptic cream. 'Patti, wait, I really don't think that now is the best moment to start going into—'

Patti dismissed him with a cheerful wave of her hand. 'Oh, shut up, Puppy! I don't want to hear any more of your silly fussing and quibbling. Leni needs to know the plan.'

'What plan?' asked Leni.

'I've bought a house. For all of us. Just around the corner, in Oxbow Gardens. I put the deposit down today. This is the surveyor's report . . .' – Patti brandished several pages, stapled together – 'and it shows that everything is perfect. There are four lovely big bedrooms, so lots of space for everyone, and a beautiful back garden for Ann to play in – just like you always said you wanted. There's a heated outhouse too, where Theo can do his music, and even a kennel for Ted – he'll be so much happier living outside. You're going to love it, my darling. A whole new house for you to decorate. A new life for us all. Isn't it a wonderful surprise?'

'I can't,' said Leni.

Patti laughed. 'Of course you can. It's all agreed. Isn't it, T?'

'Well, not exactly, I didn't know you were going to go ahead and—'

'No,' said Leni. 'I can't.'

'Why not?' said Patti.

'Because I'm in love with Roddy Riseborough, and I'm leaving Theo.'

The truth came out quite calmly and clearly, and speaking it eased the tight, constricted pain in her chest. She turned to Theo, who stood, immobilised, with a wisp of cotton wool in his hand.

'I'm sorry, T. I didn't mean to tell you this way.'

Patti made a sharp choking noise. She rushed from the room. The whole house seemed to shake as she hammered up the stairs.

Leni and Theo stood looking at each other.

Chapter Twenty-Eight

Answer the phone, goddamn you. Answer the fucking phone.

Voicemail again. Roddy slammed his mobile against the desk, then buzzed Pam for the third time in as many minutes. 'Well? Why haven't you got hold of her yet? Keep trying her landline. No, not her fucking mobile – I'm trying her fucking mobile, so what's the fucking point of you trying it too? Keep me informed. I want updates every five minutes until you get her.'

He buzzed Pam once more. 'Sorry, Pam. Sorry. That was out of order. I just really need you to help me here. I'm begging you.'

He stalked over to the window. Pressing his forehead against the glass, he tried to regulate his breathing. Far below in the street, a small crowd of people had gathered. He knew that they were waiting for him.

Roddy lifted the sash, letting a gust of cold air into the room. He stuck his head out and looked down. A straight drop of four storeys. What if he were to end it now? Climb out onto that crumbling sandstone ledge. Stand high above this sick, hateful city one last time.

Then an elegant swallow dive, hurtling faster and faster toward the idiot ghouls below. He'd be a flying hammer, arms spread wide, swooping down to smash their stupid empty heads into the ground. Blessed extinction, taking as many as possible of them with him. That would be the way to go, if only he had the balls.

Oh Leni, please. Please, my sweet Leni, please pick up.

Where was she, where was she when he needed her? Why had she promised to be there for him – a vow she'd sworn barely twelve hours ago, on the beach at Honolulu – if she wasn't prepared to keep to it?

His stomach heaved. Jesus, he was going to be sick. He dived towards the metal wastebasket beside his desk and retched into it, but only managed to bring up a little phlegm. A sour taste left in his mouth, and no relief. If only Leni was here, she would hold his head for him. She'd soothe him and make everything better.

But Christ-the-fuck-Almighty, what was the stupid cunt doing? It was 10.35 a.m., and he knew she kept her phone with her constantly. Faithless, heartless, that's what they all were, in the end.

His desk phone buzzed. He lunged and missed, knocking the receiver to the floor, then grabbed it and clutched it to his ear.

'Yes? Oh, thank God. Yes, yes – put her through, stop talking about it and just do it . . . Leni? Leni? It's me. I need you here, now. At the office. Yes. Something has happened. No, I'll tell you when you get here. I'll send a taxi straight away, ok? You're coming – you're definitely coming? Ok. As fast as you can. Don't make me wait.'

~

The anonymous rape claim against Roddy had been made on Twitter at 3.16 a.m. The first he knew about it was when he arrived at work. His first morning back at the office, after days spent writhing at home. Crisp pink shirt, silk handkerchief, fingernails immaculately trimmed. Let the pantomime resume.

Jackie was waiting for him in the lobby, even more

wire-tense than usual. Immediately he knew something was off because she looked so thrilled to see him. She was exuding some kind of frenetic delight, the excited smirk on her face unsuccessfully suppressed behind a veneer of pained concern.

'I've been calling you since just after six this morning,' she said. 'We have a big problem.'

'I keep my phone switched off until I arrive at the office,' he said. How unpleasantly shiny she was, up close. 'Healthy work-life balance, Jackie. You should try it.'

'Probably not a good idea to be the wise guy today, Roddy. And let me rephrase that. *You* have a big problem.'

She chivvied him into a meeting room where the blinds were closed. In the half-light she showed him the series of tweets on her iPad.

> *It is time for me to speak my truth. In 1994, Roderick Riseborough, then a police officer in the RUC, now editor of* The Sentinel *newspaper, forced his way into my home and brutally raped me . . . I have never spoken of this before because I was afraid of what he would do to me . . . This man is evil, he is a danger to women and he must be stopped . . . I am taking my file on this case to the police today.*

There was no signature attached, just an anonymous name: @TwoWomen. Impossible to make anything of that. It had been sent to *The Sentinel*, the BBC and five other media outlets.

His first reaction, when he read it, was to snort in disbelief. 'Ah, this is a hoax. Some kind of nutty wind-up.

Look – there's no details; it's all completely vague. I mean, 1994 – so this person was supposedly raped, by me, at some point in that entire year, but they can't quite remember when? Come on. Come *on*. This is a nut-job with a grudge, I'm telling you. Could be something to do with that cross-border smuggling hit we did last week – you can be sure that ruffled a few tail feathers. Or the Jed Carney business. What I'm saying is, it means nothing. We've had stuff like this before – well, not exactly like this, but you know what I mean. The bastards don't like us digging up their dirt, so they try to cause trouble. Forget about it, Jackie. You know how it works.'

'I'm afraid I can't forget about it, Roddy. This is an extremely serious allegation. It's out there now, and it's already been retweeted many times. In the circumstances, I felt obliged to alert the Wallaces immediately. I tried to notify you first but as I said, I couldn't get through. I've arranged an emergency conference call in the boardroom in' – she checked her watch – 'nine minutes from now. You're a bit later into work than expected.'

He wanted to sound assured, imperturbable, but the first cold tentacles of fear were stirring in his guts, getting ready to coil and grip.

'Brilliant, Jackie. This just couldn't be better timing for you, could it? What a perfect weapon in your dirty little war against me. Are you sure you didn't send those tweets yourself?'

Jackie's small chin puckered grimly, like the arse of a pygmy shrew. 'I'll be reporting that outrageous suggestion to the Wallaces also.'

'Great. Wonderful. Do that. You're the victim. But what about me? I'm the target of this ridiculous, stinking lie and yet somehow, I'm the one to blame, and I have to account for myself.'

'You deny the allegation, then?'

Roddy didn't answer, except to leave the door of the meeting room swinging shut in her face.

He went up the back way, using the emergency staircase which came out beside his office. He didn't want to see anybody. A cleaner with a rattling mop and bucket gawped at him as he raced past her, going two steps at a time.

Could it have been Jackie? Could it? Certainly, she hated him enough. But Jackie was careful too. Roddy didn't know how social media worked, but presumably it was possible to identify users who concealed their details, in cases of malicious criminal accusations like this. Surely Jackie, prim and principled Jackie, would never risk being exposed in such a way?

If it wasn't Jackie – and he really thought that unlikely, despite his throwaway dig at her – then he had no idea who it might be.

In 1994 . . . Who was he seeing then? Could an embittered former lover have suddenly decided that she had it in for him? Early to mid-nineties – that was a plentiful time, what with the added pull of the uniform. Many fish had been thrown back and left bobbing in his wake.

God, his brain was reeling. He was in shock. He could barely remember what happened last year, let alone liaisons from decades back.

What about that mouthy political hack from Dublin, with the awful hot peppery breath – the one who bred Angora rabbits in her spare time? Widely known as a ballbreaker, but surprisingly suggestible once you worked out how to handle her. She had always struck him as semi-deranged. Godetia, yes – Godetia Hinds. Could it be her? She was a good bit older than him, probably pushing her late sixties by now. Maybe she was afflicted with some sort of dementia that caused her to hunt down old boyfriends and try to annihilate them.

Who else had he dumped, back then? There was Marsha Townsend, Karl's wife. With the little alcohol problem. He had let her down hard. But she sent him a Christmas card from herself and Karl every year – Season's Greetings from Nova Scotia. It couldn't be her.

No, he was right first time – always go with your initial judgment, it so often turns out to be correct. Skulduggery, this looked like, and skulduggery it would prove to be. The whole message was hick, cobbled together, so clearly a put-up job, written by somebody who wanted to ruin him and knew that this was the easiest way to do it, given the 'current climate', as Jackie would put it. The rape claim was incidental, just a means to an end. But who, and why?

Well, innocent until proven guilty, that was the main thing. Even Mitch and Sean would have to recognise the most fundamental principle of law and justice.

Jackie chaired the video conference call, as of assumed moral right. The Wallace brothers were gentle and deferential towards her, as though she was the living incarnation of all the women who had been raped, ever. And of course she took the opportunity to advance her own anti-Roddy agenda. 'I mean, I keep wondering about the significance of that Twitter handle,' she said earnestly. '@TwoWomen. What is the victim trying to evoke here? Perhaps, God forbid, she's indicating that more than one woman has been harmed?'

'Invoke,' said Roddy. 'Invoke, not evoke. Don't you think the right choice of word is so important in our industry, Jackie? And whoever sent this shit isn't the victim – I am.'

That remark didn't go down at all well with the assembled company, he had to admit.

Reputational damage, that was the Wallaces' sole concern. Not whether Roddy had or had not committed a heinous sexual crime. When he tried to protest his innocence, he was immediately shut down, because his actual guilt or otherwise was simply not on the agenda. He was toxic to the corporate brand, in his current accused state – and so he must be removed. No discussion, no debate. He would be stepping aside while a thorough investigation took place. Jackie would act up as editor in the interim.

The lawyers were drafting a statement as they spoke, Sean said, which would be simultaneously issued to key media organisations and published on the *NewsWest* social media accounts at 10.00 a.m., GMT. Even through his confusion, Roddy noticed how crises invariably brought out maximum pomposity in Sean. 'GMT' – what other time zone would they be using, West fucking Africa Time?

Sean's long grey nose kept twitching every few seconds, as he was talking. Ah – there it went again! Possibly some kind of stress tic? Allergies? While Roddy was observing this, the conference call concluded, with the strict instruction issued that he must leave the building this morning, no later than 11.00 a.m., GMT. The entire meeting had lasted sixteen minutes.

Once he was alone in his office again, terror grabbed him and backed him against the wall. All his confidence was gone. *Lawyer up*, his brain gibbered, *you need to get lawyered up*.

Walker Gamble, the family solicitor – that's who he should call. He must have his number somewhere. Roddy hadn't spoken with Walker since the Judge died. In fact, he was by no means sure that Walker himself was still alive. Didn't he read somewhere recently that the old man had clocked it . . . shit, yes, he had! Some kind of Law Society memorial thing, his name had been on the list. No, Walker wasn't going to be much help.

Oh God, oh God.

A libel lawyer, that's what he needed. It was his own good name he had to defend, his own reputation. Who was that bloke, the flamboyant libel guy that all the politicians used, what was his name – Cruddas? Yes, Tom Cruddas. Best in the business – with prices to match, no doubt. Fuck it. He'd pay anything to make this go away.

Allies, supporters, friends: that was what Roddy needed most of all, and that was exactly what he hadn't got. There was nobody to stand alongside him.

Except one person.

~

It was 10.55 a.m. when she burst through the door, looking terrible: ghost pale, with circles under her eyes that were so purple they looked like bruises, and wearing a raincoat poppered up the wrong way.

'Oh, Christ, no, that will never do,' said Roddy. 'They'll think I've been beating you up. Hang on.'

He yanked the door open again and propelled her down the short staircase, towards Pam's desk.

'Pam, will you please help Leni here get tidied up.

Have you any make-up or something, I don't know? Just . . . get her spruced. We'll be leaving in five minutes.'

Pam was staring at something on his jacket. He glanced down and saw a long string of saliva clinging to the lapel. Nasty. Must have done it when he tried to boke in the bin. Brushing the drool off, he went back to his office window and peered down again. The crowd was bigger now, and some people had opened umbrellas. A brief burst of rain rattled against the glass. The weather was breaking at last.

Roddy turned away from the window. For comfort, he laid a hand on the back of the pheasant on his desk, and a few dusty feathers dislodged themselves and floated down. He'd seen a pheasant lying in the road this morning as he drove to work – a beautiful male, flecked golden wings vibrant, flash of white at the throat, the military green neck slumped and broken below the scarlet eye mask. Even so, it was much more alive than this dead brown thing.

Leni returned, wearing a garish shade of pink lipstick – he should have known better than to ask Pam for assistance on that score – but at least with her coat buttoned correctly. Madness to be doing this, madness to have brought her here, especially when the Wallaces were bound to realise that she was on *The Sentinel* payroll. That's if Jackie hadn't informed them already – no doubt she was on to him there, too. But the truth was that he couldn't do this alone.

'What's wrong?' she asked, coming up close, great soul-sucking eyes crawling all over him. 'I didn't expect to hear from you so soon. There's loads of people outside – photographers, TV cameras—'

'I know. There's no time to explain in detail.

Somebody has made an extremely damaging allegation against me on the internet. A rape claim. Obviously, it's a lie. I've decided to step aside as editor while I fight the claim. We have to leave the building, now. I need you to walk out beside me. Can you do that for me?'

She showed no sign of hesitation. 'Yes, Roddy. I can do that.'

'Good.' Having her here was helping. It was making him feel more decisive: somebody to perform for, someone to take charge of. He lifted his old brown trilby from the hatstand and put it on, adjusting it to the correct angle. The trilby always gave him an extra dose of chutzpah, and by God did he need it now.

He held out his hand, and she took it. 'Ready? Let's get this done.'

'Don't you want to bring anything with you?'

He glanced around the room. 'No. There's nothing here that I want.'

Pam was crying openly when they passed her desk. Roddy kept his gaze fixed on the lift doors on the far side of the newsroom. Too late, he realised that they should have gone the back way, down the emergency exit stairs. Here now, however. Bad, but no worse than Stalingrad. He put a little limp, almost imperceptible, into his stride.

The most eerie thing was the sudden hush that their presence created. The usual noise level in the newsroom was like a Chinook taking off – the same deafening mechanical chatter. More than once, especially as deadlines approached and the decibels rose, Roddy wished he had a pair of ear-protectors. Today? Absolute quiet. From the corner of his eye, he saw heads bent over desks, as though in prayer or profound contemplation. Spineless cowards. He didn't sense much sympathy, if any, until just before they reached the lift, when Martin Sharkey shambled over, gave him a brief squeeze on the arm and then quickly turned away again.

Roddy and Leni said nothing to each other in the lift, just stood there, hands interlocked, descending. Leni seemed to understand that it was better not to speak.

They crossed the marble lobby, and he stepped back politely to allow her to go through security first. The automatic glass gates swung open once for her, and again for him.

'Mr Riseborough,' nodded Wilfred, the obese security guard, whose animal body odour continually permeated the lobby. Today Roddy found the familiarity of it oddly moving. Wilfred's poignant sweat. He nodded back, as though this was any ordinary departure, any ordinary day.

They stepped out of the building into a deluge. Dripping umbrellas swarmed up the steps towards them, microphones thrusting from beneath, the wet black snouts of cameras shoving and clicking. A barrage of questions were brayed in his face.

'Mr Riseborough, what do you have to say to—'

'Can you give us your response to the claim that you brutally raped—'

'Have you resigned as editor of *The Sentinel*, Mr Riseborough, in the light of this historic rape allegation? Mr Riseborough?'

He towed Leni through the melee, forging a path for her. 'No comment. Except to say that I am innocent.'

That was when they should have climbed into the waiting car and been whisked away, but Roddy had never been the object of the media mob before, only a gleeful participant and in his agitation, he hadn't thought of arranging transport.

A delivery lorry was double-parked outside the sporting goods shop next door, its tailgate down. In the absence of any better plan, Roddy yanked Leni into the road behind the truck. Immediately they found themselves up to their ankles in a muddy, leaf-strewn torrent. Horns blared as they splashed and wove their way across to the other side. All the cars had their lights on; the morning was as dark as a December dusk. It occurred to him that his trilby would be ruined for good. Suede brogues too.

Roddy made a sudden right turn down Queen's Avenue. He'd thought of somewhere they could hide.

'Where are we going?' gasped Leni, hair plastered to her face.

'The club. We'll be there in two minutes.'

Roddy glanced behind and saw that a photographer in a ludicrous yellow rain cape was following them. From the bouncy gait and distinctive rotund shape, Roddy guessed it was Dave Morse from Picarama, a press agency frequently used by *The Sentinel's* rival, *The Daily Northern*. Fat meddling bastard.

'Roddy, who's that with you?' he yelled. 'Who's the girl?'

'Ignore him,' Roddy muttered. 'Just keep walking, as fast as you can, and don't look round.'

Never had he been so glad to see Matthias, the dour, patrician doorman at the 1921 Club. He ushered Roddy and Leni inside, out of the battering rain. Behind them, they heard Matthias's stern murmur, rebuffing Dave, and then came the sound of the portcullis-like gate closing.

'You go to the ladies' cloakroom and hang up your

coat, Leni,' said Roddy. 'I'll dry off a bit too. See you in the bar in five minutes.'

He deposited his own overcoat, scarf and sodden trilby in the gents' cloaks. When he came into the bar she was seated on a low chair by the fire, holding her thin hands up to the flames.

'Cold?'

She nodded. The waiter brought them the two double whiskeys on the rocks that he'd ordered.

It was decent of her, he supposed, that she let him finish his drink in peace, before she began talking and asking questions.

'I'm sorry I was so hard to get hold of earlier,' she said. 'A lot of things have been happening at home. But I'll fill you in on the details later. You have enough to deal with now.'

'It's alright. You got to the office in time. That's all that matters. So, well, thank you. For coming to my "rescue".' He felt his mouth twist sardonically.

'I was glad to do it. It means a lot, that you came to me.'

He didn't tell her that there was nobody else.

'So . . . could you tell me what exactly happened? This . . . rape claim. You found out about it this morning? What did it say?'

'The claim was only made this morning. On Twitter. In the early hours.' He sighed. 'I don't want to talk about it. Look it up online if you want the gory details.'

'I can't – my phone's dead—'

'Christ,' he muttered, 'do I have to do everything? Here.' He tossed his own mobile into her lap. 'Go on,' he said, seeing her hesitate. 'Just type my name in. It'll all be there.'

He watched her face as she read, the serious, perplexed frown. Then a wave of hot red washed up over her throat and set her cheeks burning, but not in the usual girlish way. This blush was darker, deeper, as if it came from old blood. And her eyes, when they met his, were full of some kind of wakening horror. She swallowed visibly.

'Do you have any idea who did this?' she asked.

'No idea whatsoever. What's wrong?'

'I have to go. I don't—' She got up and left, mid-sentence, tottering across the bar, and pushing her way out through the brass handled double doors, which stayed swinging for several seconds once she'd departed.

Chapter Twenty-Nine

After Leni told him she was leaving him, Theo did not stop crying all night. He was openly broken. Every time he looked across the kitchen table at her, the tears welled up again. Although he was hoarse with weeping, Theo didn't raise his voice once, through all the hours that followed. There was something childlike and pure about his pain. It was so clean and honest and transparent.

Leni herself felt almost nothing. She was numb, as if in suspended animation, waiting until Mr Riseborough was ready to get back in touch and bring her alive again.

Theo asked her hardly anything about the affair. Instead he fixated on the house in Oxbow Gardens, as though that was the true reason that Leni was breaking up with him. Maybe the enormity of what she'd done was too much for him to take in, all at once.

He kept telling her that he didn't know Patti was going to go ahead and actually buy the house. It was only an idea, he'd thought; he was going to talk it over with Leni once the right moment came. He wasn't hiding anything from her; there was no deception. But when he came home from work yesterday, at teatime, Patti told him she'd put the deposit down. 'That's honestly how it happened,' he sobbed. 'Please, you've got to believe me. I didn't lie to you. I would never lie.'

'It's okay, Theo,' said Leni. 'Really. None of this is your fault.' But then he'd go back to the beginning and start the explanations all over again.

Leni wasn't sure what time it was when Ann woke;

her mobile was still out of power. Since it died in the boatshed at Honolulu last night, she'd had no chance to charge it. Theo went upstairs and carried Ann down, and after that he managed to gather himself together enough to discuss some initial plans.

It was Leni who suggested he take Ann to Ballyhornway for a few days. Having Ann there would be good for him, and Bill and Dorothy could help look after her, so he could have some time to himself when he needed it. They could talk again at the weekend, and take it from there.

Leni made some tea while Theo phoned his mother – she could hear Dorothy's dismayed clucking tones – and then, sounding slightly more composed, he called Gav and arranged to take some temporary leave from work. Leni offered to drive them to Ballyhornway, because Theo couldn't face the thought of doing it himself, but at this, Theo began to sob again and said that would be even worse.

So Bill came over, looking awkward and strained, and loaded Theo, Ann and a few hastily packed bags into his Audi estate. Dorothy was at home, he said, making waffles with maple syrup for them, getting the heat on in the spare room. To Leni, it was all as unreal as a dream. Even Ann's tiny starfish hand waving out the back window of the Audi didn't break her.

She grieved for Theo, in a remote kind of way. She was aware that she was the sole source of his anguish, but it couldn't be helped. Collateral damage. Regrettable but unavoidable.

After Theo and Ann left, Leni closed the front door and sank down on to the stairs. Patti hadn't emerged from her room since fleeing the kitchen. Leni hoped she would stay up there as long as possible. Last night, she had found the strength to stand up to her mother, something she'd never done in her life before. But she feared Patti's response to this act of treason.

There was nothing to do now except sit and stare at the floor.

Beside the welcome mat was the tile that had been damaged the day that Patti's photograph, encased in its wooden crate, was delivered to the house.

Leni traced the hairline crack with the tip of her toe. Strange to think that if it hadn't been for the arrival of that delivery, and the sudden mad need for escape that it prompted, she might not have agreed to meet Mr Riseborough at the 1921 club. And then none of this would have happened. The champagne wouldn't have been spilled; she wouldn't have wept; he wouldn't have held her, and life would have continued much as normal.

But no, it had to happen. It was the union of two souls, something of cosmic significance, ordained by the stars – that's what he always said.

The plastic plug for the landline had fallen out again, she noticed. The tiny clip on its side, which was supposed to keep it in place, was partially broken. Using her fingernail to open the sprung slot in the wall fitting, Leni pushed the plug back into place. Almost instantly, the phone began to ring. It was Pam, sounding agitated, who put her straight on to Mr Riseborough.

Moments later, leaving the house, she'd shut the door as quietly as possible behind her, so as not to disturb her mother.

~

Now that she was back at Isthmus Avenue, Leni didn't care how much noise she made. She kicked off her wet shoes and dropped her bag and keys.

'Mama!' she yelled. 'Come down here. I need to talk to you.'

She listened, breathing hard. No response, not even the distant creak of a floorboard.

Could Patti have gone out? No. Leni knew her own house, and she knew it wasn't empty. Her mother was here. She could feel her presence, somewhere above.

'Mama!' Her voice reverberated through the house. 'Okay. If you're not coming down, I'm coming up.'

Passing the nursery, Leni heard a faint rustling sound. The door was ajar, and she pushed it open.

Patti was sitting on the floor, surrounded by crumpled pink tissue paper, tiny baby clothes and flimsy pieces of lingerie. The raided storage box lay empty on its side. From their place on the bureau, Ann's row of stuffed elephants, bears and penguins stared down at the scene, as if appalled.

'Found your stash,' Patti slurred. Black kohl had smeared into the delta of criss-crossed lines beneath her eyes. She looked like some kind of malevolent, shock-haired reptile.

'You're drunk,' said Leni.

Patti laughed, a dry snicker. She picked up a see-through lace bra and held it against her chest. 'Sexy. Think it would suit me?'

'I know what you did, Mama,' Leni said. Her rage was so intense that the words came out in a choked-sounding whisper. 'I *know*. It was you. You made up that story about being raped and put it on Twitter. Two Women. I know what your horrible photograph is called. Did you think I wouldn't realise? Or were you too pissed to care?'

'I have no idea what you're talking about, darling,' said Patti, enunciating each word carefully. She sat with a fixed little smirk on her face, tearing a wad of tissue paper into shreds. Leni was revolted by her, but she was no longer afraid.

'Oh yes, Mama, you do. Revenge: that's what you wanted. I spoilt your plan for the new house. You couldn't bear the thought of me going off with Roddy, having a happy life. So you tried to punish me, by destroying him. It's so obvious. You may as well admit it.'

Patti said nothing. She kept on ripping up the paper, shaking her head as though what she was hearing was too fantastical to believe.

'I really thought you'd changed,' said Leni. 'But it was all a big performance, right from the start. You had nobody else left, so you decided to worm yourself into my family. Make yourself indispensable, charm us all to death. "Dear, devoted Granny P, so generous, so kind, so loving, so fun. How did we ever manage without her? She must never, ever leave us." And it almost worked! You nearly pulled it off.'

'You've gone round the twist, darling,' said Patti. 'You don't know what you're saying. All I wanted was to make you happy. Give you a proper family home with a garden for Ann to play in. It's not my fault if you threw everything away for some random old creep.' She tossed a handful of the torn pink paper in the air and closed her eyes as the pieces fell around her.

'It was him, wasn't it?' said Leni. 'Roddy. He was the man who said you moved those bodies. The women in the photograph.'

Patti's eyes flicked open. She became very still.

'Yeah. I thought that would get your attention. No wonder you had a meltdown when you heard he was my boss, that day at Magill's. Spinning that pathetic sob story about Patti, the poor oppressed artist, fleeing to Berlin. I get it now. You were terrified I would find out the truth about who you are, what you're capable of doing. Because you did do it, if Roddy said so. I believe him, not you.'

Leni stared at her mother, shaking her head in wonder. 'I mean, to take a photograph of something like that is bad enough, but to actually interfere with a – a dead person, a corpse – the body of someone who was alive, just moments before? And call it "art"? And say it's brave, and *beautiful*? What's wrong with you? You're not human – you can't be—'

'Leni. You don't understand. It was all a very long time ago. There was a war going on. I was a different person. We have to move on now, forget about the terrible things that happened in the past. Think about the children, make life better for them. That's why I bought you a house with a lovely garden for Ann, like you always said you wanted for her—'

'Stop talking about the fucking garden. Just stop, alright? And anyway, it was you who said that, not me. Pushing your own agenda, as usual. God, why didn't I see it? Facts – what actually happened – these things mean nothing to you. You don't give a shit about the truth. You certainly don't give a shit about me, or Ann, or Theo, or anyone. All you care about is yourself. What Patti wants, Patti gets. But not this time.'

Leni began gathering up the Babygros and bras and torn bits of tissue paper. She lifted the storage box and dumped the lot in, then stood squarely in front of Patti. 'I want you to leave my house. Now. Take your obscene photograph with you. I'm going to call Roddy and tell him who made the false rape claim against him.'

'Leni, no! Please! You can't – I have nowhere to go—' Patti's huge blue eyes were imploring. She darted forward and grabbed Leni by the leg. 'Please, Leni, don't do this, I'm begging you . . .'

Leni had a powerful urge to kick her mother in the face. Anything to rid herself of the white-haired little troll clinging to her shin. 'No. I don't care where you go. Just get out.' She tried to prise away Patti's fingers, but her grip was too strong.

'I did it for you,' Patti was mumbling. 'It was wrong, I know, a bad mistake, but really, I did it for you. I had to show you what a monster that man is—'

'Yeah, so you made up a lie that he raped you, and now everyone thinks he's a rapist, thanks to you. Who's the monster here?'

'But it's true that he's dangerous, Leni – that man is a danger to women! He's a danger to you.'

'You are a danger to me. Not Roddy.'

'Leni, please—'

'Let go of me. I don't want your hands touching me. Let go!' Leni, sickened beyond endurance, wrenched herself loose. Patti screamed in pain and began to cry.

A sudden surge of guilt checked Leni's anger. 'I'm sorry I hurt you,' she said, in a quieter tone. 'I didn't mean to be rough.'

Patti gazed up at Leni, still sobbing piteously and nursing her frail wrist. It was a pathetic sight, like an abused child trying to find trust again. Leni felt her own resistance begin to weaken. But then she noticed that there were no tears on Patti's face. It was completely dry.

Chapter Thirty

'Slow down and tell me again. You're saying that *your mother* made this crazy claim against me?'

'Yes. I'm so sorry – she did.' Leni was pacing up and down the living room as she spoke into the phone. Outside, Marta walked past, struggling to keep hold of her red umbrella against the wind.

'But why would . . . Wait, who is your mother?'

'You know her. Knew her. When she lived here. Patti Barbour.'

'Patti Barbour,' Roddy said slowly. '*Patti Barbour* is your mother? Christ. I never thought of her. She dumped me, as I recall. Why the fuck is Patti Barbour accusing me of raping her?'

Leni explained. She told him everything that happened, from the time she arrived home last night, to the moment in the 1921 club this morning, when she realised what Patti had done, and why. She had to stop several times and repeat herself, because Roddy kept interrupting.

'And she's admitted this, that she made the whole thing up, out of spite?'

'Yes. Pretty much.'

'What do you mean, "pretty much"? Has she or hasn't she?'

'No, she has. She said it was a bad mistake.'

'And where is she now?'

'Gone. I don't know. I threw her out of the house.

I couldn't stand her being here anymore. Everyone's gone. Theo and Ann too.'

'Jesus! *Jesus*. I'm struggling to take this whole thing in. So she . . . because you . . . because I . . . Fuck! Your mother is clinically insane.'

'Roddy, what actually happened, back then? With you – and Patti – you never said you were in the police—'

'There was no reason to tell you. It's a part of my life I'd rather forget. And Patti – she was just a fling; it only lasted a few weeks. She upped and left one day; didn't tell me she was going. Then I read in one of the London papers that she was in Paris, or Berlin, or some such. Never saw her again. Jesus, I can't believe that she's done this – turning on me, after all this time—'

'But this thing about the bomb – she said you were going to expose her, try to ruin her, for touching the bodies. Was that true?'

'Ruin her? God, no. I mean, she knew that I knew. I told her I did. She'd been seen.'

'By you?'

'No, not me, another cop I knew – he was a DI at the Blackwater station, one of the first on the scene. Spotted her pulling at a dead woman's arm. At first, he thought she was trying to help the woman. Then he saw her crouch down with a camera. Snap. Fairly fucked-up, obviously. But I never threatened Patti, I had no intention of going public. It wasn't done. You heard a lot of squalid things in those days, and you just kept them to yourself.'

'I don't understand. If she didn't leave town because of you, then why did she—'

Roddy interrupted. 'No, Leni, that's enough! We have to get our priorities straight here. My job, my fucking job – that's what's on the line! I'm going to call Dublin now.

I'll tell them that the tweet was a hoax, by a mentally ill person with a grudge, who has now been identified. No, not with a grudge, the Wallaces don't need to get into all that old Blackwater stuff, let that lie. Maybe I should speak to Tom Cruddas first. Yep, that'd be best, I think. Get the legal perspective.' He seemed to be talking more to himself than to her.

'Okay,' said Leni. 'I know that's all really urgent. But could we get together later, maybe for dinner or something, now that everything is out in the open? Or even tomorrow, if you're too busy today?'

'No, Leni. Not today. Not tomorrow. Not next week. I told you when you came to the house last night, and I thought you understood. I need time to myself. I can't tell when, or if, that might change.'

Leni didn't reply.

When, or if.

'Leni, are you there? I'm just thinking, possibly I might need you to sign a statement, some kind of affidavit, about your mother's admission of guilt over this claim. But we can do that by post, if necessary. No need to meet face-to-face.'

When, or if.

'Do you hear me? Leni, are you there?'

When, or if.

'Alright, I'm going now. Bye, Leni.'

If.

~

Leni was very tired. It was starting to get dark, but she didn't feel like turning on any of the lamps. She climbed onto the sofa under the bay window. It was still raining hard. Her cherry tree had lost the last of its leaves and was standing in a pool of muddy water. Someone's blue recycling bin had blown over and pieces of newspaper were flying around like limp, water-logged birds. Her head felt heavier and heavier. Eventually she couldn't hold it up anymore. She crossed her arms on the back of the sofa and laid her cheek against them, the way she used to do in primary school, when the long sun-bleached curtains were drawn and the teacher told them to put their heads down on their desks for a rest. She remembered the soft, sure tick of her watch, so close to her ear, and the sharp crease in her sleeve, firmly ironed in by Granny June.

When she woke, it was completely dark. Dry waves of dusty heat were rising from the radiator beneath the window, and her throat felt parched and sore. She looked out and saw the Skoda parked at the kerb, and for a brief, sleep-addled moment, she thought that Theo had arrived home from the garden, as usual. Then she remembered. Theo and Ann were in Ballyhornway, under Dorothy's wing, being comforted by waffles. Patti was God knows where.

Oh, but Ted, Ted – what about Ted? She hadn't seen him all day. Did he even get his breakfast this morning? His heart pills?

Ted was curled in a tight ball in his usual place, under the kitchen table. He didn't stir when Leni came into the room, nor when she turned on the lights and called his name. So she knew, even before she touched him, that he was gone too.

She sat beside Ted's body for a long time, thinking. Then she decided to walk to Magill's. The rain had stopped at last, and it was a cold, clear night. In the sky she saw Orion, the hunter – the three bright stars of his belt, and the curve of his bow, pointed heavenward. On the way, she texted Roddy to tell him about Ted. But she knew now that there would be no reply, and so she was not surprised when none came.

Chapter Thirty-One

It was going to be alright. Everything was going to be alright.

Roddy got word before he'd even approached the Wallaces, while he was still in confab with Tom Cruddas. The insane bitch had apologised and withdrawn her allegation, using the same Twitter account on which she'd made the original claim. Had admitted it was all completely untrue and written under the influence of alcohol – to which, as she said, she had 'unfortunately succumbed, after a long period of abstinence, due to sudden family breakdown.' She added that she was seeking urgent medical help.

Tom Cruddas fingered his wattle, as Roddy mentally dubbed the loose folds of fat above the lawyer's collar. He seemed disappointed. He said they should still pursue Ms Barbour on defamation and malicious falsehood grounds, although he conceded that the swift retraction and full admission of guilt might considerably reduce potential damages. He urged Roddy, at the very least, to pursue the libellous idiots who blithely retweeted the rape claim, clueless as to whether it was true or not. Tom also recommended cutting up rough with the *Daily Northern*, for some highly intemperate language about Roddy's 'alleged proclivities' that it used in an editorial. But Roddy didn't want to take any of it further. It was over. He was free.

The Wallaces, perhaps cognisant – a favourite Cruddas word – of their own unjust treatment of a now demonstrably innocent Roddy, as well as the wider public standing of *The Sentinel* and *NewsWest*, had performed a swift reverse-ferret shortly after the apology emerged, publishing a jubilant headline the next day: 'Our Man Vindicated'. Mitch had even sent him a bottle of Knappogue twelve-year single malt, with his compliments. And that was enough for Roddy. He wasn't a vengeful man, although he did savour the image of Jackie putting together that particular front page.

It was reassuring, too, that Leni wasn't going to be a problem. The day after their last conversation on the phone, she had emailed him a formal letter of resignation from her position at *The Sentinel*, including the additional role he had offered her as a columnist in the *Style* section, and he hadn't heard a peep from her since. When he called Mitch, to thank him for the whiskey, he made sure to mention that the young woman who had been seen accompanying him from the building was just a temporary worker, a trainee sub with whom he'd had a meeting scheduled that morning. Sympathetic to the dreadful position he found himself in, she had immediately offered to lend him her moral support. She had however since moved on, and was no longer on *The Sentinel* payroll. Mitch had merely grunted and advised him to keep his nose clean. To which his immediate rejoinder had been: 'Oh, it is clean, Mitch. Scrupulously. And shall remain so.'

His conscience wasn't troubling him about Leni at all, because he was so certain that the end of their relationship was the best thing for her. Sad to hear about the old dog, of course. But she would soon patch things up with Moominpapa – because of the kid, and because Theo was clearly the kind of pant-wetting pussy who would excuse a wife's infidelity once he'd snivelled and wailed about it long enough. Probably he'd end up blaming the patriarchy, not Leni.

And then the Moffetts would once again be the blissfully happy family in the photograph she had first sent him. Well, maybe not *blissfully* happy, but together – reunited, a functional unit again – and that was all that anyone could hope for, wasn't it? It was far more than Roddy had himself.

Bizarre – beyond bizarre – to think that Patti Barbour was Leni's mother. She'd never mentioned that she had a daughter. There had been no sign of an infant in her chaotic split-level flat on Fitzhugh Street. No toys or games, no child-rearing paraphernalia; nothing he'd noticed anyway. He remembered Patti's patchouli-scented bedroom, which you entered through a kitsch beaded curtain with Frida Kahlo's face painted on it.

And Leni looked nothing at all like her mother, there was no physical clue to their connection – Leni so big-boned, so compliant and dreamy, Patti so tiny and feral and fierce. That ginger colouring of Leni's must have come from the father, whoever he was – and he could have been anybody, Roddy reflected, because Patti was known to be a great fucker of men. Not that he blamed her for that – in fact at the time he'd found it quite intoxicating: her frank appetite, her shameless expertise.

He'd met her one autumn night at the Tavern, a small bar near the cathedral, where he occasionally drank. Patti had been thrown out for smashing a full bottle of red wine on the floor – one of her favourite party tricks, it later transpired, and a habit that had seen her banned from many pubs in the city. The barman had twisted one arm behind her back and frogmarched her off the premises. Roddy watched with undisguised interest from his stool at the bar. She'd aimed a slap at the side of his face with her free hand as she passed him. 'Curiosity can be fatal, haven't you heard?' she hissed. Her peroxide-blonde hair was shaved so short you could see the shape of her skull under the silver prickle of hair.

Roddy had slipped from his stool and followed her. At that time, the Tavern still had a security cage, a sort of metal porch with a reinforced outer gate and a buzzer you had to use to get in; there had been a couple of rather messy murders on the premises in the 1980s. The barman had opened the gate and pushed Patti through it, then turned on his heel, almost bumping into Roddy. The gate clanged shut. Out on the street, Patti was singing at the top of her husky voice, clearly high as a kite. After a moment, Roddy recognised the song. It was 'Under My Thumb', by the Rolling Stones.

'I love that song,' said Roddy, smiling at her from inside the cage.

'Yeah? Bet you don't know all the words,' said Patti. She pushed her face up close against the metal mesh and stuck her tongue through one of the holes.

'Yes, I do,' he said. 'Watch me.' He'd proceeded to deliver his best Mick Jagger impression: hip-thrusts, pouting, everything. Patti laughed so hard that her black eye makeup poured in ribbons down her cheeks.

'You'll have to come out here with me,' she said. 'Because I can't get in there with you.' To demonstrate, she hit the buzzer several times. The barman came to the door again, and seeing that it was Patti, he gave a grim shake of the head and walked away.

'Patricia Majella Barbour,' she said, once Roddy was standing out in the street in front of her. 'Notorious international artist. Censored in my own country.'

She held out her hand, and Roddy took it and kissed it.

He knew who she was, of course. Everyone did. It was the Blackwater Street bomb picture that had made her name. But what nobody else knew was how far she'd gone to get her shot.

Jim Torrens had been really shaken by what he'd witnessed, and he was no stranger to carnage. Jim was the closest that Roddy had to a friend in the force. Another loner, just like him – ironically, that's what drew them together. Of course everyone thought they were a couple. Jim was the only other cop who'd heard of Nietzsche, not that German philosophy did him any good in the end.

'Never seen anything like it,' he remembered Jim muttering. 'Fucking unreal. Body parts everywhere. I'm thinking: no survivors. Couldn't be. Then I glimpse someone moving. Smoke clears a bit and I see her – this wee grey figure stumbling around. So small I thought she was a kid at first. She's bending over a victim's body, and then she starts pulling at them – like she's trying to help them, you know – haul them out of the rubble. Though God knows they were beyond mortal help. I'm standing there, stunned – can't move, can't say anything. Shock, I suppose. It was only when I saw the flash of the camera that I realised – fuck me, she's taking pictures.'

Jim took another gulp of vodka before continuing. 'One of the women she photographed, Maura O'Neill – she'd been in the shop getting her hair done. Second wedding anniversary. Cut and blow-dry. Table for two booked for dinner at the Chimney Corner. After the blast, Maura had no face left. Blown off completely, crown to jawbone. Yet this . . . this devil . . . she's not bothered by that. Not a bit of it. You'd think she was arranging a fashion show. If you'd seen her, Roddy, scuttling about in the dust and gore and muck. Like a . . . a grave rat, or something. She's worse than the bastards who planted that device. At least they had a cause they're fighting for, whatever you think of it. What's her cause?'

Privately, Roddy had thought that Jim's morbid fixation on this episode was a symptom of his PTSD-induced alcoholism, complications of which would carry him off less than a year later. Even the Christmassy scent of marzipan would send him diving for cover – in Jim's poor misfiring brain, it smelt identical to the plastic explosives the Provos used to make their bombs.

And of course what Patti had done was appalling, by any moral standards. But it was precisely that bravura disregard for the most fundamental rules of life and death that made her so fascinating to Roddy. He'd resolved to speak with her if he ever ran across her, which was not unlikely given the small size of the city. And now he had.

He'd been in awe of Patti: her insouciance, her wildness, her insatiable drinking. The drama she created wherever she went. The mouth she had on her – she'd say anything, to anyone. When she was there, you couldn't look at anybody else in the room.

None of his usual techniques had worked with her. She would not be harnessed and the more she resisted, the more he craved her and wanted to possess her. One night, in bed in her flat, he tried a new tactic. He cuddled up next to her tiny ear, kissed it, and whispered that he knew what she had done in Blackwater Street. To make it sound more impressive, he left Jim out of the story and said that he'd seen her himself. There was no threat on his part, no condemnation – he'd simply thought that if he told Patti he knew her secret, it might bind her closer to him.

Her whole body had gone rigid. He saw a muscle twitch in her temple. But then she laughed her brash, careless laugh: 'No, you didn't, darling. You couldn't have. Because it never happened.'

She fucked him harder than ever that night, with a violence that almost frightened him, as Frida Kahlo on the curtain looked the other way. He'd left early the next morning for his shift, and that was the last time he saw her – curled up asleep on top of the covers, adorable, like a little naked skinhead. When she didn't respond to any of his calls, he'd gone back to her flat. He knocked and knocked for ages, and then the landlord came down from upstairs and said she'd done a midnight flit.

He wasn't entirely surprised. Patti was always complaining about how bored she was in Belfast, what a philistine shithole it was, and how as an artist she could have a much more stimulating, fulfilled life elsewhere – in an enlightened society that was capable of understanding her art. To hear her talk, she was forever on the cusp of departure.

She had never fully succumbed to him. She was never his, and by leaving when she did, she never would be. What did she look like now, he wondered. Was there anything left of that blazing blue drop-dead stare?

Roddy smiled. Now that the rape threat had been neutralised, he could allow himself to marvel at Patti's atrocious nerve, which had obviously not diminished with time. Only Patti Barbour would come up with such a crazy, reckless, kamikaze plan.

It had certainly woken him up from the maudlin state he'd fallen into after the demise of his relationship with Leni. Thanks to Patti, he felt alive again. Ready for the next adventure.

Really quite chipper, as Mummie would say.

Chapter Thirty-Two

Patti was standing at the private taxi rank outside the Metropolitan Hotel, wearing a black leather jumpsuit and studded biker boots. She looks like a creature from another planet, thought Leni. Her mother's hair was the palest peroxide blonde, no longer white, and razor-cut across her brow at a sharper angle than ever. Beside her on the kerb were three overstuffed suitcases, one partially unzipped and keeled on its side, as well as several bulging plastic bags. Propped against the tallest suitcase was a large rectangular object which looked as though it had been parcelled up roughly in a bedsheet. Leni knew what that was.

As soon as Patti spotted Leni approaching in the Skoda, she began to wave and beckon, flagging the car down like one of those airport marshals with the fluorescent bats who guide planes on to the stand. Leni braked and pulled into the rank.

'I can't park here, Mama! It says taxis only, and I'm blocking the entrance. I told you I'd park on the street and pick you up at reception.'

'Oh, there was a slight misunderstanding with the management,' said Patti airily. 'Ridiculous fuss over nothing, really, the damage to the suite was negligible – anyway I decided it would be so much nicer to watch for you outside. It's fine, darling!' she added. 'Don't look so worried! It's Sunday morning – nobody about. Just put your hazards on, it'll only take us a moment to get loaded up.'

There was a queue of irate taxis behind the Skoda, horns blaring, by the time Leni packed all of Patti's luggage into the car. She had to disconnect the back seat and lay it flat to fit everything in. The sheet-wrapped parcel sat on top of the cases, wedged against both front headrests.

'This isn't safe, you know. I can't see out the back,' said Leni.

'Never mind, we don't have very far to go, do we? It's so wonderful to see you again, darling. It feels like an eternity since we've been together.'

'I think the journey will take about forty-five minutes. I've never driven there before.'

As the car left the city and picked up speed on the dual carriageway, Patti took a pack of cigarettes and a lighter out of her bag.

'You can't smoke in the car, Mama.'

'Not even a very quick one? I'll open the window.'

'No. Please put them away.'

'Okay, darling. You're in charge.' Patti adjusted her sunglasses, pushing them higher up her nose. 'Terribly bright morning. Awful glare. Oh, Leni, I can't wait to be home again.'

'Only if you do what we agreed,' said Leni.

'Of course I will. I said I would, and I'm a woman of my word. It's going to be extremely difficult – I mean, who knows how he'll react when he sees me. And I do wish he knew we were coming. Just turning up unannounced like this – it does seem rather . . . And he might not even be at home . . .' Getting no reply, she glanced across at Leni, who remained stony-faced and resolute at the wheel. 'But if that's what it takes for us to be together, darling, I'll do it. I'd do anything you asked me, to make things right with us again.'

Leni had told Patti that if she apologised in person to Roddy Riseborough, she would allow her to return to Isthmus Avenue. And then, when the house in Oxbow Gardens was ready, Patti and Leni would move in there, together. Refusing to give any explanation, Leni told her mother that she was no longer involved with Roddy Riseborough, and that she had resigned from *The Sentinel*. There was no question of her rebuilding her relationship with Theo. Isthmus Avenue was going on the market, and she wanted to move out as soon as possible. Theo was staying with his parents for now, with Ann, and had extended his leave of absence from work. He was being more reasonable than she had a right to expect, said Leni, and they were talking about a plan for shared custody.

But first must come this apology. Only if Patti was willing to do that – as proof of her total contrition – could Leni manage to forgive her mother.

Patti had resisted at first, protesting that she had already apologised to Roddy publicly, on Twitter, and asking what was the point of it anyway, if he and Leni had already split up? But Leni had been immovable. It was that, or nothing.

The road from Ardpatrick to Honolulu looked completely different in the daylight. In the car, the hilly rises and falls spooled easily away behind them. They passed the house where the dog had menaced her that awful night, and Leni caught a glimpse of him now, lying peacefully under the birch trees in the sun.

Patti, who had been silent for a while, said: 'I can understand you being bored with Theo, you know.'

'What?'

'Theo. He's missing something. He's not really a man, is he? Not what I'd call a man, anyway.'

'I told you I don't want to discuss Theo.'

'No problem, darling. I just want you to know that I'm with you. I'm on your side, always.'

Leni didn't reply. They were getting close now, travelling smoothly along the road that followed the shore. The morning was so calm that each of the far islands had its own motionless reflection in the lake-like water. A scolding blackbird shot out in front of the car and disappeared into the tawny reeds.

'Your skin is looking amazing, by the way, Leni. No trace of the rosacea at all – it's perfect.'

'Thanks.'

'Been using a new kind of cream?'

'No. I haven't been using anything.'

Silence again. They turned a bend and the causeway came into view. The tide was out, exposing the blackened timber legs that supported it. Thousands of tiny worm casts dotted the muddy sand.

Leni slowed down and put on her indicator.

'You'll come with me, won't you, darling?' For the first time, Patti sounded frightened. 'You won't make me do this on my own, will you?'

'No, Mama. I don't want to speak to him. I have nothing to say. Anyway, the whole point is that you do this on your own.'

Leni concentrated on piloting the Skoda across the causeway, making sure to avoid the biggest holes, and then they rattled over the cattle grid and on to the island. The fuchsia bushes that arched over the drive were still in flower, dripping with tiny red lanterns.

Leni parked some distance away from the house, behind the old boathouse, and left the engine running. She didn't plan on staying long.

'Well, he's here,' she told Patti. The Jeep was in its usual spot, drawn up beneath his bedroom window.

'My God, what is this place?' muttered Patti, peering up at the house. 'It's like the ghost of the Space Age.'

'This is Honolulu,' said Leni. 'And now it's time for you to keep your promise.'

'I – I don't think I can, darling – he'll kill me—'

'You must, Mama. Or else you're not coming home.'

Patti picked her way over the lawn, her boots leaving a trail of footprints in the pale frosty grass. Leni watched her. She looked back once, pleadingly, but Leni nodded at her to go on.

Her mother walked up the front path and rang the doorbell. More than a minute passed. With obvious relief, Patti turned towards Leni in the car and mimed a helpless shrug: he's not answering. Leni flinched. Behind her mother's back, the door had swung open.

Leni couldn't see Roddy, but she saw Patti launch into a series of plaintive gestures, a kind of dumb-show of entreaty, ending with fingers clasped as if in prayer. The apology, she presumed.

Now was the precise moment that Leni had to act, while Patti was distracted at the door. She'd calculated that she had thirty seconds, perhaps less, to haul her mother's luggage out of the car. Any more than that, and the advantage of surprise would be lost. She was determined to make a clean, quick getaway.

Abandoning Patti at Honolulu, dumping her on Roddy's doorstep, felt necessary to Leni. She'd been willing to tell any amount of bare-faced lies to get her mother here, because it was so clearly the right thing to do; a form of justice as much as revenge. It was a way to finally put the past behind her.

And yet Leni hesitated. She knew that there could be no going back once she'd done this. She would not be forgiven. It would be goodbye to her mother, for good.

If she didn't act now, though, it would be too late. Leave it any longer and Patti would be sitting in the car beside her, the triumphant martyr, ready to be taken home. And that wouldn't fit in with Leni's plans at all.

Come on, she urged herself, *do it. Pop the boot, sling her stuff out, and go.*

But she didn't move.

Up at the house, Patti was still talking to Roddy, who remained out of sight. Leni realised that her mother's whole demeanour had changed; all the nervous tension was gone. Her hip had found a casual resting place against the door frame, and one hand had snaked up and was moving sensually through her hair. Now she was actually laughing.

Then Leni saw her mother straighten and become very still. She seemed to be listening intently. Patti nodded, took one furtive glance over her shoulder, and stepped into the house. The door closed behind her.

~

The breath that Leni must have been holding, unaware, escaped from her lungs with a rush.

Incredible.

No, it wasn't incredible. It was entirely predictable, in fact, now that she thought about it.

Patti and Roddy had, once again, shown Leni exactly

who they were. Cannibals, both of them, without care or conscience.

Alright, then. Let them devour each other.

There was no need to hurry. Leni was sure that Patti wouldn't be coming back any time soon. She hauled her mother's belongings out of the boot and piled them on the drive. Without the fast getaway – the little drama of transgression and escape that she'd planned – it seemed like a rather pathetic thing to do.

But then Leni smiled. She had a new idea. She dragged the suitcases and the shopping bags on to the grass, leaving only the big sheet-wrapped object lying behind the Skoda on the tarmac.

The car was still running, and Leni got in and put it into reverse. As it rolled backward, she felt a muffled bump beneath the wheels, and then another. Giggling in disbelief at herself, at the audacity of what she was doing, she climbed out to take a look. There was a wide grey tyre-mark printed across the sheet, but the thing inside, which she remembered was printed on metal, seemed to be intact.

Well, she wasn't going to give up at the first attempt.

Leni bumped the car back and forth, becoming quite absorbed in the task. The rocking rhythm was strangely soothing. And then, on the eighth or ninth pass, came the sensation, and the sound, that she craved: a definite, delicious crack.

When she examined the parcel, unwrapping just enough of the sheet to check, she saw a long, jagged fracture running across the top corner of the photograph, between the sky and the bombed-out brickwork. Leni stepped into the Skoda. She executed a neat three-point turn, avoiding the mess on the tarmac, and drove away.

She was going to Isthmus Avenue, to have a shower and change her clothes, before taking a taxi to the airport. The flight to Berlin was not scheduled until 5.05 p.m., but she wanted to arrive at least three hours early – she'd heard that the queues for security could get very long.

The two thousand pounds that Magill had given her would keep her going for a few weeks, she thought, if she was frugal. In the room she'd rented on Revaler Strasse, in Friedrichshain, part of the old East Berlin, there was only space for a narrow single bed and a fold-down desk. But that was fine, it was all she needed.

She was going to Berlin because she wanted to get away for a while, and it was the first place she'd thought of. The irony of choosing that particular destination wasn't lost on Leni. But she'd resolved to stay no longer than a month. There was Ann to come back for. Unlike her mother, she'd promised she would return.

Outside the cottage that stood opposite the Honolulu causeway, a teenage girl in a denim jacket was sitting on one of the painted white rocks. She looked expectant, as though she was waiting for someone. Leni gave a merry wave as she drove past her, and the girl smiled shyly and waved back.

It really was a wonderful morning. Beyond the islands, the sun was turning the water to beaten silver. A small plane cruised overhead in the blue. Leni glanced in the rear-view mirror. She saw the teenage girl, still sitting on her rock, patiently waiting. Then the road turned inland, away from the shore, and the girl was gone.

~~~
~~~

Printed in Great Britain
by Amazon